THE DARK NARCS

THE DARK NARCS

PAUL MAHONEY

THE DARK NARCS

Windy City Publishers
www.windycitypublishers.com

Published in the United States of America

ISBN:
978-1-953294-25-8

Library of Congress Control Number:
2022903314

Cover Image by alexkoral/Shutterstock.com

WINDY CITY PUBLISHERS
Chicago

In memory of my long-time friend,
an original dark narc.
Detective Norman S. Pressley
Denver Police Department.

RIP, brother.

AUTHOR'S NOTE

THIS IS A WORK OF FICTION.
Resemblance to real people, places,
and events is coincidental.

Only in my mind is it all real.

1

FATHER'S DAY 1987 WAS SUNDAY the twenty-first of June. Frank Sullivan celebrated the weekend by taking his travel baseball team to Pueblo for a tournament. It featured some of the best 18-year-old baseball players in Colorado and some from Arizona and California as well. Sullivan's team didn't win it, but that wasn't really the point anyway. These were showcase tournaments where projected college and pro players showed their wares. Several of them had been all-league with their respective high school teams, a few had been all-state and one, Luther Pride, had won the Golden Arm award as the best high school pitcher in the state. Luther had also been an all-state basketball player his last two years at Manual High School.

Frank Sullivan was a sergeant with the Denver Police Department, assigned to a street drug enforcement unit. He joined the police department in 1970 and, while still a rookie, volunteered to coach in the fledgling Police Athletic League. He was even depicted in full police uniform in a community relations poster that year, coaching a young Black boy in a football uniform. The heading read: "If we could choose."

Since his rookie days, Sullivan had continued to coach baseball because of his life-long love affair with it, and over time he was able to see that his coaching efforts had, in general, helped a number of kids. If nothing else, it may have lessened their fear and dislike of cops. By 1987 though, Sullivan was only coaching the so-called elite baseball players 18 and up. These teams were pretty much made up of the best high school players, most of whom had just finished their senior year. No longer was he working with the average troubled kid who needed help staying in school, who just needed something to do after school, or who would benefit from dealing with cops in a positive way.

His team in 1987 was really good and Luther Pride was the star. Sullivan had gotten to know Pride while working off-duty at high school basketball games. He had encouraged him to give baseball a try and, as Sullivan had suspected, Pride was a natural. He could throw a ball in the mid-nineties, hit with power and run. He had started playing summer ball with Sullivan after his sophomore year in high school and since then they had become close. In June of 1987, Luther Pride was drafted in the MLB amateur draft in the second round by the Montreal Expos. Nobody in Northeast Denver had a brighter future than Luther Pride, and he was a community hero.

On the Monday *after* Father's Day, Sgt. Sullivan was back on duty. At that time there were four Denver policemen assigned to night narcotics enforcement. In addition to Sgt. Sullivan, there was Detective George Crowe, Detective Leon Messenger, and Detective Mike Lodi (pronounced like the Credence Clearwater song and the California town of the same name). They were all baby boomers. Messenger and Crowe were Black, Lodi and the sergeant were white. Messenger and the sergeant had fifteen and sixteen years on the job, respectively. Crowe had nine and Lodi, who was hardly ever called anything other than Lodi, had seven. Until recently, there had been only three night narcs: Sullivan, Messenger and Crowe. The other officers in the narcotics bureau referred to them as the "dark narcs," in part because they were the only narcotics personnel working straight nights.

All of these four were well-respected, but none were considered "super cops." What they had in common, and what made them a highly effective team, was their willingness to work hard and their love of the job.

Since January 1986, there had been an increasing number of complaints indicating that Jamaican nationals were dealing drugs in Northeast Denver. There had also been several homicides known to be drug related. Hostilities were rising between local dealers and Jamaicans. It was at this point that Lodi was added to the team and Sullivan had been promised even more men soon.

In addition to that, since June of 1986, Denver had become one of several American cities experiencing a raging street crack problem. The death of Len Bias, the Maryland basketball star and the number one pick of the Boston Celtics in 1986, had marked the beginning of a nationwide crack epidemic. Entire neighborhoods were being taken over by crack dealers and buyers in a matter of days and weeks. Denver, Los Angeles, Detroit, Kansas City, and Milwaukee were among the cities hardest hit.

The job of a narc, or police narcotics detective, had evolved significantly since the late Fifties when heroin and marijuana dominated the street drug scene and users were squeezed for information that could lead to the arrest of the source or the dealer. If they didn't cooperate and they had tracks, or needle marks, on their bodies, they went to jail for illegal use. After *Mapp v. Ohio (1961),* narcotics enforcement was complicated and slowed down by the requirement that evidence be legally obtained in order to be admissible in court. In short, that meant that a search warrant, based on probable cause, would be required in many cases, whereas that had not been the case before.

In the Sixties, all sorts of "new" drugs hit the street and one other major change occurred. The majority of users and dealers were young and white. Then in the late Seventies when cocaine became the thing, dealing was very clandestine and the focus of local law enforcement was to arrest the major players, the suppliers, whenever possible. This made the job of a narc a little more prestigious and desirable.

The mission for Sullivan and his team was neither prestigious nor desirable to most. Plain and simple, it was to attack the street problem in response to the complaints from citizens and their elected representatives. The rampant, out in the open dealing, and its attendant violence, was perceived as a threat to law abiding citizens and businesses, especially in Northeast Denver, which encompassed several predominantly Black neighborhoods. Those citizens and their elected representatives demanded police attention.

The undercover detectives dressed for work in blue jeans and T-shirts or whatever else made them comfortable and inconspicuous. They were assigned nondescript, city-owned or leased undercover vehicles. Many of them were seizures from previous cases. The dark narcs employed a number of investigative and enforcement techniques, but relied heavily on search warrants.

Unlike traditional detectives assigned to crimes against persons or property, narcotics detectives initiated their own cases; they were not handed an offense report to investigate. They acted on intel (intelligence) gathered from informants, citizens, and patrol officers; they prioritized targets based on the threat of violence, quantities being dealt, and numbers of complaints, and went after the criminals. Most other detectives and sergeants in the narcotics bureau were not volunteering to work crack and Jamaican cases. That was predominantly because it was a nighttime job; it was street level drug dealing and, if you wanted to catch them, you had to be on the street at night. And there was pressure for results. Perhaps most importantly, small amounts of drugs were usually involved and nearly all of the dealers were armed and confrontational. Likewise, many of the buyers were high and jittery and unpredictable. And as a group, they were also desperate to varying degrees. Most narcotics investigators preferred to work on cases that would net the so-called, higher-level dealer.

On this Monday night, June 22, 1987, all four dark narcs arrived at the office before seven p.m. for the start of their shift. It was a warm night in Denver for June and there was another stack of complaints on the sergeant's desk when the team arrived. The detectives had their desks in an open bay shared by all of the narcotics detectives and vice officers. Sergeant Sullivan had an office in a separate space next to the captain's office. It had no door on it and it was shared with the other street narcotics sergeants.

Usually, the detectives would sit around Sergeant Sullivan's desk at the beginning of the shift and discuss the plans for the night. This night was no different.

"I have to meet an informant at 23rd and Welton," said Lodi, "and I'd like Messenger to go with me to see if we can set up an introduction."

Sullivan asked if they needed any more help and Lodi said no.

"In that case I think George and I will go over by District 2, and check out those places on Jackson and then go down by Manual High School and look at some of those Jamaican houses we've got complaints on," said Sullivan.

Crowe added, "Good idea, those places on Jackson are supposed to be crazy, people all over the streets flagging down traffic and trying to sell rock. Ain't no way to tell whose selling and whose buying. I've already answered two more calls from

District 2 officers begging me to do something. They say that uniforms drive by in the marked car and everybody disappears, and as soon as the cops leave, it's like ants on a meat skin again."

"I got a call from Jeff Ryan at ATF (Bureau of Alcohol, Tobacco, and Firearms), and he told me that they'd be able to assist us on these Jamaican cases and these crack houses as well, if weapons are involved, and if we want to file the cases in federal court," said Frank Sullivan. "He's supposed to get back to me, because he would like to assign a couple of his people to work with us, especially on the Jamaican cases. ATF in other parts of the country is working lots of those cases from the weapons angle, especially on the East Coast."

After some more discussion about the proliferation of crack houses, it was agreed that maybe they'd all get back together in a couple of hours. Lodi and Messenger would probably grab something to eat on their way to East Denver. Crowe was married and had supper before work as did Sullivan. Leon slapped a hard high five on Sullivan and said, "All right, Sarge, we are gonna kick some ass tonight brotha," as he and Lodi left the sergeants' office.

"Whatever you say, Leon," responded Sullivan, "just don't hurt me man." At that Leon laughed loudly.

Sullivan, as the sergeant, was charged with all of the daily personnel bookkeeping. He was also responsible for approving all warrants, buys, and other operational plans. However, he was in charge of veteran officers who were in an assignment that they liked and were good at, and supervising them was easy. They respected him and followed his leadership without reservation; at the same time, they felt confident in giving him their input on decision-making and in running their cases the way they thought best. This was important to Sullivan to whom selfless teamwork was the cornerstone of effective supervision. Sullivan was a sensitive person who went out of his way to treat people right and was not an authoritarian leader. He was able to inspire people to quality work and productivity.

Detective George Crowe was a soft-spoken, kind, Black man with an amazing memory for people's names and faces. He was not effective undercover because he didn't have any desire to disguise himself, to pretend he was something he was not. He was accustomed to carrying himself with a military bearing and he was a big man. He had no qualms about being in a unit charged with investigating almost exclusively Black drug dealers. He saw them as a threat to the community and he had faith in the system and looked on his job as an opportunity to effectively and fairly do the job that needed to be done. Crowe had spent four years in the Air Force and was still a reserve in the National Guard.

George Crowe made a couple of calls and checked some addresses on the NCIC/CCIC (National Crime Information Center/Colorado Crime Information Center) computer. Sullivan finished what he had to do and then they left the office together. They took the elevator from the third floor down to B2 where Sullivan's undercover vehicle, a light blue '82 El Camino, was parked. They left the garage, went north to Colfax and headed east, working their way north as they went farther east.

They made their way to the 3500 block of Jackson Street, which had been the subject of numerous complaints lately, and which, by the way, was just around the corner from the District 2 patrol station. It was dusk and several people lurked in the shadows, emerging to check out passing cars and to scrutinize the occupants. Shortly it would be dark, and activity would pick up.

"I can't figure out what's going on with these crack houses, Sarge," said George Crowe, "seems like overnight a regular street will turn into a mess of crack heads and dealers. Here on Jackson there are four or five of these little multi-unit places that are vacant and they are overrun with dealers. Some of 'em don't even have power—they run a flimsy little extension cord from one house that has it. That's where people disappear to when the cops drive by, those vacant houses. I'm looking into who the owners are and then I'm gonna' contact them."

Sullivan grunted then added, "We'll get nowhere jumping these guys out here and making buys from unknowns; it's a waste of funds—unless we're willing to jump them right away and settle for one little chicken-shit sales case."

The sergeant started driving out of the area and headed south toward 29th Avenue. It was about nine o'clock. He made a right turn from Colorado Blvd. onto 29th, when Crowe's radio, set to the District 2 channel, announced a call on a shooting at about 28th and Franklin. The dispatcher sent two marked cars and stated that an ambulance was on the way as well. Shortly thereafter, the dispatcher contacted Zebra 20 (Sgt. Sullivan) on the secure channel and told him that the uniform officers wanted him to respond to the scene of the homicide as there was somebody who asked to see him right away. Sullivan responded that Zebra 20 and Zebra 22 (Detective Crowe) were on their way. Sullivan stepped up the speed of the El Camino, probably a physical impulse or reaction to the unsettled feeling in the pit of his stomach. It was a nervous sensation that he had grown to interpret as a sign that he was about to be tested in some way. It wasn't totally dissimilar from the feeling of being on deck and watching a hard throwing pitcher work to the guy at bat.

"Zebra 20," called the Channel 2 dispatcher.

"Zebra 20," responded George Crowe, answering for Sullivan, whose hand-held unit had slipped between the seats and out of his reach.

"Zebra 20, Sarge, you'll be the ranking officer from the Investigations Division. Let me know what you need after you get there," stated the dispatcher.

"10-4," responded Crowe for Sullivan, "he hears you."

2

WHEN SGT. SULLIVAN AND CROWE arrived in the area of 28th and Franklin, the street was full of bystanders. Shots fired was not uncommon in the area, although much of the surrounding area, especially to the east, was a well-established Black middle class area. Three marked cars were on the scene as was the ambulance. George Crowe worked his way quickly inside the perimeter to check it out. As he made his way to the center of the crowd where the ambulance crew was working feverishly, Crowe came across Luther Pride in the crowd, wearing his Montreal Expos baseball cap.

"Hey, Detective Crowe, remember me, Luther? Is the sarge with you?"

"Hey, Luther, yeah, he was right behind me getting out of the car. What happened? Did you see this?" It dawned on him that Luther was the person who had requested that Sullivan respond to the scene, but Crowe barely slowed down to hear the response as he moved toward the uniform officers, standing near the attendants working on the body on the ground.

"Yes sir," was Luther's response who then added, "I'll talk to you and the sarge when you get done."

Sgt. Sullivan made his way to the crime scene, nodding to Luther as he passed him in the crowd. He was temporarily in charge of the scene until the homicide detectives arrived, then it would be their task. He purposefully backed up from the body, being careful where he stepped, and called dispatch. He told them to send homicide detectives and the medical examiner. He called for an additional marked car to help with perimeter security and then switched back to the undercover channel and called for Zebra 23 (Lodi) to respond.

The crowd of bystanders had grown to forty or fifty people, and Sullivan and George Crowe walked to the edges of the crowd looking for familiar faces. At first they recognized no one but Luther, so they started addressing the people as a group and asking if anyone had witnessed the shooting. Nobody raised a hand or volunteered information, including Luther who knew he would talk to Sullivan after things settled down a bit. Then Sullivan recognized Eleanora Mathews in the middle of the crowd. She gave him a subtle signal that she would talk to him later. He had gone to Catholic high school with her in Denver. It had been more than that; they had dated and gotten close, but they hadn't seen each other for years. He was a little stunned seeing her there.

Among the crowd were a couple of local TV news trucks that had been monitoring the police scanner and had hustled to the scene. They were waiting outside the perimeter to talk to anybody from the police who would give them any information.

Two homicide detectives, Lola Mathis and Al Lopez, arrived, waved off questions from the media, and went directly to Sgt. Sullivan for information, as he was the ranking officer on the scene. He told them that nobody had been identified as a witness other than possibly two people that he knew and with whom he would talk later.

"Okay, that would be good if you'll take statements from them if applicable, and we can interview them later if they have something useful," stated Detective Mathis. "Do you have any idea who the victim is yet?" she then asked.

"No, I don't know if she had ID on her or not," was Sullivan's response. "One of the kids that I've coached for years was here and he asked the uniform guys to call me. I think he may have something important to tell us. As soon as this calms down and the crowd dissipates, I'll get him in the car and talk to him."

Zebra 23 (Lodi) had arrived at the scene and had been briefed by Detective Crowe. He explained to Crowe, though unnecessarily, that he had left Detective Messenger at headquarters because he worked so much undercover in the area, that he didn't want to be burned.

Crowe responded, "Oh no, we don't want him here now."

"You know this has something to do with the drug house down on the other end of the block. They're Jamaicans and word is they are dealing hand over fist. Too goddamn bad we haven't been able to make a case on them yet. All the uniform guys that work the area have been telling me about them, but I haven't made any buys yet." Lodi went on, "I will though, unless this shakes everybody up and they shut down. They're gonna' know that the heat will be on them and that it will come from us."

Sullivan approached the two standing away from the crowd but still inside the perimeter. The sergeant explained that the victim had not been identified as yet, but that she was a Black female about eighteen or nineteen years old.

"As soon as the homicide dicks tell me it's okay, that they don't need me here for anything more, I'm going to find Luther and arrange to meet him somewhere away from here, maybe over behind Manual, and we can talk. George is with me and I want you to talk to him as well, Lodi.

"And an old friend of mine was in the crowd also, and I gave her my card, and she will get ahold of me in a little while I'm sure." Just then Sullivan's pager sounded and he guessed the number to be that of potential witness, Eleanora Mathews.

"Maybe that's her now. I'll call her when we're done here."

The team only had three cell phones and the sergeant hadn't assigned himself one, opting rather to assign one to each of the detectives. In theory at least, they had more informants and more need for a cell phone than he did, although in fact, he worked many cases on his own and had two or three informants who called him regularly.

"Look, here's what I want to do. After we talk to Luther, I want you to see what you have on the drug house up the street, talk to your informants and get what you can. Then, in a little while, we'll meet over at Manual again in four cars, do some late night surveillance on this place, and see if we can't jump a few people and turn something up."

Sgt. Sullivan checked with the homicide detectives to see if they needed anything else. They indicated that it was pretty much under control, that there were no witnesses who had come forth yet. It was then agreed that after Sullivan had talked to his informants, he would report back to them. Sullivan and Crowe then made their way through the crowd and subtly let Luther know, when they passed him, that they wanted him to meet them behind Manual High School, less than a block away.

When Sgt. Sullivan and George Crowe drove to the darkest part of the Manual High School parking lot, they found Luther Pride waiting for them in his black 1975 Chevy II Nova. Lodi drove up shortly thereafter.

"Hey man, am I glad to see you all in one piece, Luther, what the hell happened over there?" These were the first words out of Sullivan's mouth and he followed up with, "Who is the girl that got killed?" Then he went on, "You know Mike Lodi and George Crowe, right?"

Luther shook his head and inhaled deeply. He rubbed his hands together as he exhaled. "The girl was Janel Robinson, the best softball player at Manual, maybe ever. I introduced her to you, Coach, at one of our games last month."

"Oh my God, of course I remember her," Sullivan replied immediately.

"Yeah, well, they killed her. She was down there in the park and one of her friends ran over here to Manual to get me to go pick her up, that she was in trouble. I was watching some of the three-on-three tournament that Red Shield sponsors every summer."

"Who came to get you?" asked Sullivan.

"Her name is Lilian Martinez. She told me that Janel was 'messing' with some of the Jamaicans who sell cocaine around there and said she was worried about her. So she and I got in my car and drove over to the corner of 29th and Franklin, and I parked near the corner. She jumped out and ran toward the corner of the park there. I took time to place my baseball gear in the trunk, then locked the car and walked over there. As I got to the corner I started into the park, I heard some commotion and then heard a gunshot.

"At first, I backed up. Kind of a wave of people backpedaled away from the crowd. I saw a girl down on the ground and I could tell it was Janel. I moved as close as I could get to her but at the same time, I was afraid, just like everybody else. No way could I tell who had the gun or what the hell was going on. After the Jamaican guys had all scattered, I moved in closer to see if I could do anything but I could tell she was dead already; they shot her in the head. I leaned over her to keep people from gawking at her and I shooed the crowd back, away from her."

"That had to be a shock. Did you see anybody running that might have been the shooter?" was Sullivan's follow up.

"Yeah, well, you guys know the Jamaican drug dealers are all over around here now. I think it was one of them. I don't know any of them but some of the guys at Manual mess around with drugs and they've told me how dangerous those guys are. I did see several Jamaicans running away, after the shots. One of them is a big Jamaican they call 'Ten' or 'Tenny.'"

"How do you know that Luther?" asked Sullivan, and then, as if added quickly so he wouldn't forget to ask, "Where did Lilian Martinez go?"

"I know that coach, because those guys are always over at the park and a lot of people are afraid of them and the kids talk about them. As for Lilian, I saw her running across the park, toward Manual right after the gunshot."

Sullivan paused for a moment, then asked Luther, "Was Janel hanging with those guys, or buying drugs from them or what?"

"I don't think she was into that but she did like flirting with them in the park and listening to Bob Marley and dancing and stuff. I don't know man, she did have a little bit of a wild side, but she was an athlete and a pretty serious student. She wanted to go to Metro in the fall and play ball there."

"Do you guys have any questions?" Sullivan asked Lodi and Crowe.

"Yeah, I do, Sarge," responded Lodi. "What did Lilian Martinez tell you, Luther, when she came to get you, other than she was worried?"

"She said that Janel was in the middle of two Jamaicans and that they were getting really pissed off at each other. She said she had tried to get her to leave but she wouldn't."

"Did Janel ask her to go and find you?" asked Lodi.

"Lilian didn't say that, she just said that she was worried and knew I was over here watching the tournament so she ran over here to get me."

Lodi followed up, "Does Lilian hang out with those guys or buy drugs from them?"

"I don't know, to tell you the truth. I mean, she hung out with Janel, so she probably does know them. I'm pretty sure Janel wasn't getting high with them, but I think Lilian was."

At that point, Sullivan decided it was best to get ahold of the homicide detectives and see if they wanted a statement from Luther right away. Detective Mathis told Sullivan to have Luther meet her in the lobby of headquarters in thirty minutes. He would rather have let Luther go for the night because he was pretty shook up about what he had seen, especially since it was Janel Robinson, a friend of his, who had been killed. Sullivan explained to Luther that Detective Mathis had asked for him to meet her at headquarters and he agreed to drive down there at once. Sullivan suggested that Luther go by St. Joseph's Hospital and talk to his mom, Gina, on the way to headquarters. She worked at the hospital as a registered nurse in the emergency room, and she might have heard something about the incident and be worried about him.

"Oh yeah, Coach, I need to do that. I'll go talk to her right now. I'll let you know if I hear anything from Lilian or any of Janel's other friends," was Luther's response. Sgt. Sullivan fist bumped him in agreement, cautioned him to drive carefully, and then walked back to where his car and the other two detectives were parked.

Sullivan, Crowe and Lodi agreed that they should try and do some surveillance on the suspected Jamaican drug house at the corner of 28th and Franklin. Lodi volunteered to try and get ahold of a CI (confidential informant) and see if they could make a controlled-buy from the place.

"I'll take George back to the office with me," Lodi added, "and he can get his own car, then we'll come back here and hang around to see what we can get. I'll get ahold of Leon and have him meet us as well."

16

3

DETECTIVES CROWE AND LODI HAD returned to headquarters and met with Detective Messenger before heading back to the area of 28th and Franklin, where the homicide had occurred, and where a group of the Jamaican drug dealers were operating. They went in their separate undercover cars and established surveillance positions where at least one of them could see people coming and going from 2811½ Franklin Street. By the time they had established surveillance, the block was clear, the crime scene had been processed and and most of the concerned bystanders and neighbors had moved along or gone inside their houses. Not too many people remained in the park at about ten o'clock on a nice summer night.

Lodi called the other two guys and told them that he had just heard from a CI, had picked him up, and was going to try and send him into 2811½ Franklin to make a controlled-buy. That meant that he would take city funds, serial numbers recorded, and try to buy a small amount of cocaine. He would also try and get some conversation about the shooting if possible. The informant indicated that he had heard that they were *Jakes* (Jamaicans) and were dealing cocaine, not crack. This corroborated information that Lodi and other detectives had received from other sources. Further information indicated that the dealers were visibly well-armed.

The informant was properly searched before going in and, just as Lodi was about to send him in, Messenger got on the air and asked if he could go with the CI. After some on-air discussion, it was decided that Messenger would go as far as the house but would wait outside where cover officers had a visual of him. That being decided, Messenger and the CI approached on foot. Surveillance observed a small man open the door of the house and allow the CI to enter while Detective Messenger waited on the porch. In a minute or two, the CI came out of the house and the two soon disappeared into the darkness across 28th Avenue.

Messenger made his way to where his car was parked in the Manual High School parking lot. The CI went to Detective Lodi's vehicle and handed him what was purported to be a half gram of cocaine for which he had paid $50.

Lodi called for the other guys to meet him in the parking lot on the south side of Manual High School. They parked in a dark spot near the building and the three detectives and the CI discussed the buy. Messenger explained that he could see in the house when the door was opened. An average-size man was at the door but he saw a bigger man farther inside the house. He and the bigger man had made eye contact. He didn't feel like his presence aroused any suspicion in either of them. From the porch he had observed that the park was clear and the streets were quiet.

Lodi then asked the CI to tell what he saw. He explained that there were only two people inside the house and that they were Jamaicans. He had bought from one of them before.

"I know the one guy, the little guy, but I don't know his name," said the informant with the code name of "Cool O," or "Coolo." He chose that as his code name and Lodi didn't bother to tell him that the same sounding word in Spanish, *culo*, didn't have anything to do with cool.

"He's a little bit friendly usually, but not tonight with the big man (pronouncing it mon, like the Jamaicans do) standing behind him with an automatic held near his hip."

Lodi asked, "Do you know his name?"

"Naw, man, I don't know his name and he don't know mine."

"Who is the big guy?" pursued Lodi, "What's he called?"

"I don't know, man, but the other guy's scared of him and wouldn't say shit about the shooting. He acted like he didn't know nothin' about it. Said he didn't hear no shots or nothin' I asked him about it."

"What did he call the big guy?"

"He didn't call him nothin', Lodi. He was nervous as hell. I don't know why; I guess he's just scared of him."

"What kind of automatic did he have?"

"It didn't look like a Glock, but I don't know what kind it was. A good one, black grips. Either a .45 or a 9mm. I couldn't stare at it. I was careful not to even look at the guy too much."

"That's okay, man, you did good. I'll give you a ride back to where you were," responded Lodi, who then handed him a twenty dollar bill with the standard promise of a good payday if the case ended up well. "We may want to come back here tomorrow when it cools off a little, so call me tomorrow at seven."

"I will. Thank you for this, man," said the CI, indicating the twenty.

"I'll see you guys back at the office in a minute, after I drop him off."

"Right on, man," said Leon Messenger. Then to the CI, "Hey, man, you think you could take me inside with you next time?"

"Oh yeah, man, but not if the big guy is there, huh uh. No way. He won't let you in if he doesn't know you. But once you're in with the little guy, and he can vouch for you, you can go back."

"All right, man, I'll talk to my man Lodi here and see what we can put together. Be cool now, man, you don't want anybody finding out what you're doing."

"Hell no!" replied Coolo emphatically.

It was after midnight by the time the three detectives got back together in the Narcotics Bureau. The evidence, the suspected cocaine, from the controlled- buy had been placed in the Property Bureau and the surveillance report had been made. Controlled-buys were used to independently corroborate information and to build probable cause to obtain a search warrant after the investigation has moved to that point. Informants have to be documented and established as previously reliable. The actual sale to the informant does not usually become a criminal case because to do so would require that the informant be a witness, thus revealing his identity, probably putting him in danger, and rendering him useless as an informant. If the officer is able to buy directly, no informants or citizens are required as witnesses, then the case is filed, based entirely on the evidence purchased and the testimony of the undercover officer.

While the others were doing surveillance and making a controlled-buy at 28th and Franklin, Sullivan went to meet with Eleanora Mathews at her home. He had recognized her at the scene of the shooting. She was a thirty-eight-year-old biracial woman, half Black, half Italian-American. She and Sullivan had attended the same high school near downtown Denver.

Eleanora lived by herself in a small brick bungalow in a middle class Black neighborhood near City Park. Once inside Eleanora's house, Sullivan gave Eleanora a hug and took a seat on the couch. The living room was comfortably furnished, had polished hardwood floors, and was adorned with family photos on the walls. One wall was lined with bookcases and a couple of barrister cabinets.

The two spent a few minutes catching up. They had run into each other here and there over the last twenty years. She knew he was working in narcotics, coaching baseball and that he had quit drinking a couple of years earlier. He knew that she was working at Mountain Bell, had not been married and that her parents were still alive and doing well. She knew that Sullivan was still single also. The good feeling of seeing each other again was mutual.

After the personal small talk, Eleanora began describing the night's scene at Fuller Park. She had gone there in the early evening to meet two of her aunts on her dad's side, for a picnic. Many of the older people had conceded the park to the younger crowd, in part due to the rise in drug dealing activity. Not her aunts however. They had lived in the neighborhood most of their lives and still enjoyed having a picnic in the park on a nice summer evening.

They had finished their picnic, were finished sharing family gossip, and discussing if Eleanora was ever going to get married. According to Eleanora, they felt comfortable; several other neighborhood people were enjoying the park. Some old timers were playing dominoes at a table not far from Franklin Street. It was a typically beautiful summer evening in Denver. There was a small crowd of younger Black men, whom Eleanora described as Jamaicans, and there were two or three young women mingling with them also. One of them, as it turned out, was Janel Robinson.

According to Eleanora's account, her attention and that of her aunts, was diverted toward that crowd as loud arguing ensued. Janel Robinson was in the midst of a crowd of taller, bigger Jamaican males. One of the Jamaican's grabbed another of them at his collar. As the one who was grabbed turned away, he came out with a pistol. Yelling and loud talking and name calling followed that, and the crowd moved, first as a crowd, and then as ten or fifteen separate, loose parts. During that second movement, a shot was heard—only one. Eleanora was not sure who fired the shot. The men started retreating helter-skelter. It was then that Eleanora realized that one of the women had been hit and was on the ground, a pool of blood forming on the grass around her head. The "big" Jamaican, whom she had seen with the gun, described as a black semi-automatic, was seen heading south and getting into a dark brown or black, Toyota or Honda. He got into the driver's side and drove away by himself, as far as Eleanora could tell.

Eleanora was pretty sure that she could identify the Jamaican with the gun if she saw him again or maybe saw a photo. But she had not actually seen him shoot the girl. When he heard this, Sullivan counseled her that she might be one of the only witnesses to this homicide and that being a witness, and testifying in a court room, might be dangerous. Undoubtedly, the Jamaican drug trafficking element was known to be ruthless and vengeful.

"Okay, Frank, take me downtown to talk to them, or call them, or whatever. I am a witness, and I want this guy, or whoever it was, to pay for what he did and then maybe all these other Jamaican thugs will leave town. Especially if you guys keep hitting them and can keep them from making money."

"I'll call them and then probably take you down there when it's convenient for them. They will want to videotape the interview so maybe tomorrow will be better for them."

"Let's do it."

Sullivan paused a minute or so and wrote something down in his notebook. And then he asked her, "Are you pretty sure the guy you saw with the gun got into that car and that he was alone?"

"I think he went down the street and got into that car but I can't swear to it. Once I looked back at the body on the ground I was frozen by the horror of it. The grass was soaked in blood."

Then she sheepishly added, "I felt sick to my stomach."

"But you are sure that they were Jamaicans?"

"There were at least seven or eight Jamaican guys there. You know, Frank, they don't hang with us American Blacks; for that matter, I think the only Americans they talk to are women, white or Black. But they are easy to identify when they talk, calling each other '*mon*', saying '*wah gwaan*' instead of what's going on, and like that."

While they were talking, Eleanora had made Sullivan a cup of coffee and he sat at the kitchen table with her and drank his coffee. She had also made him a grilled cheese sandwich that, after politely refusing at first, he then accepted and ate enthusiastically.

"Outside of this, how you doing, Frank? You look a little tired, but still handsome as ever."

"Yeah, right, Eleanora. You're the one who hasn't changed much—you'll probably look the same forever."

Eleanora then responded, "Yeah, the difference is, I looked old in high school and look about the same now." Then she added, "All that working out you do, and all that time you spend outside has been really good for you. Plus, the baseball helps reduce the stress of being a cop. Right?"

Sullivan answered, "Let's be honest, I look better since I stopped drinking three years ago; that's what has really changed in my life. I think the working out is part of it too, and of course I love coaching baseball. I need diversions away from the job; especially now. This street narcotics work is intense. But you know, we have a good thing going. The guys I have, Crowe and Lodi and Messenger, we all get along and go out of our way to look out for each other. Believe it or not, we think what we are doing is making life out here better and we all love this job. There are a lot of people out here who are fed up with the street drug dealers in the hood and they want us out here, 'serving and protecting.' But then there are a whole bunch of people, cops included, who think we are wasting our time on a victimless crime."

"I know you guys are making a difference, Frank. We want to keep our neighborhoods safe, grow the Black middle class, have good schools in the neighborhood—really, everything else that people want in any neighborhood. Some of these areas are getting pretty run down. Well, you already know that, but that's where all these crack dealers are."

Sullivan responded, "Hey, we've had some areas where they move into a place and within two weeks the whole block is infested with dealers and crackheads, and they're not at all discreet about it. They're loud and jittery and they make people nervous and scared. And then everybody is complaining to us and their council person, the district attorney, the mayor's office and anybody else who will listen. All those complaints end up in our office and we try to fix what's broken."

They both sat at the table for a minute looking at each other. Eleanora was thinking of ways to keep him in her house a little longer. She lived by herself and she was happy, but she liked Frank Sullivan sitting at her kitchen table.

4

ELEANOR MATHEWS HAD A CRUSH on Frank Sullivan in high school and they went out for a while. They usually went to the movies together at the art deco theaters downtown—they felt comfortable there. That was in 1966. Things were changing a little then, but white boys and Black girls dating was a rarity. Sullivan never took her home to meet his parents, though he had thought that his mom would really like her. But he had met Eleanora's mom and dad when he went to her house to pick her up. Her dad's name was Victor and he was Black; his wife Carmen, Eleanora's mom, was white. Her family were North Denver Italians and she had eight brothers (some reportedly with ties to the North Denver mafia) and sisters. They were all good looking people, but the women in the family were stunning. Victor had also grown up in Denver and had attended Denver University on a football scholarship.

Victor Mathews was a "man's man" and Sullivan liked him right away. The first time he showed up at their door, he had asked Sullivan to sit down and talk to him, while he waited for Eleanora. As they sat in the Mathews' living room the first night he was there, Mr. Mathews informed Sullivan that he was a little worried about letting his daughter go to a movie with a white boy. He then made it clear that he had done a little background on Frank Sullivan and was a satisfied that he was a "good kid." What he was worried about was what other people might think and choose to do when they saw them together. He suggested to young Sullivan that he and Eleanora not hold hands and that he not put his arm around her—just walk along as if they were together but not *together*. Mr. Mathews nodded toward the kitchen where his wife was and told Sullivan, "I know a little about getting through this type of thing, Frank, take my advice."

As Frank Sullivan sat there in Eleanora's kitchen, all those years later, he thought of Eleanora's parents, of the complexities of race in America and how that had been the determining factor in his relationship with Eleanora. It had all been new to Frank and he had chosen to suppress his feelings for her, rather than deal with the every-day challenges that would confront a biracial couple. Eleanora had grown up in a mixed-race relationship, with all its difficulties, she had not been so intimidated. He was a little downhearted as his thoughts turned to young Janel Robinson now in the city morgue and his job as a policeman trying to keep the streets safe.

After a minute or two, he shrugged his shoulders, took a deep breath and stood up. He took Eleanora's right hand in his and squeezed it gently. Then he told her that he had to get going, and thanked her for the sandwich and coffee. But before he left, he borrowed her phone and called Detective Lola Mathis to tell her that he was on his way to headquarters to talk to her and her partner. He gave her a quick rundown on what Eleanora had just told him. He would write a statement for them, and he told her that Eleanora had agreed to go down to headquarters the next evening at six o'clock for a videotaped interview.

Sullivan left Eleanora's house and headed to headquarters to meet with the homicide detectives. There was not much traffic at about midnight and it only took him a few minutes to make it to headquarters from the City Park area. He was anxious to talk further with them about the information that he had received from Eleanora Mathews. When he got there, they were glad to see him and quickly informed him how important

Luther Pride's statement had been also. They went on to talk about what a great young man he was, the statement he had given, and how Luther had talked about his coach, Sullivan, in glowing terms.

"Oh, definitely, he's one in a million in character, athletic ability and everything else. He's been playing baseball with me for the last few years and I've gotten really close to him and his mom—his whole family really. Did he seem to be nervous about being a witness?" Sullivan then quickly added, "He should be a little bit. Some of these guys are dangerous for real."

"No, he didn't seem at all nervous about anything, but he was admittedly upset about Janel Robinson being killed," was Detective Lopez's response. "And he gave us a good description of someone who was possibly the shooter, the one he called 'Ten' and some of the other people who might be involved or at least be witnesses. He didn't know any names other than 'Ten' and he didn't actually see the shots fired."

"Did he tell you about Lilian Martinez?"

"Yes, he did, Sarge. He doesn't know where she lives but we're going to run that name and see what we can find out." Lopez then added, "He did mention something else that he said he forgot to tell you."

"What was that?"

"He said that Janel Robinson drove an old Datsun station wagon, like a 1975 Datsun, yellow in color. It was given to her by her uncle who has a garage somewhere. He says it's a sweet little unit. Anyway, he thinks she must have had her car with her at the park. So we put out a BOLO (Be On the Look Out) and a District 2 car was dispatched to do a concentric search of the area for a few blocks every direction. They called me and said that they saw nothing matching that description."

"Oh, man, that *is* important. I wonder if Lilian Martinez has the car. If she and Janel were friends, maybe they came together in Janel's car. And when everything went to shit, she took off in the car. She would have needed the keys of course, but maybe she already had them." As he said this, Sullivan was thinking that as soon as he got to the office, he would ask George Crowe to get to work on finding out about Lilian Martinez, either on the computer, or in the huge Vice/Narcotics card filing system that contained thirty years worth of contact and arrest information.

The homicide detectives informed Sullivan that they had interviewed and received written statements from twenty people or so, but only one admitted to seeing anything that might be important. Most were reluctant to talk at all and made only terse statements committing to nothing. A somewhat reticent, elderly Black man named Herman Hale did report seeing a newer, dark brown Toyota leave south on Franklin after the shooting. It appeared that only one person was in the car and it may have been the same person who did the shooting, so said Mr. Hale. Unlike Eleanora or Luther, he did not give a description of the shooter, only the car. The description of the car did, however, match the description given by the other two.

"I know Herman Hale," said Sullivan, then he continued, "you're talking about a sixty-something-year-old Black man, bald with glasses? He drinks a lot."

"That's about right. He'd been drinking tonight but he wasn't drunk," stated Detective Mathis, "says he can be contacted down at the hardware store on the Points most afternoons except Sunday." "The Points" referred to the Five Points section northeast of downtown Denver, historically an African-American neighborhood.

"Hey, he's pretty sharp even when he is drunk, but he's nearly always drunk," Sullivan said, off-handedly. "If you want, I can run him down and talk to him some more. I know him from way back, from my days in District 2. I don't know where he lives now but I see him down in the Five Points area all the time. I can find him and he'll talk to me. Back in the day, he and I shared a few drinks after an extra job I had. He likes me."

"All right, Sarge, we'll keep that in mind. We're going to need some help on this. We don't know the whole drug scene out there like you guys do. That is, if it even is drug related." This was said by Detective Lopez as he looked at his notes, who then added without looking up, "And I'm sure it is.

"The other thing is that the victim may have been alone. Is that normal, did she hang out with those people who killed her, was she a user, was she the intended victim? These are things maybe you can help us find out," Lopez continued.

Sullivan told them that he would find out as much information as he could and that he and his team would put pressure on the dealers in that area and find out who did this and why. Neither of the detectives knew Sullivan well, only by reputation and that was good. He was known to be serious about his profession, a good man who socialized with other cops infrequently, but who was well-liked. The unbelievable amount of cases and arrests that the dark narcs initiated was impressive and spoke volumes about him and his team. Likewise, before going to narcotics, he was the General Vice Sergeant, and his team excelled at the street work and the investigations alike, and the people who worked for him swore by him. Those who didn't like his intensity or insistence on productivity—they went somewhere else to work.

Sullivan wrote a statement regarding his role at the crime scene, gave the detectives his pager and office numbers, and agreed to pass on anything he and his team developed.

It was one o'clock in the morning when the sergeant joined his men in Vice and Narcotics Bureau. George Crowe was working on the NCIC (National Crime Information Center) computer and the DPD (Denver Police Department) database trying to find out what he could. He was already doing what Sullivan was going to ask that he do: see what he could find out about Lilian Martinez and Janel's car. Messenger and Lodi were going through old cases trying to identify the people selling drugs at 2811½ Franklin.

When Sullivan arrived, all four of them had an informal debriefing. On his way down the hall from the Homicide Bureau, he had detoured down one floor to the Traffic Investigations Bureau, where there was an honor system snack bar. He grabbed four FatBoy ice cream sandwiches, left a five dollar bill in the box and headed back up to his office.

As they sat there eating their ice cream, they discussed the events of the night. While they talked, Sullivan typed the nightly activity letter. It detailed what the team had accomplished on that shift and was then sent to the captain in charge of the bureau as well as the Division Chief of Investigations. Most evenings when Sullivan came to work, there was a copy of his letter of the previous night returned to him with notes from the D/C and or the captain. It was their way of acknowledging the work that was being done.

This night's letter explained that they spent most of their time assisting on the homicide and that it was almost certainly drug related. It also mentioned continuing to investigate drug dealing locations in the area, while not revealing that a controlled-buy had been made at any certain location(s). Finally, the letter explained that his team would be actively trying to assist the homicide investigators in finding out who killed the young woman, a recent Manual High School graduate. This they would do concurrently with developing information on the dealers and other crooks in the area. In this sense, Sullivan and his team were, what amounted to, primary intelligence sources. Vice and Narcotics detectives knew street players and had informants. Therefore, when other detectives had unidentified victims or unknown suspects, they would often contact the narcs and the vice detectives for information. In fact, nearly all the current information on Jamaican drug dealers that the Intelligence Bureau had, whose job it was to gather intelligence, came directly from reports originating in the Vice and Narcotics Bureau, specifically, Sullivan's team.

During their meeting, the possibility of getting Detective Messenger inside the house on Franklin through Lodi's CI was discussed. They also kicked around ideas on how and why the shooting had happened. The prevailing sentiment was regret that they had not raided and closed down the Jamaican drug house at 2811½ Franklin before tonight. Perhaps if they had, this shooting would never have happened and the girl would still be alive.

After the meeting, they all finished what they were doing, cleared off their desks, and headed home for the night.

5

FRANCIS CHARLES SULLIVAN JR. WAS born in Denver after World War II. His father, Charles Gerard Sullivan, had been born in Boston at the end of the first world war. He grew up in the depression, went to work in the Civilian Conservation Corps after high school rather than going to college and studying math and engineering as he had hoped to do, joined the army, and then moved to the Army Air Corps. He went on to earn the Distinguished Flying Cross (DFC) in WWII as the Flight Engineer of a B-29 crew in the South Pacific. Frank's grandfather and namesake, Francis Charles Sullivan, had been a foot soldier and Purple Heart recipient in WWI and suffered the rest of his life from the effects of being gassed during that war.

Francis, or Frank as he was called, had been raised in East Denver near Stapleton Airport and educated in Catholic and public schools in Denver. He had been named after *his* grandfather, and both his father and grandfather called him junior, when he was growing up.

He had been raised in the Catholic faith with the Latin Mass, had been an altar boy, and he took his faith seriously. He had had fleeting thoughts of becoming a missionary priest when he was in high school. His father subtly discouraged him, hinting that celibacy might be a difficult lifestyle, maybe increasingly so, as the newness of priesthood wore off.

What had appealed to Sullivan about missionary work, as much as anything, was the travel, and the chance to see the world and learn another language or two. And he wanted to be of service and be a force for good in the world. Between the age of fifteen, when he entertained the idea of missionary priesthood, and the age of nineteen, he learned that his father was right, that a life of celibacy was probably not for him.

So when he graduated from high school, he went to college at newly founded Metropolitan State College in Denver. He graduated at age 21 with a degree in Law Enforcement and Criminology, and joined the police department. Times were changing: the civil rights movement, including the urban riots of the late Sixties and the anti-war demonstrations and unrest, had forced change on the police. Frank Sullivan and his contemporaries were the "new breed."

He was not married. He had been close to getting married at different times but had not ever been ready to commit. He spent most of his off-duty time coaching baseball, fishing, woodworking and reading. He enjoyed cooking and baking and his mom had taught him a great deal about both. He lived in a modest brick house in South Denver, not far from Washington Park.

Frank Sullivan grew up Irish-Catholic *and* alcoholic. He had started drinking regularly when he was a junior in high school and had continued drinking until he was almost 36 years old. Living in the narrow margin between drunk and functionally sober, he drank everyday but somehow avoided being arrested or killed while driving under the influence. Although he didn't drink on duty, alcohol *had* effected his performance on the job and his reputation. He remembered when he was a rookie, hearing one old-timer on the job tell another, "There use to be nothing but ass-holes and drunks on this job and there are very few of us drunks left." To a certain extent, that had been and still was true. Some of the good guys, the sensitive guys, dealt with the stress of the job by drinking, and sooner or later it was detrimental to them, many becoming alcoholics, some ruined their careers and their lives. The ass-holes, whether they drank or not, didn't seem to let the job get to them.

Through what he considered "divine intervention," Sullivan stopped drinking on July 10, 1984 and went to Alcoholics Anonymous. He had always been good at following instructions, and he followed the mandates of A.A. and the advice of his fellow drunks there to the letter. He was capable of being rigorously honest with himself; within months he had turned his career around and was getting glimpses of the contentment possible without alcohol in his life.

The first thing that Sullivan did on Tuesday morning, June 23, 1987, as he did every morning, was to have coffee. He woke up thinking about Janel Robinson being murdered and immediately thanked God that Luther Pride had not gotten to the park a couple of minutes sooner than he did. He knew that Luther would have tried to save her if she was in the middle of something.

After his coffee, he went for a little run, did fifty pushups and sit-ups and took a shower. Running had become a meditative routine for him. It was roadwork; he was an awkward runner due to a lower body deformity, possibly the result of a mild case of polio when he was a kid. He was the personification of the Nike slogan "Just do it," so he just did it, and while he was doing it, he allowed himself to work on his mental and spiritual health. He didn't run everyday, but he ran three or four miles, three or four times a week.

When he got home, after he cooled down, Sullivan called his young baseball players to remind them of the game on Wednesday evening and to let them know that Luther's friend, Janel Robinson, the excellent Manual High School softball player, that many of the other players knew as well, had been killed last night.

Then Sullivan called Detective Lopez who was in the Homicide Bureau at headquarters, working on the case. "What's going on, Sarge?" was how he opened the conversation after finding out who was calling for him.

"Nothing much, Al. I was wondering if you had talked to Janel's parents yet?"

"Yeah, Sarge, we had a car go by her address last night and give her mother the notification, and we are going out to her house to talk to her in a little while. In fact, your boy Luther gave us her address. The mother was understandably heartbroken. Luther says she's a single mother who works two jobs and that Janel was her pride and joy, "the light of her life." The father is not in the picture, we don't think. His name is Arthur Robinson and, again according to Luther, he has a record. We haven't run him yet but we are going to. Luther informed us that Arthur Robinson may also be involved in selling drugs. Have you heard of him?"

Sullivan's response was, "I have not, that I remember, but I'll check our files when I go in later and see what I can find out. I was also wondering if you had located Lilian Martinez yet, or Janel's car?"

"No. We have not had any response on the BOLO (Be On the Lookout) and have not had time to look for her yet. Would you guys have time to help us out and look for her? I mean, there were two more homicides last night in Southwest Denver and our whole unit is swamped."

"Yeah," said Sullivan, "that's what I was thinking. I'm going to call the lieutenant and let him know that we are going to spend some time on this in conjunction with our Jamaican investigations. He'll get it; the drug dealers and the violence out there go hand in hand. Once he approves, we'll get on it and try to find Lilian Martinez and Janel's car."

"Thanks, Sarge."

"No problem, I'll keep you up to date on what we find out."
As soon as he disconnected from Lopez, Sullivan called Lodi
on his cell phone. It was one o'clock in the afternoon by then.

Lodi was forty years old, had never been married and was a
person who stayed pretty much to himself. His full name was
Michael Lodi but he had become one of those guys known by
just one name—Lodi, like Ali, Bono and Dylan.

He had joined the police department when he was in his
early thirties, was an outstanding patrol officer and within
four years had been promoted to detective. Sullivan had been
an instructor at the academy when Lodi came on the job, and
he had recognized that he was a special recruit. He had military experience that he didn't speak about. Since joining the
department he had completed his college degree and was in the
process of getting a Masters degree at the Colorado University
Denver campus. Lodi had been in the Vice and Narcotics
Bureau about a year when he joined the dark narcs. He was
nearly always in the office when Sullivan got there at night to
start the shift and was usually still in the office working when
everybody else left for the night.

When Sullivan called Lodi on his cell phone Tuesday afternoon, he was already in the office. "Hey, Sarge, what's going
on?" And then he added, "I'm in the office. I thought I'd look
into Lilian Martinez a little bit and see what I could find out.
I saw George Crowe in court and talked him into coming
over here with me and seeing what we could find out about
Janel's car. He said he worked on it a little bit last night but
hadn't really gotten too far. We thought that if we can get an
address on Lilian, we'll go out there and see if we can find her.
Of course, if we do, we'll get ahold of the homicide dicks and
they can interview her."

Sullivan smiled to himself, wondering if he was even needed as a supervisor with the crew he had. All three were reliable self-starters.

"You've been reading my mind again haven't you, Lodi?"

"Oh god no, that's the last place I want to be," Lodi said as he laughed. "But I'm glad you were thinking about it too."

"Well, I talked to Lopez in Homicide and he asked me if maybe we could help them out by finding Lilian Martinez. Finding Janel's car was something I was thinking about asking George to do, believe it or not. You know, he's amazing when it comes to finding stuff out on the computer."

"Oh, I know he is," said Lodi. "Plus, this is a good case. I think if we work it from all angles, we can end up with the big Jamaican dealer that your boy Luther was talking about; that's what I want. I want to put that dope dealin' son of a bitch in jail. If we get him for selling coke *and* murder, all the better."

"I agree," was Sullivan's response, "I'm going to check on Leon and just let him know what you guys are doing and tell him that if he wants, he can go in early and help you. I think he tries to see his kids after school some days so he may not be able to come in early."

"Okay, Sarge, I'll let you know if we find out anything."

"Thanks, Lodi, see you later on."

Sgt. Sullivan then called Leon Messenger. He had known Leon since his days as a patrol officer in District 2, Northeast Denver. Messenger came on the job two years after Sullivan and they were about the same age. He became a policeman when hiring qualified minorities and women was a priority. He had always rocked a big afro and it had gotten even bigger since he was working in plainclothes.

Leon was a big man, 6'3" or so and 240 pounds. He was gregarious, loud and happy, and hungry most of the time. He was the best undercover officer on the job at that time. He was cool and had a line of rap that never went out of style; it had saved him on several occasions. Leon was a Black man committed to making a difference in the white man's world. He loved being a cop and was convinced that he could conform to the rules and regulations of the police department and not sacrifice anything of himself in the process.

"Hey, Sarge, what's goin' on, man? Is everything okay?" Even on the cell phone, Messenger's voice was resonant and enthusiastic.

"Heck yeah, Leon. I'm just calling to see what you've got going on and to see if you want to come in early. George and Lodi are in the office already, trying to do some more work on that homicide from last night. I know you were going to try and do a warrant tonight, how's that looking?"

"Oh yeah, man, it's good, man. I was going to come in a little early and try and get out there, make sure there was some activity and then let you know. I have to pick up my boy from a recreation center where he's playing in this football skills camp. After I drop him off at the house, I'll come into the office. But if it doesn't look good out there tonight, I'm gonna' wait, man. I want to get these *em effers* good."

"Sounds good, Leon, I'll see you down there in a little while. My boys have a quick practice at South High at four o'clock and then I'm heading in. Thank you, brother."

"Naw, man, thank *you* brotha."

When he finished talking to Messenger, Sullivan put his work gear together in a black leather bag. His baseball gear was already in a locked tool box in the back of the El Camino. He had authorization to use the undercover vehicle for the baseball activities since it was sponsored by the Denver Police Athletic League. Sullivan put everything he needed in the El

Camino and headed to a dive bar close to his house, known as the Kentucky Inn. He had known the owner for years and had even been known to drink in the place back in the day. In fact, he had celebrated his first St. Patrick's day on the job in that bar in 1970, a day after he was sworn in. There were still some cops, mostly old-timers, who frequented the place. It was just a little bit on the seedy side but it was dark and cool inside, and they did have good food.

6

"HEY, LARRY," SULLIVAN SAID AS he walked into the Kentucky Inn, addressing an old-time cop who was in there off-duty.

"Hey, Sarge, how you doing?"

"Pretty good, just going to get a quick bite and then head over to South High and give my team a workout."

"I read about that pitcher you've been working with. First-round draft pick, is that what I heard?"

"Second-round, Expos," responded Sullivan, then added, "His name is Luther Pride. I was a little surprised but I was thrilled he went that high. There have been scouts at all of our summer games and all his high school games since last year. He's just gotten better and better. He throws in the low-to mid-nineties and his control is getting better all the time. Plus, he's a great kid, Larry. His mom is a single mom, his dad was killed in Viet Nam, and its just so cool how things are working out for them. They're awesome people."

"He played at Manual High School, right?" Larry asked, adding "Manual is not known for baseball talent—good for them, good for Denver."

"It sure is. Especially as those neighborhoods over there are being taken over by drug dealers and the citizens are up in arms. We're over there every night. Last night a Manual girl was killed in Fuller Park. She had been a helluva softball player herself and was a friend of Luther's. In fact, he was there when it happened."

"Oh hell, man, you've gotta keep him away from all that shit. His whole life is in front of him."

40

Sullivan nodded an affirmation and headed to a booth across from the bar where Larry was sitting, then ordered a club sandwich and iced tea. While he waited for his food, and then between bites, he made notes in his notebook to remind himself what his goals for the rest of the day were. Included on his list was to admonish his players to be careful: don't drink, don't smoke weed, stay humble and keep in mind only bad things happen after midnight. He knew that they would listen, even if they didn't comply religiously to the letter of the law. There's much more to survival than being tough. Next on his list was to find Lilian, and after that, to find Janel's car. He hoped that Crowe and Lodi were already well on their way to taking care of those matters. The last thing on his list was to go past the Mountain Bell office downtown and pick up Eleanora, then take her to headquarters to give a statement to Lopez and Mathis.

Luther was playing catch with Eddie Duran, the teams number one catcher when Sullivan arrived at the South High practice field. Luther was on the bullpen mound going through his pre-game-day warmup routine. Sullivan had a quiet conversation with him while he threw to Duran. He wanted to know how Luther was feeling, if he had thought anymore about signing a pro contract, and if he had heard anything about Janel's murder. Luther told Sullivan that he wanted to pitch Wednesday's game, because it would be his last as an amateur. He had called the Expos scout Fergie Malone and told him that he wanted to sign the contract Thursday morning at his house before his mom went to work. He wanted Sullivan there and his grandparents as well.

"Do you know for sure what the signing bonus will be?"

Luther responded that it would be $72,000 and that he would be assigned to their rookie team at Bradenton, Florida, in the Gulf Coast League.

"Oh, that is fantastic!" was Sullivan's response, "You have to be thrilled."

"I am. And so is my mom. She can't stop crying she's so happy for me, and she says she's going to use some vacation days to watch me when I'm scheduled to pitch for the first time."

"That is great news, Luther, I am really proud of you." Sullivan then stopped the other players warming up and gave them the good news. Everyone of them gathered around Luther to congratulate him. When the team resumed warming up, Luther informed Sullivan that he had heard nothing new about what happened to Janel or her car. Neither had he heard anything from Lilian Martinez. It was apparent that talking about Janel made him mournful, and he stopped throwing for a minute while he put his head down and rotated his arms and shoulders, stretching them. Then he regained his composure and resumed throwing. He focused solely on the catcher and he was throwing hard. Then, after five minutes or so, he signaled to Eddie Duran that he had had enough.

After a quick ninety-minute practice, and after he addressed the boys, making the points he had planned, thinking of their safety, Sullivan got his gear packed up and headed to the office. Getting his mind off of Luther Pride's big contract was difficult. This was good news for a community that had been hit hard by a downward trend in the economy, street-level drug dealing and an attendant rise in crime, most notably *violent* crime.

He arrived at 14th and Champa, and Eleanora was waiting for him by the side door. "Oh, I love this truck, Frank. It's so you. It reminds me of when we were kids and you picked me up in that '58 Chevy truck that you had. Mmm was that sweet."

"This isn't half the truck that was but I do like it too. I bet you never thought we'd be having a 'date' like this, did you?"

"I never thought we'd have any kind of 'date' again. What a waste too; we were perfect for each other, still are, I think. But I'm good with my life." She then batted her eyes and looked at Sullivan, saying in her faux sexy voice, "Most men can't take their eyes off me, Sergeant."

"I get that Eleanora. I know how they feel." Sullivan then laughed a little and drove in silence for a few minutes. Then asked her, "Are you ready to give them a statement?"

"Oh yeah, I'm not worried about it at all. Will they bring me back to work when we are done?"

"They will," replied Sullivan and, "I'll call you when you get home and we can talk about it. He added, "Thanks, Eleanora," as he left her at the Information Desk in the lobby to be escorted to Homicide Bureau.

The entire team was present in the Vice and Narcotics Bureau when Sullivan got there. The four of them gathered in his office to discuss their agenda for the night. As previously discussed with the sergeant, Messenger mentioned that he had typed a search warrant for a place at 30th and Gilpin and wanted to execute it tonight. Lodi and Crowe were aware of it too of course, but their standard procedure was to discuss everything planned for the night, as a team, so that everybody was on the same page.

Because of the department policy regarding high-risk search warrants, Messenger considered it best that Metro/Swat do the entry, in accordance with that policy. It was agreed that he would call Metro and see if they could help with the entry at around nine o'clock. When the meeting broke up, he and Crowe would go look at the address and see what the activity level was.

Lodi informed Sullivan that he and Crowe had found a possible home address for Lilian Martinez. Lodi suggested that he and Sullivan run by the location and see if they could find her. The address that Lodi had was around 38th and High Street. When they were close, they called a uniform car, explained what they were doing and asked that they watch the back door while Sullivan and Lodi approached the house from the front.

The front door was answered by a late thirties female dressed like she was about to go out for the night. Sullivan and Lodi identified themselves, and the woman introduced herself as Sofia Martinez.

"Is Lilian your daughter?" asked Sullivan.

"Yes, she is, why do you ask?"

"Is she here?" asked Sullivan.

"No, she is not. I haven't seen her all day. I was gone last night and when I got here today she wasn't here. I don't really know where she is."

"Where were you last night," Sullivan continued, "if you don't mind my asking?"

"I do resent your asking." Then after a pause and an irritated look, she continued, "I went to Blackhawk with a friend and we had too much to drink, well, *he* did anyway and he was driving, so we spent the night up there at the casino. Why are you asking me, has something happened?"

"Well, we are looking for Lilian; we'd like to ask her a few questions about a friend of hers. We are concerned about her. Have you talked to her today?" Sullivan looked past the silhouette of Sofia Martinez in the doorway as he said this. He saw a shadow move in the hall behind her and he gently pushed next to her into the house, while asking her who else was in the house.

"That is my mom; she lives here with us. Mom, come out here for a minute, the police are here asking about Lilian." As the woman came forward into the living room, Sofia Martinez introduced her as Ana Lujan, her mother.

"*Mucho gusto*, Señora Lujan,¨ responded Sullivan, after hearing Sofia explain to her mother in Spanish why the police were there.

"No, I have not talked to her today and when I got home my mother told me that she had not seen her since last night. That was around noon when I got home and she still has not been here. Since she finished high school, she has been staying away from home a lot. Who is the friend that you want to ask her about?"

"Janel Robinson." Sullivan did not elaborate.

"That's who she has been hangin' out with lately, staying at her house sometimes I guess. I've only seen her a couple of times but she seems all right. I mean, she wants to go to Metro in the fall, but I don't really know her. And Lilian is ready to be on her own, and I hope she goes to Metro too," Sofia explained, referring to Metropolitan State College.

"Well," Sullivan began, "Janel was shot and killed last night at the edge of Fuller Park. Witnesses say that Lilian was with her and she has not been seen since."

"Oh my God, where is she? Did she see it happen? Was she right there?"

"She was right in the middle of it and was last seen leaving the park," was Sullivan's response. Sofia seemed to be processing the unsettling news with her eyes closed and her left hand covering her mouth.

Lodi then interjected a pair of questions for Sofia. "What other friends does she hang out with? Did she and Janel have other common friends?"

Sofia Martinez waited before responding. "Yes, she did, and I know that they had been flirting with some of the Jamaicans that hang around the park. Lilian told me that. She likes their music and the way they talk. She says that they are cool in a way that the boys at school are not. I don't know any names though. I mean, she mentioned some of them but I don't remember what they were."

"Sofia, does Lilian have a car or did she and Janel usually go places in Janel's car?"

"No, Sergeant, she does not have a car. She doesn't have a license but she does know how to drive. I just don't have money for a car and insurance and all that. I was planning to help her to get her license now that she is out of school. She use to walk to school and she takes the bus most other places."

Sullivan and Lodi looked at each other. "Is there anything else?" seemed to be the mutually unspoken question. Sullivan then emphasized that there was no indication that Lilian was hurt or in danger—other than that which goes along with being a witness to a homicide. Then he added that they were looking for her as a witness to the shooting and the surrounding events. He thought that Sofia seemed nervous—maybe she was on her way out and was expecting someone to pick her up. She probably didn't want the cops in her house when that person showed up.

After giving Sofia Martinez their cards and asking her to call them as soon as Lilian returned home, Lodi and Sullivan turned to leave.

"I will, and I want you to call me if you learn anything more." Sofia then wrote down her number on the back of an empty envelope and handed it to Sullivan.

"She's dead," blurted out Lodi as they stood alone by his vehicle.

"Not so fast," replied Sullivan. "She might be in on it in some way, and laying low now—maybe even in that house on Franklin."

"No, I'll bet you ten bucks they knew she was friends with Janel, they took her somewhere, had sex till they were done with her and then killed her," was Lodi's response to that.

"So you think she was a witness and they killed her to keep her mouth shut?"

Just then Zebra 21 (Messenger) was calling for Sullivan on the radio.

"Go ahead, Leon," was Sullivan's response on the secure undercover channel.

"Yeah, Sarge, this thing is looking good, man. I called Metro/Swat and they will meet us in our office at nine o'clock for a briefing."

"Good deal, Leon, we'll see you down there in a little while. Lodi is standing here with me so he knows too."

"Right on."

7

WHEN SULLIVAN AND LODI ARRIVED at their office, some of the Metro Swat guys were already starting to gather there for the briefing. Sullivan and the other three dark narcs met in his office to quickly go over the case. Then Sullivan briefed the Metro officers on the facts of the investigation, followed by the Metro sergeant who detailed their entry plan.

The target was a suspected Jamaican drug dealer; he was known to be armed; and he was dealing cocaine in powder form, not crack, as was the *modus operandi* for these Jamaicans. He had not been identified positively, but it was thought that his first name was Radcliffe, or maybe that was his last name. Detective Messenger had been in the house and he had seen a shotgun. Because of the weapons information, and the fact that the evidence could be easily destroyed, the on-call judge had signed the Immediate Entry provision on the search warrant.

As planned during the briefing, three of the dark narcs covered the back of the house as Metro entered the front door courtesy of two officers wielding a battering ram. An unknown male was encountered, reaching for the shotgun in the corner of the room. He recognized that it was a police raid and that he was hopelessly outgunned, so he dropped the weapon, following the commands of the first officers to enter the house.

Another unknown male ran through the house and barreled out the back door into the gunpoint reception of Lodi and Crowe, with Sullivan on the opposite side to create a funnel of fire if necessary. He was searched and a Glock 9mm pistol was taken from him as were several hundred dollars. He had not had time to go for the gun in his waistband, as he was quickly subdued and handcuffed. Part of the plan was for Detective Messenger to remain out of sight until any prisoners were taken away from the house. This was because of his undercover potential in these Jamaican cases.

Once the house had been secured, it was systematically searched by the narcotics officers. A uniform car had been called to transport the two prisoners to headquarters. After the prisoners were out of the house, Messenger made his way into the house through the darkened backyard, wearing a black, hooded sweatshirt. The search yielded a few ounces of cocaine, a Remington 870 shotgun and about $2,500. At headquarters it was learned that the man arrested inside the house was Radcliffe Edison, age 33. He would be charged with Possession of a Controlled Substance and Sale of a Controlled Substance based on the undercover-buys made by Detective Messenger. Outside the residence, Robert Grant, age 30, was arrested for possession of the 9mm automatic and was charged with CCW (Carrying a Concealed Weapon), a city ordinance violation.

The suspects were advised of their rights at headquarters by Lodi and Crowe. Edison didn't appear to be in the country legally and would be held for INS (Immigration and Naturalization Service) to determine his immigration status.

Radcliffe Edison, who was also known as Edison Radcliffe, was polite and almost friendly, while disavowing any knowledge of the gun, money or cocaine found in the house. He said he did not live there but said he was living with a friend whose address he did not know. He, however, was the same person who had sold a gram of cocaine to Detective Messenger on two occasions and, as a consequence, he would be charged with the sale of a controlled substance, two counts. He did not see Messenger at the time of his arrest, nor at headquarters, so he was unaware that he had sold to a cop. Allowing Edison to know Messenger's identity would be delayed as long as possible. For that reason, Detective Crowe would file the case as the investigating detective and would attend the preliminary hearing as the case officer. It was likely that a plea bargain would be arranged and that Edison would never know of Messenger's identity as a cop. Therefore, Messenger's valuable role in investigating the Jamaican cases could continue.

Robert Grant, arrested at the rear of the house, was not a Jamaican; Robert Grant was not his real name. His real name was Lorenzo Walters, and Detective Lodi took the time to interview him. Although he was only arrested for CCW, he was a convicted felon, and the charge of "Weapon by a Previous Offender," for which he might land in county jail, could also be filed. He was currently on parole for Aggravated Robbery and a parole violation could send him back to prison. For these reasons, especially the last one, Lorenzo Walters was anxious to tell Lodi what he knew about Jamaican drug traffickers.

Detective Lodi had been raised in Missouri, spoke with a middle-America tone and had a "common man" attraction when he wished to let it show. Lorenzo Walters had not previously known Lodi but, realizing he was in a fix and that he needed to get out from under the pending charges, Lodi appealed to him as trustworthy. In his mind, he stressed the fact that he was giving up information on armed Jamaican drug dealers, not African-Americans. It was an important distinction to him. He was in touch with what was happening on the street and knew of the animosity that existed between Jamaicans and American Blacks, due in no small part to the air of superiority that the Jamaicans flaunted.

Lodi began his interview with a formal Miranda advisement that he and Walters both signed and dated. Lodi wanted Walters to tell him about the Jamaican drug dealers at 28th and Franklin and those involved in the murder of Janel Robinson.

"Look, man, I know how this works." was Walters' lead in, then he continued, "What do you want to know?"

"Well, what I want is something that will lead me to the big Jamaican here in Denver and then a case against him. We have a case against you, and it's cut and dried, but if you give us something good, I'm sure the D.A. will drop the case against you and we will talk to your parole officer and get that aspect of it worked out." Then Lodi looked him straight in the eyes and asked, "So what is it, Lorenzo, how are we gonna' make this work?"

"Ah, man, well, I don't know all the Jamaicans that are dealing, and they come and go. You know they bring the shit in from Miami a kilo at a time and then sell it off by the gram. They maximize the risk by doing it that way but, man, they be making money like a mutha'.

"They ain't really all working together, but they all know each other, you know, and they keep their distance from us local Blacks. They don't trust us and we don't trust them, but for some reason I have been able to get in a little bit. I know two places where I can go right now and buy a gram of cocaine, no problem. I mean, you know, I don't want to be no witness or nothin', but I can make a buy for you if that's what you want."

"Okay, that's a start, where are those places?"

"Well, there's one over at 16th and Lafayette. I don't know the exact address but it's the apartment building on the corner, The Lafayette Arms it's called. Apartment number 2 on the first floor. Then the other one is the one at 28th and Franklin, second door from the corner, across the street from the park.

Now those two, I have seen some of the same people at both of those places and I have been to both of them a few times, See, I can't get no fuckin' job so I've been buying cocaine from these places for other people who are scared to go there themselves. They know I carry a gun and can take care of myself.

"But don't get the wrong idea, I wanna' change my ways and get my shit together. I'm workin' on gettin' my GED and I'm almost ready to take the test again. In the meantime, I have been applying for janitorial jobs and such and have the forms signed, so that I can show them to my parole officer. I don't wanna' go back to prison. I might have something pending at St. Luke's/Presbyterian on the night shift, janitor work, but hey, it's something anyway and I have done that kind of work."

"Well, I get what you're saying. If you can help me get into these two places then you can move on. Can you give me any names?"

"McConnell, is what they call the guy on Lafayette. The big cat on Franklin, is called 'Big', 'Big Ten', 'Tenny', 'Mr. Big'. They don't seem to call each other by regular names too much—it's mostly nicknames."

"By they, you mean the Jamaicans, right?"

"Uh huh."

Detective Lodi was reluctant to ask leading questions of Walters that would let him know how much he already knew, and he didn't want to ask him directly about last night's shooting in the park. He made a few notes, but what he was really doing, was taking a minute to see if Walters would volunteer information.

And it worked.

"Hey, you guys heard about that shooting last night? The one in Fuller Park? I'm sure you did."

"Yeah, we did, the homicide guys got a hold of us to see if it was drug related, or what we might know."

"Oh hell yeah, man, it was all about drugs. From…"

"Wait a minute, were you there? Or how do you know?"

"No, I mean, I wasn't there, but I went to the house on Franklin late last night and talked to the little guy there, and he told me that several Jamaicans were there and a fight broke out and some American girl was shot. He made it sound like there was an argument and it just happened. Not like they were trying to kill her."

"What do they call the little guy?"

"They call him 'Pea' or 'Peahead' or some shit like that."

"Did he act like he knew who the girl was?" And then Lodi added, "Did he say what she was doing there?"

"All he said was that she and another girl were partying with the Jamaicans. He said she was some young girl that'd met some of the Jamaicans on the streets and in the park and stuff." Then Walters continued, "Who was she anyway? He didn't tell me her name and I haven't heard yet?"

"Her name is, well was, Janel Robinson. She just graduated from Manual High School and was not the drug type. In fact she was a good softball player and a pretty good student. The other girl with her is named Lilian Martinez and we still don't know what happened to her."

"Oh, okay, well I don't know her. But I mean, these dudes are cold-blooded and hateful. Nothin' surprises me."

Lodi responded, while scratching his beard, "That's the way it seems. So if you want to work this off, here's the way it's going to be. You give me enough information to make three drug cases on these Jamaicans and your case will go away. Like I say, I'm sure the D.A. will be okay with that. Now, if you can give us the shooter and others involved in the shooting, then that might be enough right there to make this go away.

"The thing is, you have to do this my way and I'll go over all that with you. You have to stay in touch with me, page me every night, until we get this done. It's either that or your parole gets violated and you go back to prison. Agreed?"

"I got no problem with that."

Lodi and the newly acquired confidential informant then went through the documentation process required by departmental procedure and discussed how and when they were going to proceed. Lorenzo Walters was released, agreeing to get ahold of Lodi on Wednesday afternoon.

8

AFTER EDISON RADCLIFFE HAD BEEN booked in the city jail, next door to police headquarters, and after the evidence had been logged into the Property Bureau, George Crowe renewed his computer search for Janel Robinson's car. Finding nothing current on the computer, he called the city impound lot just on the chance that it was there. It was. It had been towed from around Eighth Avenue and Kalamath Street in the early morning hours on Tuesday. It had been involved in a hit and run accident a few blocks away and the driver abandoned the car, in traffic, where part of Eighth Avenue merges into southbound Kalamath.

George Crowe called Detective Mathis in Homicide to report his findings and she asked that he look into it for her. Then he called the Accident Investigations Bureau and got the details of the hit and run. They expressed no interest in doing a search warrant on the car. As a result, Detective Crowe took the information and typed a search warrant for the vehicle, adding to that information the fact that the vehicle belonged to a homicide victim and was taken from the scene by unknowns, possibly the killer(s). He called the on-call assistant D.A. and they approved the affidavit. He then called the on-call judge for permission to bring the warrant to be signed, explaining why the warrant needed to be executed immediately.

The on-call judge that week happened to be a World War II veteran who had been a B-17 pilot, a recipient of the Purple Heart and the Distinguished Flying Cross. He was a fair and well-respected judge who had spent time as a prosecutor in the sixties, then a County Court judge, before being appointed as a District Court judge. He signed the search warrant after reading Crowe's affidavit and wished the detective good luck with his case.

Crowe was on his way to the pound when Detective Messenger called him on the radio. "Hey, man, I'm starving, man. Why don't you pick me up on the way and we can go to Popeye's before they close. I need something to eat."

"All right Leon, I'll meet you on B-1 (first parking level at Police Headquarters) in about five minutes and after Popeye's you can go with me to the car pound and we'll do this search warrant."

"Thank you, my brotha,'" was Messenger's heartfelt response. Being a big man, he didn't go too long without refueling and had no aversion to fast food or any other kind of food unless it was overly spicy. "I'll even buy yours," he added.

The search of Janel's Datsun at the car pound was undertaken only after the crime lab technicians had processed it for fingerprints, hair samples, blood samples, etc. They were not thrilled to be called out to the pound in the middle of the night to do what they thought could wait until the next day. But they did it.

The back hatch of the station wagon had been damaged in the accident and had been wired shut before it was towed to the pound. Apparently, the driver of Janel's vehicle had run a red light and had been partially broadsided by a van. There were blood stains and drips in the back of the station wagon and whether they were there before the accident, or resulted from an injury caused by the accident, was unknown. Also found in the back of the vehicle was a braided silver bracelet, the type of piece often associated with Native American jewelry. It was a small bracelet, more than likely belonging to a woman. That and registration paperwork and personal items possibly belonging to Janel Robinson were inventoried and placed in the Property Bureau as evidence.

Crowe called the homicide detectives to inform them what the processing of the car had revealed. They asked that Crowe have the car put in a secure cage when they were finished processing and searching it, and they would follow up if necessary.

Back at headquarters, Sgt. Sullivan had written the search warrant report. It served as an after action report, and one had to be made, by the supervisor, after a search warrant was executed. A copy had to be forwarded to the Chief of Detectives Office and a copy sent to the Civil Liabilities Bureau.

After finishing it, he took a copy to the homicide detectives for their information. He then spoke with Mathis and Lopez regarding Eleanora Mathews' statement. They informed him that it went well and that they took her back to work when they had finished. It was exactly the same as what she had told Sullivan last night. As Sullivan started to leave their office, Mathis walked out and started down the hall with him, stopping about half way down and touching Sullivan on the arm.

"I noticed that Eleanora is crazy about you, is there anything between you two that would hurt our case if she were a witness. It's not my intention to pry but you know what I mean. You know what these defense lawyers will do if they can find a potential conflict of interest, especially a juicy one like a prosecution witness and a police sergeant."

"Hey, I appreciate your bringing that up," was Sullivan's response. And then, "We are friends since high school, we dated in high school and I know her parents. I've seldom seen her since we were kids and it is a coincidence that she was a witness in this case, and that I was on the scene to see her there. If I had not been there, she still would have made herself known to you as a witness. There isn't any dirt here, but truth be told, I'm crazy about her too. Nothing to worry about. And as you can see, she can handle herself verbally and will not be easy prey."

Lola Mathis studied Sullivan as he talked. She had seen him around and had heard stories about him but she had never worked a case with him. She knew that he had been offered more prestigious positions, like Homicide, but had turned them down to stay in Narcotics, "runnin' the streets." She found herself really enthused that he and his team were helping them on this case. "Okay, that's all I wanted to hear. Thanks, Sarge."

"No problem, Lola, I'll see you later."

Sgt. Sullivan was about to leave his office and head home at about two-thirty a.m. on Wednesday morning. He had written the nightly letter, emphasizing the search warrant results—money, drugs, guns and two arrests, and mentioned further work on the homicide investigation. He commended Detective Messenger. Then his office phone rang.

"Hey Sullivan, this is Lieutenant Gallegos in the radio room (Police Communications Center). Take it for what it's worth, but we just received a call from an unknown male threatening to kill you and one of the detectives on your team. We pulled the call and transcribed it for you, if you want to come and pick it up. I know you guys have been kicking ass and taking names lately and you never know—they could be serious."

"Thanks, Lieutenant, I'll be right up there to pick it up. Maybe we could listen to it together. Also, you probably already did this, but we'll need a statement from the clerk who took the call."

"I'm all over it; she's writing it as we speak and one of the dispatch officers is writing a Threats Offense Report. I'll sign it and send it through."

"Okay, I'll see you in a minute, Lieutenant."

Sullivan paused a minute, wondering who it was who called. Veiled and implicit threats were part of the job. But this was the first time he remembered that somebody made it formal, and officially recorded, by calling the police dispatcher. He and his team had made some enemies but he could not think of anyone likely to call in a threat, knowing it would be recorded.

Sullivan then made his way to the radio room on the fifth floor and met with Lieutenant Gallegos in his office.

"Hey, Frank, how's it going? Here's a copy of the Threats report and a statement from the civilian agent who answered the phone."

"Thanks, L-T. What did she say about the caller?"

"Well, as you'll see in the report, it was a deep-voiced male with a foreign accent, possibly Caribbean, clear accented English, but not American English. He named you by name and Crowe, is it?"

"Yeah, George Crowe, good man. He's worked with me for a while. No other names mentioned?"

"No, just you two by name. You'll see when you read the transcript, he's threatening you guys for 'arresting our people.'"

"Okay, that probably is a Jamaican then. Any caller ID or anything?"

"Unfortunately not."

Sullivan and the lieutenant chatted a while longer and then he thanked him and headed back to his office. He added a couple of quick lines to his nightly activity letter and forwarded copies of the reports pertaining to the threats through the chain of command.

9

ON WEDNESDAY AFTERNOON, SULLIVAN GOT his Elite Eighteen (eighteen years and older) baseball team ready for their baseball game at All-City Stadium near South High School in Denver. They were playing a team from Boulder that had several All-State high school players recently graduated. But the only player who had been drafted, let alone drafted as high as the second round of the baseball amateur draft, was on Sullivan's team—Luther Pride. He was going to pitch his last game as an amateur and sign a professional contract the next day. The Expos' scout who was responsible for getting him signed wanted him to skip his last amateur game. But Luther and Frank Sullivan were too close, and Luther wanted to play one more game with his teammates, most of whom were truly elite players themselves, and Luther had become close with nearly all of them.

Luther's mom, Gina Pride, was there with her mom and dad. Luther's dad had been killed in Viet Nam when Gina was carrying Luther. She had never remarried and her parents had been a big part of Luther's upbringing; they had been a strong, positive influence in his life. They lived close to Luther, and his mom and he ate dinner with his grandparents at least twice a week.

Gina was a strong woman, a registered nurse, and a sharp-witted, assertive person. Over the two plus years that Sullivan had coached Luther, he and Gina had become good friends. The three of them had gone out to breakfast or dinner many times, especially on weekend road trips.

"Hey Frank, are you able to make it to our house tomorrow morning for the signing?" Gina asked this from the fence while Sullivan stood and watched Luther finish warming up in the bullpen.

"I would not miss it for anything. Not only that, I would really like to go see him the first time he pitches in A ball. I'm pretty sure I can't get any time off right now, but you should go down there to Bradenton, if at all possible."

"Oh I'm way ahead of you, Frank; my dad wants to go too if he can. I can't believe the ball player you have turned him into. And that bonus! Did Luther tell you about that?"

"Oh yeah, he sure did. The thing is, it's you and your parents who have made Luther what he is today. He's a terrific young man who is blessed with extraordinary athletic ability, but you guys raised him right. I have just been blessed to have coached him for two or three years."

Just then their conversation was interrupted.

"My goodness, Sarge, who is this gorgeous sista' you are talking to?" Detective Messenger followed this up with a hearty laugh and a "oh man."

"C'mon, Leon, this distinguished woman is Luther Pride's mother and she's very careful about who she is seen with." Sullivan then came close to the fence separating the playing field from the spectators and reached up over the fence to give Leon an easy high-five.

"Thanks for coming out, Leon, let me introduce you to Gina Pride." Then looking to her, he said, "Gina, this is Detective Leon Messenger one of my long-time friends on the job and one of the guys I work with now. Definitely one of the good guys. I'm surprised you two have never met."

"Pleased to meet you, Leon, I have heard Frank talk about you many times. All good."

"Ah man, I hope so, he's my main man."

"Hey, Leon, watch this kid throw a little bit even if you can't stay too long. He's really good. Think Bob Gibson." Then he added, "I have to get ready to coach and do my thing so I'm going to leave you two but, Gina, introduce him to your mom and dad. He'll get a kick out of them and their old school ways."

Sullivan then put on his coaches hat for the next two hours and took care of business. Luther pitched three perfect innings, striking out four. Sullivan took him out of the game, and players and fans and coaches of both teams gave him an ovation and handshakes and high fives.

When the game ended and before going to work, Sullivan confirmed that he would be at Luther's house at ten o'clock in the morning for the ceremonial signing of Luther's professional baseball contract. As he drove to headquarters to get back to his "real" job, Frank Sullivan put his mind into "official" gear and started thinking about what needed to be done tonight.

Coaching youth baseball gave him some separation from the confrontational reality of aggressive police work. It was his job and that of his team to take action and to get results. Entering into it also, were complex socio-economic and racial issues that were none of their making. It was his responsibility to see that the mission was transparent and that no hidden agendas were fostered. They were an action unit, responsive to citizen complaints, and performance evaluation was based on results. There was immense pressure, because of the underlying issues, to do everything by the book. They were doing an unheard of number of search warrants requiring scrutiny of intelligence information to ensure accuracy, carefully written affidavits detailing probable cause to support the warrants, flawless execution of the warrants so that no mistakes of location or identity were made, and diligent preparation and presentation of the case in court. Close wasn't good enough. Getting the address wrong was unacceptable. The number of weapons being recovered on these warrants was unheard of and his team had a flawless record—no officers shot, no suspects or innocent bystanders shot. It wasn't like baseball where an error, once in a while, could be tolerated. Every night had to be errorless. And tonight was just another night.

The other three team members were already at the office when Sullivan arrived, as was the lieutenant, who worked days but would often wait around for the dark narcs to come in so he could pat them on the back, offer moral support and pass on any department news or changes affecting them. His name was Hugo Connors, about 6'5" tall and strongly built. He had been a narcotics detective, and a good one, and was a good lieutenant. He let his troops know how much he appreciated the work they were doing and that they were doing it at night, when it was most needed and most dangerous.

On this night, Connors wanted to talk to Sgt. Sullivan and the rest of the team about the threats report that had been made the night before. As he explained, only the sergeant and George Crowe were mentioned by name, but the department was taking it as a threat against the "dark narcs" because of their work against Jamaican drug dealers specifically. His main point in addressing the group was to remind them to be especially cautious and to look out for each other, even more than usual. His presence, at their informal roll call, let them know, as their friend and their commander, that he was not taking the threat lightly by any means, and that he was concerned for all of them.

After the lieutenant had his say, he stood around while the team had their nightly planning meeting in the sergeants' office. George Crowe reported on what had been found in Janel's car from the search of it at the pound. Lodi reported that he had talked to Sofia Martinez and that she had still not heard from Lilian and that she was now worried. Lodi shook his head and muttered to himself after saying this, and then out loud he said, "Can you imagine that her daughter was hanging out in the park with drug dealers, "flirting" with them and only just now after two days missing she is worried? I mean what the fuck?!!"

"Yeah, man, she has to know more than she is letting on," was Leon's two cents worth.

"Way more," was Crowe's contribution. "but the thing is," he added, "what is she not telling us? If we could get her to open up and talk to us, we might be surprised what we'd find out. She might know where Lilian is and who she's with. I bet she's shacking up with one of those nasty fuckers. Lodi, if you want, I'll go with you to talk to her, and maybe together we can convince her to be more open with us."

Sullivan then chimed in, "That's a good idea if you two can do that. And you know something, we really don't know much about these guys. Where do they hang out? What clubs do they frequent? Are there Jamaican restaurants that they go to? Let's start putting that kind of information together. We really don't know anything about them except where they are dealing. Let's keep our eyes and ears open and see what we can learn. Find the legitimate Jamaican community here in Denver. Maybe it's not in Denver, maybe it's in Glendale or Aurora.

"Leon, what would you think of trying to work on this and maybe going into their restaurants or clubs—undercover? It's possible you can develop sources in those places as well. I mean, we are always so busy it's hard to make this a priority, but I think we should do what we can."

"Right on, Sarge, I'm all in man, I think it's a great idea. I'll look into it and see what I can find out about their whole scene."

"All right, you other guys, talk to your informants and I'll talk to people I know as well, as far as Jamaican clubs and restaurants go. What else for tonight?"

"If we could, I'd like to have Coolo go with Leon one more time and try and get into the place at 2811½ Franklin. This time we can wire Leon. What do you think, Leon?" That was Lodi's input.

"Hell yeah, brotha', let's do it, man. What time do you want to do it?"

"Let me see if I can get ahold of Coolo, but probably about ten-thirty or so."

"Right on," was Leon Messenger's response. Then he added, "I'm gonna' work on some paperwork from last night's case in the meantime. Lemme' know, man."

"I will, I'll call him now and try to set it up, but then George and I will run out there and talk to Sofia Martinez."

Sullivan then, by way of concluding the meeting, added, "Okay, let's do it!"

Hugo Connors, who was still in the meeting, listening and observing, commended everybody for their effort and again reminded all to be safe. Then he patted Sullivan on the shoulder and headed home.

Lodi went to his desk and dialed the number he had for Coolo and was waiting for an answer when homicide detectives Mathis and Lopez walked into the Vice and Narcotics Bureau and approached Lodi at his desk. Lodi hung up the phone and acknowledged their presence.

"Hey, guys, what's going on, got another homicide you need some help on?" Lodi asked them jokingly.

"Well, have you solved the other one for us yet?" asked Detective Mathis.

"No, but we'll probably have it solved tonight," responded Lodi, in the same half-kidding tone Mathis had used for her question.

"Well, please hurry up because now we need help on another one." She was now turning serious and added, "We got a call from District 2 officers on a DOA (dead on arrival) at 16th and Lafayette. They had been called by an anonymous caller who stated to the 911 operator, 'There's a dead *mon* in apartment 2, or words to that effect. When they got there they found a bloody mess in apartment 2. Looks like a Black male in his twenties shot in the head. He'd been dead a day or two at least; we'll know for sure when we get the coroner's report. Had an ID in his wallet saying he was Darnell Coolidge."

"Holy shit, I was just trying to call him. He's been working for me on these Jamaican dealers. I was starting to wonder what happened to him, because he was supposed to call me yesterday and I haven't heard from him. He took Leon to the Jamaicans at 2811½ Franklin and was going to take him back, tonight maybe, and get him introduced so he could buy directly from them. Son of a bitch, I can't believe this."

"He had your name written on the back of a twin quinella ticket from Mile High Kennel Club from a while back. It had a bunch of numbers under your name; it's probably your phone number in disguise." Detective Mathis pulled out her notebook and read off about fifteen numbers. As she and Lodi looked at the numbers together, Lodi discovered that his phone number was indeed hidden sequentially, with a number in between each correct number.

"So was your informant staying at that address or what? There was no furniture in the place, no paperwork, nothing at all. Nothing in the fridge, no toilet paper in the bathroom. It was a dirty mess, like somebody had been living there but they were careful not to leave anything." Mathis looked directly at Lodi and Messenger standing next to his desk before adding, "Somebody executed him Lodi, shot him right in the forehead—twice—point blank almost. It was a horrible mess, powder burns around the wounds, blood on the walls, blood all over the floor; nobody should die like that. Bullets exited and went into the wall."

By this time, the whole team, including Sullivan, was gathered around Lodi's desk picking up the gist of the conversation.

"You know what this might mean, Leon?" Lodi asked rhetorically. Then followed up, "If they made him as an informant, it may be that it's because he took you there and they have you made as a cop. No way you're going back in there, huh-uh. We need to figure out something else."

"Man, that's awful news. It makes me sick to think about. But it shows you how bad these dudes are. I liked the little guy too; he was cool, he was trying to get his life together, I think." Leon shook his head slowly when he finished what he was saying.

"Well, that guy from last night's warrant was telling me about that place—Lafayette Arms Apartments, an ornate old building. I drove by there when we finished last night and it looked pretty quiet then. That guy's supposed to call me in a little while so I'll see what he has to say. Maybe he's already heard something about it. I won't be surprised if he knows something, or at least knows that it happened.

"What I want to do, and I'm sure the homicide guys agree with me, is find out who did these killings and what's behind them. Janel Robinson and my man Coolo, were they killed because they were believed to be snitches or what?" Lodi was obviously rattled by the news.

"That's why we're here talking to you guys—these hits are drug related and we need all the help you guys can give us. So whatever comes up, let us know, and the sooner the better; maybe that there's more murders to come. That reminds me, any more on Lilian Martinez, has she been located, or is she another victim yet to be discovered?" Detective Mathis appeared to shudder as she said that, and then she hung her head.

Lodi spoke up again, "Well, George and I are going to go out there right now and talk to her mother to see if she won't open up more about Lilian and her relationship to the Jamaicans. I just have the feeling that she knows a helluva lot more, and grandma might know something, so maybe we should talk to her too. If she has something good to say, maybe I'll call you, Al, and you can interview her on the phone in Spanish."

"That'd be okay, I'll be in the office working on this paper-work so just call me and, if need be, I'll go out there and talk to her in person."

With that, Mathis and Lopez started making their way back to their office.

Lodi and Crowe grabbed their gear and headed out to interview Sofia Martinez. Leon Messenger went back to the typewriter to work on the case from last night. Sgt. Sullivan went into his office and called Luther Pride to check on him.

10

SULLIVAN WAS RELIEVED TO HEAR Luther's voice when the phone was answered.

"How's it going, Luther?"

"Hey coach, I'm doing fine. I am packing some of my things because I'm supposed to leave here and be in Bradenton on Saturday. My mom and I went shopping this morning to get some new clothes and stuff that I'm gonna need. Then tomorrow after the signing, we have to go to the bank and take care of a few things. You know, I've never had a checking account before."

"Sounds good. Hey, one of the reasons I was calling was to find out if I should bring some food tomorrow."

"I think mom has it covered, between her and my grandma they'll have some good stuff I'm sure, but I'll ask her when she gets home at eleven-thirty and tell her to call you if she needs something. She's even more excited about this than I am."

"Heck yeah, but she is going to miss you like crazy when you are gone. She's gonna need some time to get used to it, but she'll be fine and so will you."

"Yeah, I know she will, and I can't wait to get started. I can't believe it! I'll be a pro ball player in the morning. First real job I've ever had."

"*Real* job, huh," Sullivan blurted out, and then after a chuckle, before ending the conversation, added, "Okay then, my boy, have her call me if she needs something. Otherwise, I'm just going to pick up some flowers for her in the morning."

69

"All right, Coach, that'll be cool, I'll see you tomorrow then. Be careful, okay? There's some crazy shit, I mean stuff, going on out there."

"Got it, see you in the morning."

His phone rang almost immediately after hanging it up. It was Eleanora Mathews.

"Hey, Frank, how are you tonight? Are you guys busy?"

"Hello, Ellie," he said, realizing he had used the nickname he called her in high school. "Yeah, we're busy again. There was another homicide, looks like it was Jamaicans that did it. A place down on 16th and Lafayette. You probably know the building, Lafayette Arms, an old, almost Victorian-looking building."

"Who was killed, do you know?"

"Yeah, it was somebody who had business with them, somebody we knew from previous dealings. And it was brutal—almost like an assassination. Homicide is trying to put it together with the one the other night and we're doing what we can to help them. We have to put some stuff on hold while we fit everything together. But hey, it goes with this job."

"Hmmm, well, I was wondering if you wanted to come by here when you get off work. I'll make you something to eat."

"I don't think tonight is a good night for me. I have to get up early and be at Luther Pride's house at ten o'clock. He's signing his pro contract and they want me to be there. Well, *I* want to be there. I love the kid and he's the best ball player I've ever been around, let alone coached. Plus he's like a breath of fresh air to me. And I'm not even sure when we're going to be done tonight. We have some stuff going on.

"But I have to admit, the idea of seeing you tonight appeals to me. I know what a good cook you are," Sullivan laughed as he said this.

"Yeah, I'm sure that's all you're thinking about Frank—my Italian cooking."

"I'm thinking about a lot of things, to be truthful. But the predominant thought is how good it was to see you the last couple of days, and to get a chance to renew our friendship, or our relationship, or whatever you call it."

"Yeah, I feel the same way, Frank. Why don't you call me tomorrow night and maybe we can get together after you're finished working if you want to."

Okay, Ellie, that sounds good, I'll call you tomorrow. Have a good night."

Sullivan hung up the phone and wondered what the hell he was doing. He was not in a relationship and did not particularly want to be in one. Didn't have the time to put into it. But yet he still had feelings for Ellie and she knew it too.

He walked out of his office and over to the fixed base radio and called to Lodi and Crowe.

"Zebra 22," Crowe responded, "go ahead, Sarge, Lodi and I are together."

"Did you guys have any luck talking to Sofia Martinez."

"We're on our way down to the office now to talk to you about it. We'll be there in five."

"10-4, see you then."

Leon had heard the radio traffic and came back to the base station, interested in what was going on.

"What'd they find out, Sarge?"

"I don't know. George just said they'd be here in five. Sounds like maybe they got somewhere with her. I sure as hell hope so. I think that somehow, Lilian Martinez might be the key to finding out who killed Janel Robinson and Darnell Coolidge too."

"Man, I hope so. I was talking to Mathis and Lopez in the hall. They think these Jamaicans are on some sort of vendetta

71

and won't stop until we stop them. And then you begin to think about the threats against us. This whole thing could be about the pressure we have been putting on them and they're trying to eliminate the snitches. But why kill the girl?"

Sullivan responded, "Did they intend to kill Janel or was it an accident, a shot intended for somebody else, maybe one of their own? Was she involved with two of them and got caught up in it? I don't know, but I'm just now thinking about something that Luther said to us, that Janel's dad Arthur might be involved in drugs himself. Maybe he has something to do with her getting killed. I'm thinking that we should try and find him and see where he leads us."

"Hey, man," responded Leon, "I'll get on the computer and see what I can find out and then go up to ID and get his record and his mug shot if he has one."

"Thanks, Leon," acknowledged Sullivan. "When the other two get back, we'll sit down and talk about it."

Sullivan followed Leon Messenger as far as the computer terminal and then he continued on, reaching into his pocket for his keys. With them in hand he approached the lieutenant's office where the confidential informant files were maintained under lock and key. He found the official file for Darnell Coolidge, aka "Coolo." He opened it, sitting down at the lieutenant's desk to go through it. He found that Coolidge had a very minor criminal record including his one possession arrest, the latest entry. His other arrests were all petty offenses and misdemeanors— nothing of a violent nature. On his IIR (Informant Information Report), Lodi had put down an address, 1125 Pearl, with a note, "Family lives here, maybe mother and sister."

Finding nothing else noteworthy, he made a copy of the mug shot and the IIR and headed down the hall to the Homicide Bureau.

Lola Mathis was standing by the door talking to two uniform officers when he entered the office.

"Hey, Sarge, what you got for me, our Jamaican suspect I hope?" She had been thinking about these two homicides, almost like she was anticipating the next, worse, deed. The wanton violence that had ripped life from Darnell Coolidge was a reverberating statement. The bad vibes were not lost on her.

"No, Lola, but this is something you may need. Let's go over to your desk."

When they got there, they were provided a modicum of privacy and he showed her the informant file. They talked about the address noted and she admitted that they had, thus far, found nothing—no tickets, no contact cards, nor other reports giving them an address for Darnell Coolidge.

Detective Mathis informed Sullivan that Lopez was tied up with paperwork, but that she would drive by that address. She would get a uniform car to meet her there and together they would notify the victim's family if they could be located. Maybe they could shed light on what he was doing in the apartment at 16th and Lafayette.

"I'll call Lodi and let him know what I find out, if anything," Mathis informed Sullivan as he left the office, nodding agreement.

When Sullivan reached his office, Messenger, Crowe and Lodi were sitting there comfortably, talking about what they had learned pursuing their two separate avenues of investigation.

"Hey, Detective Sergeant Sullivan, let me get out of your chair, man, we've got some good shit to tell you, especially these two." Leon Messenger spoke jocularly, then persuasively as he pointed to Crowe and Lodi.

When all four were seated, Sullivan informed Lodi that he had made some copies of Coolidge's informant file and had passed them on to Detective Mathis. "They had nothing, as far as an address goes, so maybe that note you made on the file will help them out. Do you remember what you put for an address?"

"Yeah, I had a possible somewhere over on Pearl Street, I think. If I remember right, his mother and sister may be living there. As far as he goes, I never did know where he was staying at any given time. It didn't matter much; he called me when he was supposed to and he almost always met me where I asked him to." Lodi then added, "I haven't really been talking to him that long, and as you know," he said looking at Sullivan, "I've only used him a few times. But I was going to use him more, to get Leon further into the Jamaicans up on Franklin, to start with."

"That's right," was Sullivan's response, adding, "Mathis is going to go out there now and get a couple of patrol officers to help her check out the address you had, so that the next of kin notification can be made."

At that point in the meeting, George Crowe brought up Sofia Martinez and the conversation that they had just finished.

"She seemed glad to see us, as if she had been expecting us to go back out and talk to her," was Crowe's response to Sullivan's question about Sofia Martinez's state of mind today regarding her daughter's disappearance for two days.

"Oh she's definitely worried now. When she saw us she came out of the house and asked if we had found Lilian yet. I think she had been drinking a little but she was not drunk. She said she had just gotten home from work.

"We told her that we thought she was not being completely honest with us and that we needed to know the truth about Lilian's relationship with the Jamaicans, and with Janel Robinson for that matter. She stood there and looked at us a minute, as if deciding whether to talk to us or not, then she invited us into the house."

"Was she alone, or was her mother there?" Sullivan asked.

"She said her mother was there," Crowe said this and then added, "but she didn't come out, maybe because she speaks very little English. I looked around a little, just to make sure the boyfriend or someone else was not there. The back bedroom door was closed and I peeked in and she was sitting on a bed watching Telemundo. While I was doing that, Sofia started complaining about my snooping around." Crowe was familiar with Telemundo as his wife was a Spanish speaker from Mexico.

Then Lodi picked up the conversation. "I explained that we were not trying to be intrusive, just cautious. When I got her relaxed a little bit, she opened up. She said that she had no idea where Lilian was, but that she did know more than she had told us.

"To begin with, Lilian has been hanging around with those Jamaicans for the last two or three months. She was introduced to them by Janel, not long after Janel had met them someplace. Lilian started using cocaine, and even though the Jamaicans aren't selling crack, they started making it for her. It was not long until Lilian got hooked. She said she didn't know if Janel had tried cocaine; Lilian had never told her much about Janel. Sofia didn't know it at the time, but Lilian had pretty much quit going to school for a while, and having no means of paying for the crack, she basically became a 'crack whore'. I hate to put it so crudely, but that, according to Sofia, is what it amounts to.

"About a month or so ago, Lilian started feeling sick and a home pregnancy test was positive. She told her mother soon after learning this because she was feeling physically sick—and desperate. Sofia took her to the clinic where the positive test was confirmed. What tests also revealed was that she had STD, sexually transmitted disease. The doctor at the clinic gave her something to fight the infection, and something to calm her as she withdrew herself from crack cocaine. And according to Sofia, she had a miscarriage."

Lodi paused at this point to take a drink of his coffee. Sullivan and Messenger both sat quietly: Messenger with his head down, rubbing his forehead with his fingertips, Sullivan looking past the others, a far away look in his eyes. Crowe then picked up the narrative.

"After that, Lilian didn't manage to stay clean for very long. And she hasn't been staying at home. She only comes and goes when Sofia is at work and her grandma is there. Her grandma will fix her something to eat, then she will change her clothes and pick up a few things and leave before her mom gets home. Her mom has caught her there a couple of times and said that she looks a little rough."

Sullivan interrupted at this point, "George, did you mention the blood that was found in the trunk of Janel's car?"

"No, I didn't. I told her that we found the car, that it had been involved in an accident and that I searched it. I described the bracelet that we found and she said that it sounded like it might be something of Lilian's. I asked her if she knew if Lilian had ridden in Janel's car and she said, "Yes." So, I mean, the bracelet could've been left in the car before.

"And I lit into her then about why in the hell she didn't come clean with us from the git-go, or for that matter call us when Lilian started hanging with them Jamaicans and got hooked on crack. Then she started crying and I felt bad. But the good part of all this is that she agreed to look through

Lilian's stuff and see if she can find anything that might identify somebody—the guy who got her pregnant for instance. She insists that she never saw any of these people and Lilian didn't give her any names or nothin."

George Crowe had a unique way of speaking. His mouth shaped words slightly abnormally, as a result of a serious childhood accident that damaged his tongue. In addition, when he was excited or trying to make a point, his voice would go up part of an octave and the modulation would continue. He did not talk much but it was easy to listen to him when he did have something to say. And he most often spoke with sincerity and honesty.

Then Lodi picked up the conversation again. "I think we need to find out if Lilian is staying at the house on Franklin. One way would be to see if I can get ahold of Lorenzo Walters, the guy from last night, and send him in there. He says he can buy from those guys."

"Hey, man," interjected Leon, "I'm serious, I can go in there. I'm not worried about them thinking that I'm the man."

"No way, Leon. Lodi's right, you're not going in there until we know more about who killed Coolo and why. If Lodi can't get ahold of the informant, let's go sit on the place a while and see if she comes or goes."

"All right, Frank, I'll try and get ahold of him now. I have a number but I don't know if it's any good or not." Lodi started to his desk to use the phone.

"Good deal," was Sullivan's response. And he turned to George and asked, "So what is it, Detective George Crowe, my friend? You think that was Lilian's blood in the trunk; is she dead? You usually get an accurate feel, or ESP, for things like this." The dark narcs tended to address each other with a false formality at times to inject a little levity into their discussions.

Calling each other detective, or detective sergeant in Sullivan's case, was not otherwise done. They all knew where they stood in their working relationships and friendships.

Crowe answered Sullivan, "Well, to be truthful, I don't think she's dead but I don't think she's hiding out with the Jamaicans either. I think they put her in the trunk, maybe she was hurt already. They were taking her somewhere, maybe to get rid of her, then she lived through the hit and run accident. When the accident damage forced the rear hatch open, she bailed out and took off running. What do you think, Leon?"

"Oh man, I have no idea, but I think if one of those guys that hangs out or deals at that house is using her just for the you know what, they wouldn't kill her for no reason."

"How 'bout you, Sarge?" asked Crowe.

"Well, I think she's alive, but unlike Leon, I don't think she is with the Jamaicans. I think she was about to get herself killed too for some reason and slipped through the crowd after the shooting. I hope I'm right, because if we can find her, she can put this whole thing together for us."

Detective Lodi walked back in just as Sullivan was saying this and asked, "Then whose blood is in the trunk of Janel's car?"

"I don't know."

"Well, while you're trying to figure that out, Sarge," Lodi said facetiously, "we can go out there and try to make a controlled-buy. I'm going to pick Lorenzo up at 23rd and California, at that loading dock across the street from Lawson Park. Then I'm going to drop him off behind Manual High School where we met Coolo the other night, and send him in. It's so hard to get close and see it but I'll watch from the parking lot at the back of the school. George, if you could get to the north end of Franklin, I think we'll be good. Maybe you could stay to the west of Franklin a couple of blocks on 28th, Sarge."

"Okay, sounds good, see you guys out there. Leon, I don't want you anywhere near that place for now."

"Right on, Sarge! I might walk down and talk to Mathis and Lopez if they are in the office. See what's new, man."

"Good idea," was Sullivan's response to that.

11

AFTER THE OTHERS LEFT THE office, Leon made a personal call. He nearly always called his two boys at their mom's house before bedtime to tell them he loved them and wish them a goodnight. He did this with the promise to see them on his next day off, Saturday.

When he finished that call, he walked down the hall to have a conversation with the homicide detectives. Both Mathis and Lopez were in the office when he got there.

"Hey, man, how you doin'? he said to Lopez, as the two shook hands. Then to Lola Mathis, "Hey, girl, everything okay?"

He continued by asking them if there was anything new on the two "Jamaican" murder cases.

"Nothing new on the Lafayette Street case, and the only thing we know for sure on the other one is that the blood in the trunk of Janel Robinson's car was not hers. Obviously, we didn't think it was but we had to eliminate her as possible source of the blood. We do not have a blood type for Lilian Martinez so we cannot say if it is hers or not. Lilian does not have a driver's license and her mom couldn't find any medical records with her blood type on it." Mathis paused then.

Leon interjected, "Yeah, you know, Lodi and my man George Crowe went and talked to Lilian's mother again just a little while ago. I think she finally opened up about Lilian's true relationship with the Jamaicans over on Franklin."

Leon then informed Mathis and Lopez what Sofia Martinez had disclosed to them about Lilian's addiction and pregnancy and her comings and goings from home. The homicide detectives again expressed their gratitude for the work that the dark narcs were doing. Then Detective Messenger asked, "But there's nothing new on the murder of the CI?"

Detective Mathis responded, "No, well, wait a minute. I did go out to that address on Pearl that you guys had. I met a uniform car there and the victim's mom is living there. So I was able to make notification of her son's death. It was pretty rough on her and I didn't begin to divulge the brutality of it. I left it at, 'He was shot and we found him in the apartment.' She didn't know anything about that Lafayette address and did not know where he had been staying, said he'd been into drugs ever since high school, had never worked much and 'probably would not have ever amounted to anything,' but that she thought that he would have liked to get off the street. She cried a little and I tried to console her as best I could. I didn't let on that he had been talking to you guys and she didn't mention anything about it to us."

"Oh man, that's tough. Imagine if that were your son, man. I hate to think about it. Drugs will kill you one way or another and they're killing a lot of brothas' out there now."

Leon then asked Detective Mathis if there was anything else that he could do for them and she said, "Not at the moment but if there is, I'll be sure and tell you guys."

"For sure, man," was Leon's response, and then, "those other guys are out there on Franklin now with an informant, trying to make a buy and to find out if maybe Lilian Martinez is in that house now."

"Really?"

"If she is, I'm sure the sarge will come and talk to you about it. I kinda' think she might be."

"Okay, thanks again, Leon, see you later."

With that, Messenger headed back down the hall to their office. Just as he was entering, he heard the fixed-base radio on the narcotics channel: "Zebra 20 to base."

It was the sergeant calling in. "Go ahead, Sarge," was Leon's response.

"Hey, Leon, the people in this place up here on Franklin won't deal with Lodi's CI. The thing is, there is quite a bit of activity and we're going to stay in the area. Lodi and George are both in good position to see the place and I'm going to be close by. We just want to get some idea of how much activity there is and possibly see Lilian coming or going."

"Okay, Sarge. If it's okay with you I'm going to stay up here and work on some paperwork. If you need anything, just call me, man; I'll keep the radio turned up so I can hear it."

"You got it."

The surveillance at 28th and Franklin continued for a couple of hours. A steady stream of customers, one every fifteen minutes or so, but no sign of Lilian Martinez. The sergeant was about to suggest that they call it a night and go to the office to finish their paperwork when a series of five or six gunshots were heard in the immediate vicinity.

"Zebra 20, are you hearing that?" Lodi was the first to get on the air.

"Yeah, Lodi, I heard it. Could you see any muzzle flash or anything to indicate where the shots came from."

"No."

"Zebra 22, I heard it too, Frank, and it sounded like it came from somewhere to the west. Maybe right behind the house in the alley. I'm going to drive there and look around."

"Okay, I just heard them dispatch a patrol car to the area on a report of shots fired—anonymous complainant. George, you look around where you are, Lodi, you stay south and east, and

I'll stay to the north. Maybe we'll see something. If not, let's head to the barn and wrap this one up."

"10-4, Sarge," said Lodi followed by a, "me too," from George Crowe.

After several minutes they called it a night and headed to the office.

When Sullivan got to his desk, he discovered a written intelligence report indicating that according to a "reliable" source, a Jamaican national named Dexter Campbell, had threatened to put a "contract" on Sgt. Sullivan and Detective Lodi. This related to their arrest of him on drug and weapons charges some months earlier. He had made bond on the case and did not show up for court. A detective in the Intelligence Bureau had been contacted by an informant who told him of the threat. The information was not current; the informant had picked it up when he had been in jail with Campbell. The informant had mentioned the threat in a "by the way" manner while reporting a current "hot tip" to the Intelligence Bureau detective, who made the report official and sent it through channels. The informant was unable to offer any more details.

Sullivan approached the detectives at their desks in the bay and informed them that another threat on "their lives" had been made and that he had received the report from the Intelligence Bureau.

"We don't want to get too carried away with this, especially since it's dated, but we don't know where Campbell is for sure. We should make a project out of finding him and putting his ass in jail on the FTA (Failure to Appear) warrant or getting another case on him if we can. Sound good? Okay then, let's go home."

"Hey, I just want to mention that I have a warrant ready for tomorrow night," Lodi informed them, and then continued,

"I'm going to get it signed tomorrow afternoon while I'm in court and then, if it looks busy tomorrow night, we can hit it. It's up at around 23rd and Downing Street."

"Sounds good, let me know. Good work, guys, see you tomorrow night." With that, the lights were turned off and the four of them headed home.

As Sullivan started driving, he realized that he was not going to be able to get any sleep if he went straight home. The killing of Janel Robinson had upset him considerably. Perhaps it was that she was a close friend of Luther's, who was almost like a son to him, or just that her young life had been ripped from her so violently. He was taking it personally.

That being the case, he chose to drive to the District 3 police station at Iowa and University and catch a quick workout. He parked the El Camino in the parking lot and went to the gym in the basement. No officers were working out at that time of day—it was about change-of-shift time. The night shift was heading home and the morning shift had just hit the street. He decided to skip the weights and instead take a fast run around Washington Park. That took him about 25 minutes and he had settled down considerably by the time he had completed it.

When he arrived home, it was four o'clock in the morning and Sullivan was able to sleep. After three or four hours, he got up, took a shower, and put on some pressed blue jeans, an Oxford shirt, striped tie and a gray sports coat. He stopped at King Soopers on the way to Luther and Gina's house and bought two dozen, long-stem red roses. When he pulled up shortly before ten o'clock, the street in front of their house was full of cars. Evidently he was one of the last ones to arrive.

He was greeted at the door by Gina Pride who hugged him warmly and then grasped both of his hands, while telling him how gratified she was that he had been put in Luther's life, and because of that, her life as well. Sullivan then shook hands with Luther's uncle, Donnie Ray, and continued to make his way through the crowd. All of his players were in attendance as were some of their parents. Finally, he shook hands with the Expos' scout who had been largely responsible for drafting Luther.

"Big day, huh, Frank. I'm happy for the teachers and coaches at Manual High School. I've just met some of them here and I'm happy for the whole community, the whole city. It's something good to celebrate." That was how Fergie Malone, the Expos' scout and former major leaguer saw it.

"It *is* a big day, Ferg. I really appreciate your getting after this and making it happen. I'm pretty sure you'll have no regrets," responded Sullivan.

"Oh I'll have no regrets," was Malone's response. "You never know if a guy's talent will get him through the minors to the big leagues, but this is a quality kid; he deserves a shot. He'll need some luck and some developing but I bet he makes it. No matter what, I'm very happy for him and his family."

A few moments later, a staged signing of the contract was performed so that local media could get some footage for the evening news sports report. It all went well and was followed by lots of handshakes and well wishes for Luther Pride and his mother. As the party was dispersing, Luther caught the attention of Frank Sullivan and let him know that he wanted to talk to him after everyone had left.

Luther followed Sullivan part of the way to the El Camino, then said, "Coach, Lilian called me last night. She could only talk for a minute she said, because she wasn't supposed to be using the phone. She said there were two Jamaicans there, and they didn't want her to leave. I asked her where she was, and she said she was in a house down around 23rd and Downing.

I could tell that someone was approaching her and she quickly said 'I have to go.' I asked if she were in danger and she said, 'I don't know, bye, I gotta' go.'"

"What time did she call you, Luther?"

"It was late, my mom was already asleep and we had stayed up quite a while getting ready for this," he said as he motioned back to the house with his left arm. He continued, "I would have called you but it was after two in the morning and I wasn't sure what to do."

"That's okay, Luther, we were gone already and we wouldn't have gone down there and barged in anyway. When we get to work tonight we'll get on it and I'll let you know. What time do you have to leave on Saturday?

"I leave early. I will fly to Atlanta, then a short flight down to Sarasota where somebody from the team is supposed to pick me up and drive me to Bradenton."

"Oh man, that is so exciting! I bet you can't wait."

"Yeah, Coach, I can't wait to get started. I'm a little nervous to tell you the truth. I think I might get to pitch a little next week, after the physicals and all that."

"Okay, well, I'll try and get back over here tomorrow, or better yet, why don't you, your mom and I and go to lunch while you guys are running errands and getting things together, before your mom goes to work."

"Perfect," responded Luther, "we'll call you."

The two shared a high handshake and a bro' hug and Sullivan headed to the El Camino. Just after he got in the car his pager sounded. He recognized the number as Lodi's. He wasn't too far from the District 2 station so he went there to return the call.

"Hey, Lodi, I was at Luther's signing deal. What's up?"

"I came in early for court and caught the judge in chambers and got the warrant signed. If I get a chance after court, I'll go look at the place."

"Well check this out. Luther said that Lilian called him late last night, early this morning really. She said she's in a Jamaican place somewhere around 23rd and Downing. I wonder if it's the place you have the warrant for. She didn't necessarily say that she was in danger or needed help, but she did say that she wasn't supposed to be using the phone. So when you go by there to scout it, keep your eyes open. It would be good to know if she's in there before we hit it."

"Yeah, but if she is in there, Frank, there's a good chance that there's a killer in there with her. Either way, we have to keep that in mind. This might be a good one."

"Okay, well, let me know what it looks like and if I need to get in there early. Otherwise, I have some things to do but I will be there around six or so at the latest."

12

1205 E. 23RD AVENUE WAS part of a duplex residence not very far from downtown Denver. It was an old building made of dark red brick. The brick needed pointing in many places, the painted concrete porch was cracked in the middle and chipped around the edges. Many years as a rental had taken its toll on the place but most of the tenant wear and tear was on the inside. Mother Nature and owner neglect were responsible for just about all of the damage to the outside.

The hardwood floors were covered with dirty carpet. The plumbing leaked under the kitchen and bathroom sinks. The bathtub was stained from rust in places, and where not, it was a grimy gray from lack of attention. All the walls needed paint, the old wood sash windows were in need of repair or replacement and the wood entrance doors showed signs of previous forcible entries. It had been a very well-built house in its day but it was fifty years old. There was no air conditioning.

On this June day in 1987, it was hot and uncomfortable inside. And there was a mix of unidentifiable smells—not good. The kitchen sink was full of dirty dishes, and pots and pans sat on the stove with food stuck to them. In one pan was a sticky vegetable mix and in the pot was a mix of dried meat and sauce. The bathroom was at the foot of the stairs at the back of the kitchen. Lilian Martinez was trying to stay in the upper part of the house in a large room with three beds on the floor. Over the years the house had been modified to increase maximum occupancy. Lilian was not alone in the house—she was a "guest."

The occupant of the house, the person who had rented it, was a Jamaican male, age 28, whom Lilian called "Bunny." She did not know his real name or actual age, only that he was from Jamaica, by way of Miami, and that he associated with other Jamaicans exclusively, except for women. Lilian was introduced to Bunny by Janel Robinson at the house at 2811½ Franklin Street two or three months earlier. Janel knew Bunny and other Jamaicans in the neighborhood from them flirting with her at a Jamaican grocery store called "JamaicanJerk," after the familiar Jamaican spice.

Lilian continued to get to know Bunny, as she would see him around the neighborhood on her way home from school. One thing led to another and she started using a little cocaine with the Jamaicans in the house at 2811½ Franklin Street. She liked the high it gave her, and Bunny liked the sex that followed her use of cocaine. The first cocaine-then-sex-parties involved Lilian and Bunny and one other Jamaican male named George Brown. She actually was attracted to George Brown more than Bunny but, after being with him only a time or two, he was arrested for D.U.I and hit and run and other traffic charges, and an immigration hold for INS (Immigration and Naturalization Service) was placed on him. She would not be seeing him again soon.

On the other hand, she started seeing Bunny every day. He was selling cocaine in quarter-gram, half-gram, and full gram decks out of the house at 2811½ Franklin Street. He would give her a quarter gram of cocaine and then have his way with her. She did not resist, but he could tell that he really didn't have a hold on her yet, so he started making her quarter-gram of cocaine into crack for her. The Jamaicans would not sell crack because the crack users were addicts, and after buying some for themselves, they would hang around outside soliciting additional customers. They would then take a little piece of what they bought for someone else, smoke it themselves and start hustling other potential customers. In no time there was an ongoing frenzy of activity outside a crack house. The Jamaican drug dealers did not want this. They used the traditional, low-profile, clandestine approach to illegal drug sales, with one notable exception—guns and violence were part of their business plan.

When Bunny started Lilian on crack cocaine, she became addicted almost overnight. She stopped going to school and then she stopped going home. She spent all day and night at the drug house. She became a crack whore. Before long she was pregnant, had a sexually transmitted disease and literally did nothing but have sex and get high.

That was in her first month associating with Bunny at 2811½ Franklin Street. Since then she had experienced brief intervals of sobriety; she had returned home occasionally; she had been treated for STD, twice; she several times reignited her relationship with Bunny who was no longer dealing at 2811½ Franklin or staying there. He had moved to this filthy little house at 1205 E. 23rd Avenue.

Now, no longer pregnant, she was trying to stay in the upstairs part of the house, away from Bunny and whoever else came and went. This, three days after she had been two feet away from a girl she hung out with, Janel Robinson, as she was shot and killed in Fuller Park on Monday night. The shooting came at the end of a Jamaican barbecue. An argument had erupted quickly, and Janel Robinson and Lilian were near the two principals. After it happened, she had been grabbed by Bunny, who had noticed Janel's car keys on the ground after she had fallen, so he pushed Lilian southbound out of the park—part of a moving crowd. Ten to fifteen people were involved in the scrum when the shooting scattered them. By the time the police arrived, all the principals had dispersed to the protection of anonymity—except for Janel Robinson.

Janel's car had been parked east of Franklin on 28th Avenue. When Bunny and Lilian got to the Datsun, Bunny forced her into the unlocked rear hatch of the station wagon and told her to stay low. He got into the driver's seat, started the old Datsun and calmly drove away from the park. Lilian had not resisted Bunny's efforts to get away from the park.

But now as she sat in this rented house farther downtown from the park, she was having a panic attack. And her anxiety had steadily risen since Monday night; Bunny had treated her as a liability since the shooting. He had been alone in the house and did not do any dealing Tuesday or Wednesday. Wednesday night he started dealing again. Up until then, all he did was smoke cigarettes and watch TV. Bunny did not do drugs. And since Monday he had not let Lilian do any either. But she had been drinking rum and coke when he wasn't looking. She ran out of cigarettes and he finally went and bought some more for her. He also brought home some lunch meat and bread and Oreos. They had hardly spoken since the shooting and she was puzzled by his attitude. Prior to Monday, he had been attentive to her needs, if only to take care of his sexual urges. Since then she felt like a hostage whose fate was yet to be determined. She contemplated trying to escape. The thought of trying to kill Bunny had even crossed her mind; she knew where a gun was kept.

She decided to go downstairs to the bathroom and try to make her face look better than it did, and to wash her mouth out and improve her breath, made foul by fear and anxiety— and withdrawal. Then she would go talk to Bunny and see if he would tell her what was going on. She would ask him if she could leave; she would tell him she was scared. As she was descending the stairs, she heard the front door open and heard the voice of the big Jamaican she knew only as "Big" or "Tenny", although she had heard others refer to him as "the Poet." He had never been friendly to Lilian. It was apparent to her that he was "the main man." He was strictly business; he had no time for small talk or grab ass, or making friends.

When Lilian heard him, she hurried into the bathroom. The bathroom door had no lock and Lilian's nerves made urgent her need to pee. When she had taken care of that, she scrubbed her face and rinsed out her mouth. Then she put makeup on her bruised face, and lipstick on her swollen lips. (Bunny had banged her face and bloodied her nose as he roughly forced her into the hatch of Janel Robinson's Datsun, fleeing the scene of the shooting.)

She left the bathroom and went to the kitchen to listen to what Bunny and the big man were saying. It's difficult when Bunny and Tenny talk as they use an earthy patois that makes it hard for a non-Jamaican to understand much of what they are saying. Lilian was able to make out the tone of the conversation though, and it seemed matter-of-fact. Lilian took it as a good sign that there was no raising of the voices and no whispering either. She realized that she was biting her nails and that her hands were sweating. She leaned back against the kitchen counter and closed her eyes. She had no idea that what was coming down next would save her the trouble of finding a way to get out of that house.

13

ALL THE DARK NARCS WERE in the office by five-thirty on Thursday evening to start their seven to three a.m. shift. This was not that unusual and nobody was complaining as they got together in the sergeants' office for a quick meeting. Lodi informed the team that he had the warrant signed for 1205 E. 23rd Avenue, that he had driven by there and scouted it, and that there was some activity. He decided to call Metro and have them do their recon, and meet at eight o'clock in the narcs' office for a briefing. Influencing the decision to do it immediately was the information that Sgt. Sullivan received that Lilian had been, and may still be, in the house; she was the x-factor in the case. She was at the least, a witness in Monday's homicide, if not a victim being sequestered against her will. And she had not been ruled out as a suspect, as unlikely as that seemed.

After Lodi updated them, they all discussed the case. It was decided that Detective Crowe would check the address again at seven-thirty and then be back in the office for the briefing.

The briefing was held in the usual manner. The narcotics sergeant gives an overview, making it clear that a warrant has been signed and that the address has been double checked. Then the narcotics detective who is the affiant gives details on the target location, including fortification, suspected occupants and weapons information. At that point the Metro sergeant goes over their entry plan that has already been formulated based on their scout observations. Modifications are made as necessary based on current and updated intel.

The streets were not very busy as Metro made their approach to the house at 1205 E. 23rd Avenue in their nondescript but oversized cargo van that could be described as a modified milk truck. It was designed for officer safety and tactical advantage without any hint of its fortification or what its intended use was. It was a cloudy evening, almost dark. As the van came to a sudden stop, the officers exited the vehicle and headed to the front door and two gunshots were heard to come from the house. There was no muzzle flash visible but the unexpected sound of incoming fire forced an instant decision by the team leader: proceed with stealth and swiftness, *or* spread out laterally in both directions and seek cover while trying to identify an armed target. The Metro sergeant chose the former and seconds later the team crashed through the front door.

Sgt. Sullivan, and Detectives Crowe and Lodi covered the rear of the house as was their assignment. Shortly after the report of the gunshots, the back screen door flew open and an "unknown male" tumbled out. Lodi stopped him dead in his tracks with a shoulder tackle that put him face down on the ground. He was patted down for weapons, and having none, he was then handcuffed.

Metro was securing the interior of the house, room by room and declared it safe. However, the Metro team leader, Sgt. Tony Marchesi, immediately got on the radio and called for an ambulance Code Ten (red lights and siren) as he looked at the body of a young female, matching the description of Lilian Martinez given at the briefing. She was breathing, but bleeding from two wounds to her upper chest/shoulder. The sergeant called for one of his men to bring the first aid kit. The team member who was the designated medic then put a compress on the wounds to slow the bleeding while monitoring the victim's pulse and breathing. The ambulance arrived within five minutes of being called and transported the victim to Denver General Hospital (DGH).

A District 2 car responded to take the suspect to headquarters. He had been advised of his rights at the scene and immediately lawyered up. When asked what happened to the woman on the floor, he responded, "*I guess you shoot her, mon, I don duit.*" A weapon, a Browning Hi-Power, 9mm semi-automatic pistol was recovered on the floor in the bathroom at the rear of the house. It was cocked and there were eleven rounds in the magazine. Two spent shell casings were recovered from the floor in the living room. This, an indication that the shots were fired from there, in the direction of the kitchen.

Sgt. Sullivan and Sgt. Marchesi stepped out onto the front porch to confer a moment. Marchesi confirmed the fact that the shots were fired before Metro had even made entry, and that no Metro officer had fired his weapon. That was Sullivan's impression as he had heard the shots before he heard the ram hit the front door. Sgt. Sullivan had taken control of the crime scene since he was the senior officer from the Investigations Division at the scene. He had informed the Metro officers that a detailed statement from each one, describing their individual actions, would be required.

Marchesi patted Sullivan on the back saying, "I gotta tell you, Frank, you guys are too much. How do you keep coming up with these wild ass cases, night after night? And you know, we work well with you guys, partly because the intel you guys put together is always right on, and we trust you. Like tonight, the only fact you didn't have was that Lilian Martinez would be shot twice as we approached the door." Marchesi laughed a little after he said it.

"Hey, man, that's something I wanted to ask you about, Tony. Have you guys discussed this kind of contingency: shots heard fired inside the target location, but not necessarily fired in your direction?"

"Well, we have discussed it *ad infinitum.* We only have two choices: either advance or retreat. In this case, I decided to keep moving forward because the shots were not directed our way—there was no visible muzzle flash. Now, I could have been wrong, but I was pretty sure that the shooting was unrelated to us, whether inside this house or next door or whatever. And you know, we work fast and efficiently, so I was pretty sure we'd be all right, and we were already committed and were all out in the open without cover. As it turned out, the shots had been fired *in* this house; we were not the target, and we found the victim half-dead on the floor. Do you think the fuckin' guy saw us and then shot her for some reason?"

Sullivan responded, "Either he saw you guys and shot her because he suspected she was the informant and, seeing you guys, confirmed it in his mind. Or, he shot her, unaware that the house was about to be hit. Like you said, you guys were on it fast. But he is the guy we thought would be here, not the big guy, the boss, but the one that sells here. It's a good hit all the way around. Hopefully, Lilian Martinez does not die and then we have a witness—but either way, this 'Bunny' is caught."

"Good deal, Frank, we appreciate you guys."

"And vice versa for sure."

Detective Lodi had asked radio to send the homicide detectives due to the distinct possibility that Lilian Martinez would not survive. Then he and Detective Crowe began a search of the upstairs, wanting to leave the crime scene of the shooting undisturbed until the homicide dicks could see it, or as undisturbed as it could be after eight Metro officers and three narcotics officers had been there.

While they began the search, Sgt. Marchesi and some of the Metro officers moved through the crowd of people that was gathering, making casual conversation. They quietly made it known that the resident of the house had shot a woman in the house. They were hoping to stop any rumors that might get started, that the cops shot somebody. It was an "old school," effective way of letting the public know what was going on without telling them much, but addressing their concerns. It was an approach based on the fundamental importance of community buy-in.

It took better than three hours, but eventually the processing of the crime scene was completed. The crime lab team processed the scene as a possible homicide and the dark narcs searched the house for evidence to support their case. In addition to the weapon, they recovered two to three ounces of cocaine in quarter, half, or full gram decks. Papers, scales and $950 were also recovered.

Detectives Mathis and Lopez had responded after Lilian Martinez had been transported to DGH. They had checked on her and learned that she was in surgery, in critical condition. Sgt. Sullivan suggested that Detective Lodi could stop by Lilian Martinez' home with a uniform car and inform her mother of what had happened. The uniform car could then transport Sofia Martinez to the hospital if she so desired. The homicide detectives were glad to accept that offer as they could then take some evidence to headquarters before going to the hospital to check on her condition.

At headquarters, Lodi interviewed Bunny while Crowe worked on the computer and ascertained that his real name was Winthrop Jensen, age twenty-seven, that he had been arrested for possession of a controlled substance in Miami and that he was also known as "Winny." Lodi's interview yielded nothing whatsoever, as Bunny refused to answer any questions and said nothing other than to tell him not to call him "Bunny."

With Winthrop Jensen still in the holding cell, Lodi, Crowe and Messenger sat at their desks, in a three desk cluster, and took a few minutes to talk among themselves. It had been another stressful night; not as much for Messenger as he had been kept away from the scene to keep himself from being seen. But for him, being on the sidelines was more stressful. He preferred to be where the action was—with his team. While they talked, Lodi pulled out a Cuban cigar, trimmed the end off with his pocket knife and then put it in his mouth, but didn't light it.

"Don't tell anybody, but I just have to have a victory smoke. You guys want one?"

"Nah, man, I ain't puttin' one of those stinky things in my mouth. What won't you put in your mouth, man?" was Messenger's laughing response.

"We don't have to say nothing, Lodi, everyone in the building can smell that thing," said Crowe, referring to the building smoking ban again.

"Aw, who gives a shit. When they do as much work as we do, they can smoke too; plus, ain't nobody here at night anyway," was Lodi's rebuttal. Then to George Crowe he said, "Let's take this guy over there and put his ass in jail now so I can smoke this cigar when we get back."

They did just that and when they returned, Sullivan and Messenger were talking about the fact that Lilian Martinez was out of surgery and in the ICU—condition still critical. Sullivan had talked to the homicide detectives who had updated him.

It was almost three o'clock in the morning by then, and when Sullivan had composed the nightly activity letter, they called it a night. Before leaving his desk, Sullivan called

Eleanora Mathews. She had worked until eleven o'clock and when she got home she made homemade biscuits; she was about to prepare sausage, scrambled eggs and gravy, if he were coming. All evening at work, Eleanora had thought about doing something special and asking Frank Sullivan to come over. She informed Sullivan of this and he responded, "I'm on my way."

14

AS DETECTIVE CROWE LEFT HEADQUARTERS, two shots were fired that shattered his windshield as he exited the parking garage onto Cherokee Street. Detectives Lodi and Messenger were following Crowe out of the garage in their cars and they saw Crowe disappear in his car as it rolled to a stop sideways in the street. Lodi immediately called it in on the tactical channel, and then on Channel 1. He pulled his car forward out of the garage driveway and stopped next to Crowe's vehicle. Messenger followed Lodi into the middle of the street.

The shots disintegrated the windshield of Crowe's undercover Toyota Camry, but he rose unhurt from the front seat and hollered at Messenger and Lodi that he was okay. He indicated that the shooter was in the back of a pickup that was heading south on Cherokee from 13th Avenue. He was wearing dark clothes and a balaclava. The pickup continued southbound on Cherokee Street.

Crowe hollered again that he was okay and frantically motioned to them to follow the suspects. Lodi and Messenger immediately took off in pursuit of the vehicle after confirmation that George had not been hit. By this time Messenger had gone to Channel 1 and put the description of what had occurred and the suspects' vehicle and route of travel out to all the area cars.

The vehicle headed south on Cherokee Street at a pretty high rate of speed and then turned west onto 12th Avenue. A District 1 patrol car happened to be about to enter the garage as the shooting happened and that car became the first car in pursuit, followed by Lodi and Messenger in their cars. As the uniform car began pursuit with red lights and siren, the truck accelerated quickly to 75 or 80 miles an hour. There was no traffic at that time of night, early morning, except for delivery trucks leaving the *Rocky Mountain News* with the morning papers to be distributed all across the metro area. Fortunately, none of those was crossing 12th Avenue at that moment.

Unfortunately, the driver of the pickup truck carrying the shooter either forgot, or was unaware, that 12th did not go through at Speer Boulevard, and that on the other side of Speer Boulevard northbound, and 10 to 15 feet below, was a straight drop off to Cherry Creek. The driver, at almost 80 miles per hour, attempted to stop but blew through the stop sign, leaving skid marks across Speer Boulevard northbound and the sidewalk next to it, and became airborne. The truck landed nose-first in the middle of Cherry Creek. The rifleman in the rear of the pickup was thrown from the truck into the concrete wall on the other side of the creek.

The cab of the truck burst into flames and the driver was consumed by the blazing inferno. By the time the fire department arrived, flames had consumed everything but the metal shell of the truck, and the tires were melting and smoking.

Sgt. Sullivan arrived at the scene of the accident seconds after it happened. Emergency vehicles and uniform officers and fire fighters were doing their part to stabilize the scene so that an investigation could take place. The radio in the El Camino played, *I Still Haven't Found What I'm Looking For*, Bono and U2 singing, "I believe in the kingdom come, then all the colors will blend into one, blend into one…" Sullivan took a few deep breaths with his eyes closed and thought about the last few minutes. Then he walked toward the edge of Cherry Creek where Lodi was standing, and asked to borrow his cell phone.

"Hey, Ellie, it's me, Frank."

"I know who it is, Frank. Don't tell me, I get it, you're not coming."

"No, I'm not, Ellie. I was just leaving the building to head your way but somebody took two shots at George Crowe, who was driving out before me. We chased them down but, before we could catch them, they crashed their truck into Cherry Creek and they are both dead. I'm gonna be here all night writing reports and trying to figure out what's going on."

"Oh, Frank, I'm so sorry. Is George all right?"

"Yeah, he's fine, a little shook up, but fine."

"Okay, I'll let you go. I know how insane it must be. I'm a little worried about *you* though. That job you are doing is crazy, non-stop action."

"No. We'll get through it. It's just crazy at this moment in time. But I will call you tomorrow and then I do have Saturday off to cool it a little. Don't worry though. I am sorry that you made food for me, but if you save those biscuits, they won't go to waste. Talk to you tomorrow, Ellie."

"Okay, Frank, talk tomorrow."

Sullivan then took Lodi's phone back to him where he was standing and looking, as Denver Fire Department crews, personnel from the coroner's office, and others retrieved two bodies and a '78 Ford F-150 from Cherry Creek.

"Thanks, Lodi."

"What the fuck, Frank, can you believe this shit? I guess the L-T was right. We have to take these threats seriously. I wonder how long it will take before we know who these bad boys were. I already ran the plate and it came back with no record."

"Okay, well it may be an old plate that doesn't belong on the truck. Tomorrow we can get the VIN off of it, if it has not been destroyed, and we can probably get a listing on it that way."

"Yeah, that's what I figured. How's George? Something like this has to scare the shit out of ya."

"He's fine, he's making a statement now and then he'll go up, and when I get there I'll figure out a new vehicle for him until his gets a new windshield. I'm anxious to know if the bullets will be recovered from the inside. No doubt, though, they're serious about getting us off their case. Hopefully, we'll learn something if we are able to identify these two.

"Oh, what about the gun? Was it in the truck?" Sullivan added.

"Well, I've been watching them all along and I told the fire department guys to be looking for it, so I don't think they have seen it yet. When they get that thing out of the creek, I'll get right on it and inventory everything that's in it, if anything survived the fire."

Eventually, the accident scene was cleared off the street and out of the creek. The sun was coming up as the last of the recovery and cleanup vehicles left the scene. Traffic patterns had returned to normal just in time for rush hour. The burned out hulk of the pickup was towed to the pound; a warrant would be executed to recover anything of evidentiary value. A Ruger 10-22 carbine with a rotary magazine was recovered from the creek. The stock had burned away, the steel was black as coal and the magazine was gone, probably melted in the fire. It was a bolt action, one of the most popular .22 rifles in production. The serial number indicated that it was an older model and that it had been stolen in a burglary earlier in the year. In all probability, it had been used as currency in exchange for cocaine.

No bullets were recovered from Crowe's undercover vehicle. All indications were that the bullets had hit the windshield on the driver's side, and skipped over the vehicle.

George Crowe had been quietly working on his statement, describing exactly what happened as he saw it. It was less important than it would have been had both the driver and the shooter not been killed in their attempt to get away. However, this attempt was part of a conspiracy, and the goal would be to somehow discover the identity of the other conspirators.

As George Crowe worked, he admitted to himself that he was upset. He had been threatened and the threat had been carried out, however unsuccessfully. He considered himself to be courageous, and rightfully so. Crowe was a Black man who had served his country in the Air Force and had continued to do so in the Air National Guard. Before becoming a cop, he had carefully considered whether he would be "selling out" Black people or could he be a force for good by working for justice inside the system? Truth is, Messenger had worked out the same conflict, as had most Black officers who had preceded them in law enforcement. No Black police officer was blind to the fact that change was needed—by and large they wanted to lead the change. They wanted contentment in their lives, a difficult goal to come by for any police officer.

None of this, however, was on George's mind. He was worried that he or one of the others would be hurt or killed unless they stopped the threat by identifying who the head guy was behind it and arresting him. Backing down, letting up on the Jamaican drug dealers, that wasn't happening. The dark narcs were targeted by the dealers because they kept the pressure on them. He decided he would talk to Sullivan and suggest that maybe they add at least two more guys to the team, so they could turn up the pressure. He also decided that he would not tell his wife about the ambush—at least not right away.

It was seven o'clock in the morning when the dark narcs gathered in the sergeants' office to summarize a crazy night and wrap it up. Crowe brought up his idea that with two more people they could increase their pressure, possibly put the Jamaicans out of business and solve at least two homicides in the process. He also made it clear that he didn't think the threat to the dark narcs would go away until they captured the head of the Jamaican drug dealing organization in Denver. Sullivan agreed with Crowe and said he would bring it up with the lieutenant at their next meeting. But the last thing he told the team before everyone headed home was, "We've got 'em on the run and we're gonna keep 'em on the run. We're on the right side of justice in this thing and we're gonna win. Let's go home."

This was greeted by, "That's right, man," from Messenger; "Well, I hope so," from Lodi, and lastly from Crowe, "Let's hurry up and do it. Those shots to the windshield were pretty close to my head."

15

SULLIVAN WENT STRAIGHT HOME AND before he had a chance to get something to eat and then go to bed, he was called by the captain in charge of the Vice and Narcotics Bureau. The captain, Juan Soto, and Sullivan had been friends since going through the police academy together. They had also played a lot of fast-pitch softball together. He was calling to be reassured that George Crowe was okay and he told Sullivan to give Crowe time off if necessary. He said that he had called Crowe personally to check on him, and that he seemed a little listless and reticent. Sullivan thanked him for calling and suggested that Crowe was shook up and tired but, in his opinion, was okay. He assured Soto that he would keep him up to date on that and everything else through Lieutenant Connors.

"By the way," Soto added, "I just heard that Lilian Martinez is fighting to stay alive, so there is still a chance we have a witness in all this mess. She may know who's behind these attempts to kill some of us. I hope she makes it."

"Me too," was Sullivan's response, "talk to you later, Juan."

"Be careful, Frank."

"Thanks, Cap."

Sullivan then fixed some scrambled eggs and toast and went to bed after eating. His baseball team was supposed to have batting practice at four o'clock in the afternoon and then play in a tournament in Boulder over the weekend. Frank was thinking about a team without Luther Pride, when his phone rang again. This time it was Luther.

"Speak of the devil," said Sullivan as he picked up the phone, "I was just this very second thinking about you, and Gina too for that matter."

"Hey, Coach, I was just wondering what was going on. Janel's mom called to tell me that Lilian got shot last night. What happened? Were you there?"

"What happened is that we were hitting a drug house down on Ogden and 23rd and just as we were making our entry, the Jamaican inside shot Lilian twice, then bolted out the back door where we snatched him."

"Who is he? Is he the guy she's been shacking up with, the one who got her hooked?"

Sullivan thought a minute about the risk of saying too much, even though he trusted Luther implicitly.

"We *think* he's the guy she's been with, the one that helped get her hooked on cocaine. He won't talk to us at all though, so we have a lot of work to do before we get this figured out. Have you heard anything new? What else did Janel's mom have to say?"

"She had nothing more to say really, but my mom and I are going to stop by there when we are out so I can tell her how sorry I am. I'll see what else she has to say. But nobody else that I know really knows those people. I mean there are some guys at Manual that are into shit, but I don't have anything to do with them. I really don't think Janel was into it like Lilian was. I'll call you after I talk to Janel's mother."

"Okay, sounds good. And give me a call if you and your mom want to grab a bite to eat. I'd love to see you again before you leave tomorrow."

"I would too, Coach, I'll call you."

When Sullivan woke up, it was two-thirty in the afternoon. He had been awakened by the phone ringing. Again, it was

Luther. He told Sullivan that he and his mom would like to meet him at the Blue Onion on East Colfax at three-thirty for a late lunch/early supper. Sullivan agreed to that; before hanging up, Luther told him that he had learned something from Janel's mom and he would share it with Sullivan in person. Sullivan immediately called one of his assistant coaches and asked him to handle practice for him and get the team ready for the games tomorrow.

Sullivan met Luther and his mom Gina late in the after-noon. Sullivan had been going to the Blue Onion for years, ever since he had worked in District 2 in the Seventies. It was a cop-friendly, Greek owned bar/restaurant, clean and dimly lit with good food at good prices. Sullivan greeted the owner Pete on the way in and they shook hands. Back in the day, Sullivan would go in the place off-duty, have a few drinks and even make some football bets with Pete. Those days were gone but he and Pete remained friends. Going in there always made Sullivan feel like he was a cop in another era or part of film-noir.

Sullivan, Luther and Luther's mom had a nice meal and talked mostly about the good times that they had shared and Luther's journey from high school ball to professional baseball rookie. Some of the conversation made light of how Luther would develop from a kid in the low minor leagues to become a star in the big leagues. Optimism abounded.

At the end of lunch, while his mom was away from the table, Luther quickly mentioned that he had talked to Janel's mom, and that she wasn't doing very well—she was pissed off. He said it had taken some convincing on his part before she agreed to talk to him (Sgt. Sullivan) or any other cop, but that she would be able to tell them who the main Jamaican was. He went on to say that she was going to tell *him* (Luther), but he told her to talk directly with Sullivan and that he could be trusted to keep her out of it. Sullivan assured Luther that he would stop and see her later in the evening.

Sullivan left the Blue Onion after an emotional goodbye with Luther and a hug for his mother along with promises to stay in touch. He decided that he would go immediately down to talk with Janel Robinson's mother LaDonna. The agony of losing a child was unimaginable to him on a personal level though he had witnessed many other people experience it during his time on the job and even before. He prepared himself to listen to what was sure to be an emotional account, and offer what consolation was appropriate while encouraging her to let it all out so that those responsible for her death could be prosecuted.

LaDonna lived near 22nd and Lafayette and it took fifteen minutes to get down there in the afternoon rush hour traffic. He notified the dispatcher what he was doing and what his location was, according to procedure and as a matter of safety.

When he knocked on her door, she opened it enough so that she could see Sullivan's badge and credentials when he showed them. She allowed him in and sat down on the couch while pointing him to a straight back chair to the side of it. She was a big woman, of muscular appearance. Her hands too were strong-looking and rough as she took Sullivan's offered hand in hers. She looked like she had been crying and she started to sob when they both were seated.

Sullivan paused to allow her time to compose herself. Finally, she started the conversation, "Nice to meet you, Sergeant. Luther has nothing but good things to say about you and the same goes for his mother. I agreed to talk to you because I want you to catch who murdered my daughter. I don't know too much, but ask me what you want to know and I'll tell you what I can."

"Well, thank you, Mrs. Robinson."

"LaDonna, please."

"Okay, LaDonna. First of all, my condolences for the loss you have suffered. I know of your daughter from Mrs. Pride and Luther and they talk of how special she was. This must be terribly hard for you. Thank you for taking time to talk to me. I want you to know that we are working non-stop, trying to catch these Jamaican drug dealers before they wreak further havoc on this community. We have done many investigations and have put lots of them in jail. Two of them tried to kill one of my detectives last night and then they piled up their truck in Cherry Creek trying to get away from us. Both of them are dead and we have not identified them yet."

"Okay, well, I read about that in the paper and all I can say is good riddance to bad rubbish. I'm sorry, but that's how I feel."

"Okay, *I* can't say that, but if you won't quote me, I will agree with you. I don't know if those two guys had anything to do with Janel's murder or not, or if she even knew them. Do you know much about her relationship with those Jamaicans who were at the park the night she was murdered?"

"Here's what I know, Sergeant: Janel met some Jamaican guys in a grocery store down by 30th and Downing; she told me about it. First, I must tell you that she and I had a terrific relationship, almost like she was my little sister. Anyway, she met these guys and a short time later she saw them in the park next to Manual High School, on her way to and from school.

"I must say too, she was a good kid. She didn't hang around with the ne'er do well kids, no sir. She was an athlete and a pretty good student; when she wasn't in school, she was playing ball—softball or basketball. She was good, man, my word was she good.

"So she comes home, all excited about these Jamaican guys she met, and the music they were playing and how cute some of them were, you know, the young ones. This was a couple of months ago at least. She would see them and they would flirt with her, but from what she told me, they never offered her drugs or anything. It was all innocent enough up until about two weeks ago. Janel had started staying away from that crowd on account of her friend Lilian who had gotten involved with one of them, and ended up hooked on drugs…"

Sullivan stopped her there, "You know what happened to Lilian, don't you, LaDonna?"

"I sure do. I'm just sick about it, but there are some things you don't know."

"Why don't you start at the beginning then?"

LaDonna Robinson paused a second then wiped tears from her eyes. "I can't believe I'm sitting here talking to the po-lice about my daughter being killed. I talked to the po-lice detectives, from homicide, I guess, and didn't really tell them any of what I'm about to tell you.

"First of all, my ex-husband, Janel's father, is a drug addict, drug dealer, thieving, useless, sorry-ass human being. Pardon my language, but I can't help it. His name is Arthur Robinson. Apparently, he has been buying drugs from the Jamaicans and owes them money. I don't know how much or why in the world they would front him anything, but apparently they did. He must have been middling deals for them or some such thing.

"Anyway, it looks like Lilian was over at the place they sell from on Franklin and 28th, and she had seen Arthur there at the drug house dealing with the Jamaicans. Then, when they are trying to find him again, Lilian volunteers the fact that my daughter Janel, the one they all be whistling at and trying to get next to, is Arthur's daughter. That was a couple of weeks ago."

Sullivan interrupted her at this point, "Wait a minute, tell me how you know this."

"How I know it is that Janel came home and told me that apparently her dad had been buying from the Jamaicans she had gotten to know a little bit. Up until that point, I don't even think she knew for sure that the Jamaicans she had seen in the park after practice and games were tied into the ones selling cocaine at 28th and Franklin and other places. But after Lilian let it be known that she was Arthur's daughter, she started getting pressure to help them find him and get their money back. She explained that she never sees her father and had no idea where he was. And she also told them that his business had nothing to do with her or me.

"Pardon me, let me back up. A couple of the Jamaicans came here knocking at the door a couple of weeks ago. When I answered the door, they asked for Janel. There were two of them and they were young, very dark and handsome. They were not impolite or rough but were clean and clear-eyed. I went and got Janel and she came and talked to them outside on the porch. I stayed inside, but I tried to hear what the conversation was about."

"And what was it about?"

"It was about Arthur; they were looking for him and wanted Janel to tell them where he was, if she knew. She told them again that he was not part of her life and had not been for years and that she could not help them. They told her that he had stole something from them and owed them a lot of money. They came right out with it: if he didn't pay back the money, they'd kill him."

"How did Janel react to that threat to kill him?"

"Well, she told them to get off our porch and quit talking about killing folks. That she had nothing to do with any drugs or drug dealing."

"Did they leave then?"

"Yes, and when she came in the house she was crying some, and I hugged her and told her it would be all right, that I would try and get in touch with that worthless father of hers and warn him. In any event, I told her to start putting some distance between her and the Jamaicans. Her argument was, that not all of them are into drugs, some are cool, and those are the ones she had wanted to get to know a little bit, maybe learn something of another culture. She liked their spicy food, and their music and the way they talked."

"The two that came to the door, could you recognize them if you saw them again?"

"Oh dear, I really don't know. Maybe."

"Okay, don't worry about it, I'll get some pictures together and bring them over so you can look at them. Did she tell you the names of any of the people?"

Mrs. Robinson gasped and closed both her hands in front of her lips, almost as if in prayer, then exclaimed, "Oh my goodness gracious, I almost forgot that. I asked her for details of what they said and she told me that those two were "just errand boys from 'the Poet." When I asked her again, she said that 'the Poet' was the main Jamaican drug dealer in Denver and that she had seen him around but he didn't know her. He wasn't one of the ones she would talk to in the park or one of those she had seen in the Jamaican grocery. 'Thank God,' I told her."

"She tell you anything about him?"

"Just that he was a Jamaican, maybe about thirty years old, and tall, dark and handsome. And like I said, he's supposed to be dangerous. But I have a question or two for you, Sergeant Sullivan."

"By all means ask me, LaDonna. I'll give you an answer if I can."

"Do you guys have any idea who killed her? Or more importantly, *why* they would want to kill her? Could it have been an accident?"

"So far, we don't know the answer to any of those questions. But when I get back to the office, I'll check with homicide and see if they have anything new. What you have given me here is going to help though, and if you learn how we can find Arthur Robinson, by all means call me." As Sullivan said this, he handed LaDonna one of his business cards that included his office and pager numbers. He encouraged her to page him anytime day or night. With that he said goodbye.

When Sullivan got back to the El Camino, he got behind the wheel and stared straight ahead blankly for thirty seconds or so. It was an intentional pause on his part to fully empathize with LaDonna as a childless mother, alone with her grief and anger. After starting the vehicle, he decided that he would drive to headquarters through Five Points and see if Herman Hale was working at the independent, Black-owned hardware store on Welton Street.

When Sullivan arrived at the hardware store, he parked in a spot right in front of the place and could see from there, Herman at the front register. "Hey, if it ain't *Father Sullivan*, where you been, Frank? I ain't seen you in two years I bet, maybe longer. Not since that night you helped me out of that jam at the 715 Club. How long's that been?"

"Well, that's been three or four years, I guess, I was still working Vice then. How you doing, Herman? It's good to see you again."

Herman finished ringing up a customer who had bought some plumbing parts and got him on his way out the door. Then he responded, "Pretty good, man, still listening to my jazz, still working here part-time and still getting me some trim, every now and then."

"Well, that just about covers it all, doesn't it?!!"

[Trim, in blues lexicon, is slang for female nether regions and is still commonly used by old timers, Herman Hale for example.]

Sullivan and Herman Hale had met in 1976 when Sullivan was a patrolman, working an extra job several nights a week, guarding one of the state office buildings during the country's prolonged bicentennial celebration. There had been threats that certain buildings might be bombed by militant dissidents and uniform police officers were hired for beefed-up security.

Hale was a night watchman at the building and he and Sullivan hit it off. To Hale, Sullivan seemed so young and innocent, and after learning of his Catholic school background, he started calling him *Father Sullivan*. Hale was a middle-aged Black man, and Sullivan was in his late twenties. Yet there existed a natural affinity between the two. Herman drank a lot (mostly vodka), and Sullivan had grown up among people who drank a lot, and within a few years was drinking heavily himself. He didn't look down on Herman for maintenance drinking.

The two had maintained an easy-going friendship for the next few years while Sullivan continued working in Northeast Denver as a patrolman. Sullivan would occasionally stop by the hardware store in Five Points where Hale still worked, and the two would talk sports and have a drink or two. Hale was a gambler who played the numbers regularly, and always played the same numbers: 7-1-5.

"So what's on your mind, Frank? I know you didn't stop by to have a drink, cause you're on the wagon. And God bless you, man, you're a lot better off in the long run. Anyway, talk to me."

"I'm here to talk about that homicide in Fuller Park the other night, Herman, the homicide dicks said that you were there."

"Yeah, Frank, I was there. I went down there to see my numbers guy and was just about to leave when it happened. I didn't see who did it but I did hear it and saw everybody scatter. I saw a big Jamaican dude with a gun in his hand and I saw him leave the park in a dark Toyota. Did I see him shoot her? No, I did not, but you know me, I'm a gambler and have spent my whole life on the street, and I would bet anything he did it.

"The thing is, Frank, you know these things as well as I do; you've worked out in this part of town for a long time. We gamble, we have after-hours joints and bootleggers, there are places where you can buy dope and get some pussy and all that. But its all part of the sub-culture; we keep it quiet and we usually don't kill each other behind it. I mean, the Greeks and the Italians do their gambling and numbers things too, man, and the white guys sell cocaine and marijuana, no big deal.

"But these Jamaicans are a different breed of cat and since they've moved in, there's a lot more violence. And they act like they are better than us. There's a lot of animosity between them and local dealers and it's getting worse. You guys need to get 'em outa' here!"

"Did you know the girl who got killed, Herman?"

"No, Frank, I did not, but I heard she was a helluva good ball player. Did you know her?"

"I didn't know her either, but you know I'm still coaching baseball, and one of my players, Luther Pride, knew her real well."

"Luther just signed with the Expos, right?"

"Right, he's a great kid and has a good chance to make it to the bigs. He'll be in Bradenton playing A-ball next week. He says that Janel was a really good kid. Do you have anything else that would help us?"

"No, man, I don't. But trust me, Sullivan, if I knew something I would tell you and I'll call you if I hear anything. Give me your number again. And you guys are on the right track trying to stop that shit out here. Otherwise, the good people and middle class Blacks will be forced to move to Aurora, or Montbello, or some other damn place, and everything will go to hell around here. Nobody will tell you that they want the cops doing their jobs in our neighborhood, but they're lying. We need the cops out here like everywhere else."

"Well, I go to the community meetings, not because I want to but because I'm ordered to, and the concerned Black citizens show up in force and demand police attention because their neighborhoods are being terrorized by armed dope dealers. They're afraid for the safety of their own kids going to school and just being in the neighborhood. And I tell 'em, we're out here every night; just keep calling in those complaints and we'll do what we can."

"You're a good man, *Father Sullivan.* I'm glad you're working in our part of town."

"Well, I've got two good Black dudes working on my team, a relentlessly tough hillbilly white cop and myself. We won't let up. You probably heard about it, but two Jamaicans tried to ambush one of my guys leaving headquarters the other night. We chased them down and they wound up dead in Cherry Creek."

"Oh man, that's some scary shit. You be extra careful, Frank, I don't want nothin' happenin' to you."

117

"I appreciate that, Herman. It was great seeing you again. I'll come by when things slow down and we can grab some chicken or a link and have a long talk."

"All right, Frank, keep your powder dry."

"Thanks, Herman, I'll talk to you soon."

Sullivan could see that Herman Hale understood the seriousness of this new Jamaican influence on local drug trafficking and its impact on the viability of the neighborhood. When he arrived at headquarters at a little before seven o'clock on Friday evening, the other three dark narcs were already at their desks, and they followed him into his office for their meeting.

16

GEORGE CROWE COULD HARDLY CONTAIN himself with the news he had for Sullivan. The shooter who had fired the Ruger 10-22 carbine at Crowe had been identified. At the morgue his fingerprints had been taken and crime lab technicians ran those through the computer revealing that he was a Jamaican male, age 28, named Glenmore Henry. With the exception of possibly dental records, there would be no way to positively identify the driver. However, Crowe had ascertained through investigation that Glenmore Henry had been contacted as a passenger in the same '78 Ford F-150 five days earlier. The driver at that time was Clive Henry, age 30. The truck had Florida plates on it that listed to Clive Henry, Fort Lauderdale, Florida, thus providing, at least circumstantially, an identification of both.

"Man, that is fantastic, George," was Sullivan's response.

"I'm having the prints run through the FBI system so maybe we'll get a picture, or more information on Glenmore. Nothing on NCIC (National Crime Information Center) for either name as far as a criminal record goes."

"Okay, if you get a picture of Glenmore, I want you to take it to Mrs. Robinson to see if she recognizes him." Sullivan then gave the other three a rundown on what he and LaDonna Robinson had discussed, emphasizing the part about "the Poet" and the two guys who had gone to her house and pressured Janel for information about her father Arthur. Sullivan then asked Messenger what he found out about Arthur Robinson. Messenger slapped himself on the forehead and said, "Oh man, I started to do that but got sidetracked and it totally slipped my mind. I'll get on that Monday, if that's okay, Sarge." He then continued, "For some reason I think I know this cat, man, from when we were in District 2, Frank."

"That could be, Leon. I don't remember the name at all, but you're going back, man; that was years ago. What I can tell you is that Janel's mom didn't mince words when describing him. She called him, and I quote, '…a drug addict, drug dealer, thieving, useless, sorry-ass human being.'"

"Hell, for all we know," interjected Lodi, "the Jamaicans already found him and killed his 'sorry-ass.'" He quickly added, "But I hope not, asshole or not. I hope we find him and get to talk to him first."

"Okay, here's the deal, let's finish up some loose ends here tonight and wrap it up early. We've already worked about fifty hours this week. I don't want to push our luck. Next week we'll get back after it."

"Hey, Sarge," Messenger started, "I want to go back into 2811½ Franklin next week. I'll wear a wire and you guys can get some place close, but I'm pretty sure I can buy there and maybe hook up with the main man."

"Okay, I'll let you know what I think about that on Monday, I'm not sure I'm going for that, man. I kinda' think we need to do some serious surveillance, maybe even install a camera somewhere inconspicuous. I still don't feel like we know enough about what's going on there. And this has been a violent week; we came about a foot from losing Detective Crowe here and I'm not in the mood to push our luck. Let's continue to put this thing together and make sure we know as much as possible.

"But like we were saying Wednesday, you going into some of the Jamaican hangouts, away from Northeast Denver, to see what you can pick up in the way of general intel will be good if we can do it. You might even run into 'the Poet' in a situation where he wouldn't be suspicious. Let's make a list of two or three main Jamaican hotspots out in Southeast Denver and Glendale, and go check them out. More than anything, it will be good to just change our game plan a little bit."

"I'll go in one of those places with you, Leon," Lodi said.

"Come on, man, I'm not taking your redneck ass with me," responded Messenger laughingly.

"You telling me they won't let white guys in there?" was Lodi's retort.

Messenger laughed loudly and he and Lodi slapped hands. Then Messenger added seriously, "There isn't anybody I'd rather have with me, man, but I don't think it'll work with these guys." Then switching gears again he continued, "Now if you were a good-lookin' chick, or even just good-lookin', maybe we'd be all right." He laughed loudly again and Lodi just shook his head.

The conversation shifted back to what loose ends they had to clear up and they proceeded to get to work. High on Sullivan's list was to go and talk to the homicide detectives. He grabbed a legal pad from his desk and walked down the hall.

Detectives Mathis and Lopez were sitting face-to-face at their desks when Sullivan walked in to the Homicide Bureau. Their desks were piled high with paperwork and both were typing. They looked up as Sullivan walked in and Lopez stood to shake hands with him. Their conversation immediately went to the heart of the matter. Janel Robinson was killed on Monday night—Jamaican drug dealers involved; Darnell Coolidge was killed Wednesday night at a known Jamaican drug house; Lilian Martinez was critically wounded in a drug house by a Jamaican drug dealer on Thursday night; and a police officer was shot at while leaving headquarters and, in the aftermath, two Jamaican suspects died in a fiery crash trying to escape apprehension. Four dead and one almost dead in four nights constituted a crime wave. Was it a rampage, a vendetta or coincidence?

The headline of the *Rocky Mountain News* late edition Friday morning had read, **JAMAICAN DRUG MURDERS SHAKE NORTHEAST DENVER.** The subtitle said, "**Ambush of detective at headquarters shatters windshield.**" The front page was visible on the corner of Lopez's desk. Sullivan had already read the story that included "man on the street" interviews with citizens in Northeast Denver who expressed fear, frustration with the justice system, and anger. Some of the anger too was directed at the police department and the district attorney's office for passively allowing drug dealing and attendant crime to take over their neighborhoods. Sullivan shook his head as he pointed at the paper on Lopez's desk.

"Yeah, why don't you guys do something out there?" Asked Lopez kiddingly.

Sullivan just continued shaking his head a little. Then he switched the subject to the pressing questions on his mind. "Anything new, Al?"

"Well, Crowe came down and told us what he had found out about those two from early this morning. Man is he lucky he didn't get killed. I wish the two guys would have survived so we could have interrogated them, or maybe made them on these other cases. But on the other hand, we don't have to worry about them getting off. They're gone."

"True. How about Winthrop Jensen, have you had any luck interrogating him?"

"We went over to the jail and talked to him. After we advised him, he told us that he wasn't going to say anything other than that it was the cops who shot Lilian Martinez. After

I reminded him that we did GSR (gun shot residue) tests on his hands that showed positively that he had fired a weapon and that his prints were on the weapon we recovered, he changed his tune a little bit. I told him that if Lilian Martinez died, he would be looking at the death penalty and the best we could do was get him life in prison.

"I don't think he realized that she was still hanging on and that she might survive. Then he said that he would talk to us if she lived but if she died it wasn't worth it. Of course, I told him that he would have to come up with something good, like giving us who killed Janel Robinson and Darnell Coolidge. He didn't say anything after I said that. If Lilian Martinez recovers, we will go talk to him again. By the way, we heard that she is getting better and it looks like she is going to make it. They said that she may get out of ICU tomorrow, and if she does, we can see if she will talk to us."

"That sounds real good; her mother will help you persuade her to talk, I think. At some point we want to talk to her also, regarding the drug case against Jensen."

"If you want, Sarge, I'll call you and you can talk to her a little bit when I do. Then we can get a formal statement later when she gets better."

"Okay, that sounds good, let me know. How about the Coolidge case, are you guys getting anywhere on that one?"

"We're getting nowhere on that one: no prints, no witnesses, no evidence except the spent rounds so far. You guys have a better chance of solving that one than we do."

"What kind of gun was it that killed him?" Sullivan asked.

"It was a 9mm," was Lopez's response, then added, "We recovered two rounds from the plaster wall where he was shot. They were distorted, but not in terrible shape, so a comparison is possible if we come up with a weapon."

"Okay, well, we took one off a guy the other night."

Sullivan then informed Lopez about Lorenzo Walters, aka Robert Grant, whom they arrested on Tuesday night leaving a house that Messenger had a warrant for. He explained that Lodi talked to him and he wanted to work his case off but hadn't done anything yet. "He's on parole for agg robbery, so it's worth checking into, I think," he said, and then continued, "How about the gun Winthrop Jensen used on Lilian, have you tested that one for a match? It was a 9mm also."

"No, not yet, I have it and it's on my to-do list, but I haven't tested it. But tell those guys to come and see me and we'll check both of them out—theirs and Jensen's. That would be something, wouldn't it, if we could nail one of these guys with those two murders? Unfortunately, the round we recovered from Janel Robinson's head was slightly disfigured, but we should still be able to match it. As long as we're at it, we'll see what we can do, maybe put the trifecta on somebody."

"That would be something. One more thing, I stopped by the hardware store and talked to Herman Hale. He's not much help but he'll call me if he hears something." And after a pause, "Okay then, Al, see you later. Thanks!"

"Thank you, Sarge."

Sullivan went back to his office and his body was feeling sore. It had been a long week and he hadn't been able to work out much. He thought of Al Lopez's mention of a to-do list and thought, "Man, we have so much on *our* 'to-do' list that we'll never get it all transferred to the 'got done' list." Then he remembered some AA basic sayings like "Easy Does It," "One Day at a Time," and "Keep it Simple," and reminded himself to "stay where his boots are." In other words, stay in the present moment. When he got into the future, even a few hours, he was lost in the mire of things he could not control—not good for him.

When he reached his office, he summarized his conversation with Lopez, then he gave the word for the guys to wrap it up and head home. Unless something pressing came up, and he had to call them out, they would be off until Monday night and they all needed the rest.

Sullivan typed up the activity letter and summarized the week's work as he and Lopez had done verbally: two drug-related homicides, two suspects dead as a result of their own negligence after the attempted murder of a police officer, one citizen shot and wounded by a drug dealer who was then arrested, and two drug search warrants executed. Guns, money and drugs seized. To some degree the streets were safer Friday than they were on Monday, but "the Poet" was still on the street.

After distributing the report, he went back to his desk and telephoned Eleanora Mathews.

She answered on the second ring. After finding out who it was, she said, "Hey, Frank, I was starting to worry about you. Are you okay?"

"I'm beat, Ellie, we've had a helluva week. Did you just get home from work?"

"I did, just this minute walked in the door and the phone was ringing. I was hoping it was you and I didn't want to miss it."

"Do you want something to eat? I could run over to Chubby's and get some Mexican food or I could come and get you and we could go to the Village Inn or something like that."

"Hmmm. Come and get me so we can go to the VI. Pancakes sound really good to me. Is that okay with you?"

"Sure, we can go to the one in Cherry Creek and we can still beat the two o'clock bar rush. I'll be there in fifteen minutes."

"I can't wait."

Sullivan grabbed his shaving kit from his desk and stopped by the men's room to wash up and brush his teeth. His dark brown beard looked a little ragged so he trimmed it up a bit and his mustache as well. And then wet his brown hair and combed it back. He splashed on some Old Spice, packed up his shaving kit and checked himself out in the mirror. He was startled by the age in his blue eyes; they looked tired and a little bloodshot. He took his shaving kit back to his desk, locked the office, and headed to the El Camino.

Sullivan was the last of the team to leave the building. He paused as he started up from the B-1 level to the street, thinking about the attempt on George Crowe's life. As he reached the street and looked southbound, he saw in the area the other three undercover cars used by his team: Lodi in the open parking lot across the street, and Crowe and Messenger across 13th on Cherokee with an eye on the exit from the police parking levels. They all met up briefly on Cherokee to the south.

"You guys are too much, work like dogs all week and then take time to cover my ass."

"Hey, man, ain't nothing gonna happen to any of us if we stick together, man," was Messenger's reply and the other two affirmed that.

"You guys are un-fuckin'-believable, ya' know that don't ya'? Don't even think about working somewhere else cause I'm not letting you go."

With that they all had a good laugh, but what they had just shared wasn't funny. It was a feel good, "they can't stop us" moment resulting from a surrender of ego and a commitment to something greater than themselves—each other.

17

AS HE DROVE OFF, SULLIVAN recognized how blessed he was and thanked God for it. Since he was a little kid, he had spent lots of time by himself and occasionally mumbling things to God was not uncommon. When he was running late trying to catch a bus, a Hail Mary or two would be in order. If he was at bat in the school yard and really wanted a hit for some particular reason, he would likely have talked directly to God. He hadn't been an outstanding student but had always listened intently when the nuns talked of matters of faith, miracles, apparitions of the past, and the presence of God in everyday life. He no longer strictly practiced the Catholic liturgy but he lived his faith daily.

He made his way to Eleanora's house, a small brick bungalow in the 2700 block of Fillmore Street, a couple of blocks north of City Park Golf Course. It was a stable, middle-class neighborhood characterized by well-built houses on nice size lots. When he got there she was sitting on the front porch waiting for him. It was a warm summer night and she was drinking a glass of white wine. She was dressed in blue jeans and a light blue Nuggets T-shirt. She greeted Sullivan on the porch steps with a hug and a peck on the cheek. He returned both and followed her inside the house. She retrieved her purse and announced that she was ready to go.

Eleanora got into the El Camino and did a quick reality check. Until Monday night she hadn't seen Frank Sullivan for years, though she thought of him often enough. Then, an innocent girl was murdered in the park not thirty feet from her, and who should arrive to stabilize the scene but her old high school boyfriend. She couldn't believe how healthy and handsome he looked to her as he and his partner strode into Fuller Park to take charge of the homicide scene. He looked taller than his six feet and two inches and not as rail thin as he once was. He had obviously been working out.

She had gone to their twentieth high school class reunion the previous year but Frank Sullivan was not there. She talked to other classmates who knew him and had seen him around, and they told her that he was doing great, that he stopped drinking and had a well-respected job as a detective-sergeant on the police department. She had been very disappointed as she had counted on seeing him there.

The last year they were in high school, they had dated for several months. Prior to that, they had seen each other around in school and had been friendly but hadn't dated. Then one Sunday, Frank went to dinner with a friend of his, who attended Mount Carmel High School in North Denver. The dinner was at the home of his friend's grandmother around 41st and Umatilla Street. His friend's mom was part of a big North Denver family named Catalina. She was one of seven brothers and sisters. The men were all big and good-looking, and the women were knockouts and looked as Italian as could be. Every Sunday the family had a traditional Sunday Italian dinner that was out of this world. Frank had been there before and got along well with the family. They teased him about being Irish but made it clear that he was welcome any time. When his friend Mike invited him, he never said no. On this particular Sunday, Sullivan's mouth dropped when he saw that one of the beautiful Catalina women at the table was his classmate from Cathedral High School, Eleanora Mathews.

As he was introduced to those whom he had not met, and while they waited to be seated, Eleanora explained that this was her grandma's house and that she was surprised that Mike had not told him that they were related. Then Sullivan remembered Mike telling him that his cousin went to Cathedral and mentioned her name, but it hadn't really meant anything at the time because he didn't know Eleanora.

Eleanora had coal black hair and dark brown eyes. She was tall and well built. Being the 1960s, it was remarkable that she neither denied the fact that she was biracial nor did she feel it necessary to tell everybody about it. She seemed completely comfortable with who she was, and who her parents were. Her biracial dad had been a college football star at the University of Denver and then a Denver fireman, and her mother was from the strikingly handsome, accomplished, North Denver Italian family. Eleanora had inherited her father's athletic grace (although she played no sports), and certainly her mother's beauty.

When she finished high school, Eleanora went to the University of Denver on an academic scholarship and studied business and Italian. She spent her last semester studying in Italy. Upon graduation she remained in Italy for three or four years. Her Italian was fluent by then. In Italy, she had predictably fallen in love with an Italian professional soccer star for Juventus in Torino, Italy. Eleanora was in Torino doing graduate studies at the University of Torino that she, and most Italians, referred to as "Unito." She was a research graduate assistant as part of her grant to study there. When her studies were complete and her romance with the soccer star had run its course, she returned to Denver and eventually accepted a management position with Mountain Bell. She had advanced to become the Operations Administrator, overseeing all off-hour operations. Hundreds of people worked under her command and she was a rising star in the company.

She had been involved with several men in her twenties and early thirties but no lasting relationships. In her later thirties, she had just about stopped dating and had pretty much decided that when she wanted a serious relationship, she would move back to Italy and have it with an Italian. Race played no role in her relationships there, and whether she liked it or not, that wasn't the case in this country.

But whatever she had, or was rekindling with Frank Sullivan was unique; she didn't think of him as white. Maybe it was just he, or the Irish Catholic factor, or that she had known him since he was a boy—he was different.

Sullivan and Ellie talked easily on the way to the Village Inn in Cherry Creek. She mostly listened as he recounted the events of the week.

"Is your job always like this, Frank?"

"No, this is exceptional. I mean, we spend our time on the street, going after armed drug dealers, so it's always dangerous and uncertain. But we found ourselves on the crest of a rising crime wave this week, unlike anything I've ever seen. We really needed this weekend."

Sullivan then told her how close-knit the team was and related how, unbeknownst to him, the three detectives had waited on the street to make sure he got out of the building safely tonight. Doing so, following a week of long hours, murders, shootings, and an attack and other threats against the dark narcs was a statement of resolve and unity.

After a short lull in the conversation, Ellie spoke up again, "Oh, how is Luther, did he leave for Bradenton yet? I read the story about him in the paper and there was a great picture of you and him and his mother. What a good-looking kid! And his mother is strikingly attractive. I'm surprised you and she haven't gotten together."

"Oh, we've gotten together many times, not like you are suggesting though, and we really like each other." They both laughed when he said that, and then he went on, "We've been on trips with the team and we go out for lunch once a month or so, usually with Luther. And her parents are great people; they live pretty close to you. They are a big reason that Luther is who he is today. I bet they read him a thousand books before he was five years old. He could read and write at five or six. Then her dad taught him all kinds of stuff about automobiles and household maintenance and gardening, not to mention how to throw a baseball. You name it, Luther knows something about it. Granted, he won the genetics lottery, but he has had three adults caring for him his whole life."

"That's how I was raised too," Eleanora said. "Not by three adults, but my mom and dad were always reading to me. Of course we didn't have TV like it is today either. Reading was my main form of entertainment. Got a library card when I learned how to read and I've had one ever since. And you know, they say that reading to a child has as much to do with how they turn out as anything you can do."

"It's obvious in your case too," Frank added. "Your upbringing has allowed you to accomplish some great things and as a result you are self-confident. Of course, you are blessed with exceptional looks and that doesn't hurt either. But that's not what defines you."

"Well, same goes for you," she replied, demurely.

"Well let's put it this way, I was raised in the Catholic faith, was taught to pray when I needed help, and trust God. I got the love I needed when it made all the difference. Nothing wrong with that. I've been dealing with my character defects since

I quit drinking and I try to turn just about everything over. Previously, I insisted on taking control when I most needed help and alcohol almost destroyed me. I'm getting better."

"You seem like you're doing great," Eleanora agreed. "I was so glad to see you the other night and to see that you are looking so good and doing so well. But you were blessed with good looks and a lot of talent too. And I'm sure your parents did the best they could."

"They did the best they could," Frank said wistfully.

The El Camino had a cassette player in it and Sullivan had been playing a Sam Cooke and The Soul Stirrers gospel tape for the past two days. He went to a soul music store in Five Points and bought it Thursday after Luther's signing. The owner of the shop was a friend of Sullivan's from a Sunday Morning League baseball team on which they played together a few years ago. He was a high school teacher who ran the music store in the evenings and on weekends. He seemed to know every song ever recorded, and when Sullivan came in asking for a gospel tape, his friend Herb had the perfect thing for him. Sullivan didn't know Herb's last name and it seemed that Herb didn't know Sullivan's first name. That not withstanding, they were friends and always glad to see each other.

The words of "Farther Along," as only Sam Cooke could enunciate them, with harmony from the Soul Stirrers, filled the El Camino just as Sullivan and Eleanora finished talking about their upbringing.

"My God, Frank, when did you start listening to gospel?"

"I started listening to gospel back in the Fifties, on the country music station, KLAK, on Sunday mornings. But I just recently started listening to Black gospel. Then I bought this the other day from my friend Herb down at All Soul Records in Five Points. I mean, I've been listening to Sam Cooke since the Sixties. I'm sure you remember making out to Sam Cooke, "Meet me at Mary's Place." But I didn't know anything about his gospel stuff. I love it, especially after an emotional week like I've had. It's painful and hopeful at the same time."

"Your love of music and poetry is why I was crazy about you in high school, Frank. You seemed to have a worldliness about you that other high school boys didn't. And I'm not the only girl who noticed it."

At about that time, they arrived at the Village Inn and Sullivan commented before getting out of the vehicle, "What you and anybody else mistook for worldliness was my extreme naïveté." He smiled as he said it.

In the restaurant, they talked some more of Sullivan's job, a little about the food at the place and the drunks coming in after a hard Friday night at the bars. Finally, they talked about themselves. Eleanora explained that she loved her job, and that working the afternoon shift had allowed her to develop her own style of management—away from the upper management cliques interested in suppressing individuality. Sullivan commented that he was in a similar situation. By taking an assignment that nobody wanted and being successful doing it as he had seen fit, he was influencing enforcement in what he deemed a positive way. His style was characterized by aggressive enforcement. High rates of attendant violent crime, armed dealers and public nuisance problems, where the safety of a large number of citizens was threatened, were a priority. They both agreed that what they really thrived on was the freedom to be themselves.

During breakfast, they relaxed into the situation, and though they hadn't spent time together in years, it was an easy date. Conversation went back and forth from the past to the contemporary—news about old classmates, to what he and she were reading, what movies they had seen recently, how much

Denver had changed, and so forth. They sat there almost an hour and Sullivan suddenly crashed under the weight of the week's activities.

When they got back to Eleanora's house, it was almost three in the morning. In the living room, they held each other tightly and kissed passionately. Then Sullivan broke the silence and the embrace, held her hands and told her he had to go.

"Could we continue this tomorrow or sometime soon, Ellie? I'm sorry but I am totally beat." He then added, "We're playing up in Boulder tomorrow at Scott Carpenter Field at one o'clock. We have a double header. I'll call you when I get that wrapped up."

"Well, I might just drive to Boulder and see what you've got without Luther Pride on the mound."

"Don't remind me, I'm gonna miss him like crazy—on a lot of levels. But even without him, I have a really good team this year."

"I'm sure you will miss him. And I want you to stay now, and I can tell you want to, but I know you must be beat." She kissed him again and said goodbye, "See you tomorrow."

"Okay Ellie, thanks for staying up and waiting for me. Great to be with you."

As soon as he began to drive home, Sullivan tried to focus on Saturday's baseball games in Boulder. He sorely needed a distraction after the week he had experienced but he was having trouble thinking of anything but the job. He hadn't even been able to give his full attention to Ellie, as much as he had wished that he could. He was preoccupied with the Jamaican case, worried about the threat of violence associated with it, and was anxious to get back to work and bring it to a successful conclusion—weekend or not. After seeing his team waiting, to ensure that he didn't get ambushed leaving head-quarters, he was sure that they were all of one accord.

18

LEON MESSENGER WOKE UP EARLY Saturday morning and called his kids at their mother's house. He had arranged to take them to their karate lessons and he planned to work out in a separate area while they were doing their thing. He cleaned up and got his workout gear together and drove from his home in Glendale to Aurora to pick up his kids. Messenger had two boys, ages eleven and nine. Leon and his wife had been separated for years but the boys regularly questioned the situation and expressed their displeasure about their dad not living with them. But just about every Saturday morning they did something special together.

The boys were aware that their dad was a police detective and often had questions about what he did on the job. He usually left it at, "I put bad people in jail, people who hurt other people." He emphasized that he was one of the good guys and so were they. They idolized their dad and often mentioned that they wanted to be cops too when they grew up.

After the boys had their class, Messenger picked up some sandwiches at the deli so that they could have a picnic in the park. He had brought a nerf football with him and the three of them threw the ball around after lunch. When they were done he took them back to their mom's house and told them that he might see them on Sunday and that he planned to take them to the Denver Zoo.

As he drove home he noticed a Jamaican grocery store called the Kingston Corner, in a small retail space at Mississippi and Colorado Boulevard. Thinking of the conversation he and the sergeant had, he decided to go in. He reached under the seat to make sure he had his off-duty weapon with him. He carried a Walther PPK off duty. He started doing it shortly after he came on the job, explaining more than once that he carried it because "it's the same piece my man Double-oh-Seven carried, man; I just had to have one. Who knows, I might even run into the ebony version of Pussy Galore someday." Then he would laugh heartily and maybe slap somebody on the back, whoever was in slapping distance.

Messenger found the Walther and shoved it into his waist band under his Hawaiian shirt after parking his undercover 1979 Chrysler Cordoba in the lot in front of the store. Messenger always dressed nicely. Today he had on some expensive beige slacks, dark sox and sandals to complement his Hawaiian shirt. It was about three o'clock in the afternoon when Messenger walked into the grocery store on the pretense of shopping for something original to take to a barbecue later. He was greeted by a nice looking young woman speaking with a Jamaican accent who told him to let her know if she could help him in any way. He said he was just looking around at the moment and then, as he was walking away added, "You know what, I'm looking for something sweet and spicy to take to a barbecue."

"Well, thank you for asking, but I have to work until six tonight. But I can recommend some delicious sauces instead." Then she burst out laughing and so did Messenger. He reached his hand out and the young woman gave him five.

"Cedella is my name," she said in less accented English.

"Norman Preston is my name," Messenger replied. "And how did I find a beautiful sista' like you in this little, out of the way grocery store?"

"Well, the beautiful sista' as you say, happens to be the owner of this little grocery. What brought you in to my little place here, Mister Preston?"

"Oh man, seriously, I'm lookin' for some barbecue sauce for one thing and some of that DG, I think it's called, ginger beer. It's delicious. Is that what it's called?"

"Exactly, mon, or should I say, man, as you do?" She asked rhetorically.

"I like how you say it, Cedella, so do you have any of it?"

"Of course we do, let me show you. And by the way the *yaadies* call me Della."

"Okay," responded Messenger with feeling, then with puzzlement "What's a *yaadi*?"

"One of my own people from Jamaica. *Yaad*, meaning home, *yaadi* then is somebody from home, you people would say *homie*, I think."

"Oh, okay, I get it, right on—Della it is. That's even prettier. Della is an awesome name for a sista."

The two talked some more as Messenger picked out some spices, some barbecue sauce, and some ginger beer. He was enjoying the music as he looked around and observed the other patrons. It was a small store, maybe a converted 7/11, but there were five or six people in it the entire time he was in there. He was being alert and realized that he probably should have told the sergeant that he was going to go in there. Even though walking into any grocery was innocent enough, there was a chance he would run into somebody related to the Jamaican criminal element, maybe somebody who knew him.

He was in the store about twenty minutes and was sweet talking Della most of the time. She disappeared into the back of the store for a few minutes and Messenger heard her talking to someone on the phone. He strained to overhear the conversation with no luck. When she returned, he met her at the cash register to pay. Messenger was content to ease on out of there as he had set himself up to return later. It seemed that Della was coming on to him, flirting with him. She was pleased when he told her that he would try and stop by and see her Monday evening.

Messenger left the store and went back to the Cordoba, put his groceries in the back seat and decided that he would find a place where he could park and watch the place from a distance. Across Colorado Boulevard there was a McDonald's restaurant in the 1100 block of South Colorado Boulevard on the west side, so he parked in the lot and went inside where he ordered some hamburgers and a large diet coke. Sitting by the window he could see the storefront of the Jamaican grocery, then he started eating one of his three Big Macs.

He had almost finished his food and drink when he saw Della leave through the front of the grocery store. She left in the company of a tall, fit-looking man and together they walked to a dark Toyota sedan in the parking lot. Della got into the passenger side as her companion got into the driver's side. Messenger was pretty sure he was the big guy he had seen through the doorway when he went to 2811½ Franklin, before the informant entered the place and the door closed. The informant was killed soon thereafter, one theory being that he was killed for that very reason—that he brought a cop to his place of business.

Messenger got up immediately, exited the restaurant and hustled across Colorado Boulevard, so that he might have a chance to get a license plate number as the vehicle left the parking lot northbound. He got lucky, caught a break in traffic both directions and got to the east side of the street. He had grabbed a fishing hat from the Cordoba and pulled it down, almost over his eyes, which he had covered with dark glasses from his shirt pocket. He stayed close to the inside of the sidewalk as he made his way down the street. There was some foot traffic that he used for concealment; it was imperative that Della not see him. He could see that she was engaging with the male because she got as close to him as the split seats would allow. She appeared to be paying no attention to anything outside of the vehicle.

The vehicle turned right onto Colorado Boulevard northbound and Messenger had his phone out. He called Detective Crowe and told him, "Hey, man, write this down, I'll explain later, BNN-455, Colorado."

"Okay, one more time."

"Baker Nora Nora, four-five-five, Colorado passenger plate."

"Okay, Leon, got it. What the hell are you doing man?" Crowe's voice modulated with excitement as he said this.

"Try and get a listing on it, would you, man. I'll call you back in a little while. Thanks, brotha."

When Messenger disconnected from his call to Crowe, he nonchalantly turned around and headed back to the south. He then jaywalked across Colorado Boulevard, dodging traffic in the process, his Hawaiian shirt flapping in the breeze. He got back to his car and took a deep breath, then another, and then he drove to a nearby 7/11 where he bought a bottle of orange juice. He stood outside the store and drank it in two or three gulps and threw the bottle away in the trash container.

When he got to the Cordoba, he made some notes about his afternoon's work. He was now sure it would become part of the investigation. He had just met a new player in the case, Della, and had possibly identified the vehicle being used by one of the main players. He may be a major drug dealer, maybe he's a murder suspect, hard to say. But he was going to get a lot of attention until he was identified and his role defined.

After he had made some notes, he paged Sergeant Sullivan and left him a message to call him when he was finished with his games in Boulder, adding that he had some good stuff for him.

It was about six o'clock when Sullivan returned Messenger's call.

"What's up, Leon, everything okay?"

"Hell yes, man, better than okay." Leon Messenger then proceeded to tell the sergeant, in great detail, what he had been doing all afternoon. He also included the information he had received on a call back from Detective Crowe. The license plate he had taken down listed to a Tennyson Cummings, at 7474 North Washington Street in Adams County, Colorado, on a 1985 Toyota Camry four-door.

"Oh man, Leon, Tennyson Cummings must be "the Poet." Get it—Alfred Lord Tennyson and E.E. Cummings?"

"That's what I'm thinking, Sarge." Messenger smiled to himself at how excited the sergeant was with the work he had done. He liked working with and for people who recognized initiative and good solid police work. Sullivan was one of those.

"Excellent work, Leon. I'm on my way home from Boulder so I'll drive by that address on my way; it's not too far off the old turnpike. I doubt if the address is any good but if it is, and the car is there, then I'll call you. If there is no such address, then we can just wait and get on this Monday night when we get to work."

"Sounds good. Oh hey, man, how did the games go?"

"We won both, five-one and seven-nothing. Even without Luther we have the best team around, I think."

"That's good, man." Then back to the subject at hand, "Like I said, Della wants me to drop by there Monday evening, so that might lead to another way into this guy, at least an introduction to him. If I can meet him, I can take it from there, man."

Their call ended and Sullivan made his way to the North Washington Street address. The location was in unincorporated Adams County in an area that twenty years earlier was home to several small farms. The farmers would take their fruit and vegetables to Denver and elsewhere in a truck and sell them either downtown on Market Street or else peddle them from the truck in various neighborhoods. Those farms were long gone now and there was no such address as 7474 N. Washington Street. Nothing even close to that. The entire east side of the block consisted of vacant lots covered with weeds, beer cans, broken glass and other debris or abandoned buildings without any address on them.

Sullivan then decided that he would drive by 2811½ Franklin Street on his way home and see if, by chance, the Camry Messenger had seen was parked there. It was, in the back, confirming that by going into the Jamaican grocery, meeting Della and doing a little surveillance on the place, Messenger had shined a new light on the case. He identified a main player in Tennyson Cummings and identified a vehicle listed to him. Sullivan considered doing a little surveillance himself and then thought better of it. This could not be rushed and he was tired after a day on the ball field.

He decided to head home and take a shower. He hoped he wouldn't have to deal with anything too critical until he got a little rest before calling Eleanora.

19

WHEN SULLIVAN WALKED INTO HIS kitchen, his answering machine was blinking. The most recent message was from Luther's mom, Gina. The previous was from Luther and the one before that was from Eleanora Mathews.

Gina Pride was calling to tell Frank that Luther had called and said he was settled in his room with a host family in Bradenton, had met some of the guys and was anxious to start playing ball on Monday. He also had asked his mother to call Frank and tell him to call him at the number he had given her. The second call was from Luther who asked Frank to call him as soon as he could, that he had some important information for him. He reminded Frank that he was now in the Eastern Time Zone and two hours ahead of Denver time. He was going out for pizza with some of the players he had just met and would be back in his room that had a private number at ten o'clock his time. In the third call, Eleanora asked that Frank call her when he got home.

It was a few minutes after eight, Denver time, so he called Luther right then. Luther answered on the first ring. After they talked about the flight and what he thought of Florida, what he thought of the guys he had met, and his living arrangements, they got to the point. Luther informed Frank that Lilian Martinez had called his home and his mother had given him the message and the number to reach her in the hospital. He had called the number, the fourth floor nurses station. Lilian had been released from ICU. His call was transferred to her bedside phone. Lilian said she hurt like hell and was nauseous from the pain killers they had given her. Lilian told Luther that she wanted to tell him the whole story about how Janel was killed and about why she had been shot. Before she could tell Luther what was on her mind, he told her that he could not be in the middle of it; he was in Bradenton, Florida starting his baseball career. Luther told her to talk to Sgt. Sullivan, nobody else, and that he would have him contact her.

Luther and Frank discussed it for several minutes. Sullivan told Luther that he was exactly right, that he should not be in the middle of it. According to Luther, Lilian eventually agreed that Sullivan should go to her hospital room, number 414, and talk to her on Sunday morning at eleven a.m. She told Luther that her mom had been sleeping in the room with her and that she would be there when they talked. That's the only way she would do it, if her mother could be present. This arranged, after some more baseball talk, Luther and Sullivan ended their conversation with the promise to be in touch soon, after Luther's first pitching opportunity, if not before.

Sullivan sat still at his kitchen table for a few minutes. He had not had time to clean up or eat or anything else when the phone rang again. It was Eleanora. He remained still and let the call go to the answering machine.

"Hey, Frank, this is Ellie. I'm sorry I didn't make it up to Boulder today to watch you guys play. I completely forgot that a friend of mine was having a baby shower this afternoon. I went shopping for a gift and then went to the shower. I think I had a little too much punch and now I'm feeling drowsy. I'm going to bed soon, but call me tomorrow if you want to get together. I'm going to go over to Mount Carmel, my mom's old neighborhood as you well know, for Mass at eleven o'clock in the morning. If you want to go together, call me in the morning. Hope…" The machine cut her off mid-sentence.

Sullivan was relieved to listen to the message. All he wanted to do was relax, maybe watch a game on cable television. He made a lettuce and tomato sandwich on dark rye bread, poured a glass of milk and turned the television on. He found the Braves/Giants game on TBS and watched some of that. It was a pitchers' duel that the Braves eventually won 1-0. Sullivan didn't know that though, as he fell asleep in his chair and didn't wake up until two in the morning, at which time he turned off the TV, brushed his teeth and went to bed.

After a few hours of restful sleep, Sullivan got up, went for a run, and got cleaned up. It was about nine-thirty when he called Eleanora and told her that he had a meeting at eleven o'clock and that he would call her when he was done, probably about one o'clock. She was in a good mood and looking forward to going to Mass and the coffee and donuts social after Mass. Hearing this, Sullivan realized that one of the things he treasured about her was her unwavering faith, and her optimism, which he thought was a consequence of her faith. It also came to mind that he could benefit from her company, a non-police presence and attitude, in addition to the amorous adventure that awaited them.

Sullivan called Detective Lopez on his cell phone to inform him of his intention to go to the hospital and talk to Lilian Martinez at her request. He explained that she had called Luther and asked him to arrange a meeting, which was not exactly true but close enough for the time being. Then he assured Lopez that he would try and get a feel for Lilian's health and disposition. Lopez was enthusiastic about it and relieved that he didn't have to respond to the hospital on his day off. He expressed complete confidence in Sullivan's ability.

Then Sullivan called Lodi and Crowe and Messenger to inform them of what he was doing. He had learned that one requisite for, and perhaps the most important key to, good team morale, was making sure that nobody felt that they were not being included. In this case, Crowe and Messenger were glad to be in the loop and happy that the sergeant was handling it rather than assigning them. They were also anxious to hear what Lilian might have to say about who killed Janel Robinson. Lodi, however, volunteered to meet Sullivan at the hospital to standby in case he was needed. Besides, he said, he was already at headquarters anyway, working on paperwork. Sullivan decided that it would be good to have him along so they agreed to meet shortly before eleven o'clock.

Lilian's hospital room was directly in front of the nurse's station on the fourth floor of Denver General Hospital. The first thing that Lodi and Sullivan noted was that an armed hospital security officer was stationed outside her room. After showing him their credentials, they were allowed to enter the room. Sofia Martinez was sitting next to the bed, trying to help her daughter sip some water. She turned and greeted the officers, "Hello, Lodi, hello, Sergeant, she's getting better and is anxious to talk to you guys."

Lilian nodded, and then added, "I feel weak so let's get this started before I need to sleep some more. They are giving me something for the pain but my mind is clear."

Sullivan then took out his tape recorder and put an introduction to the interview on it, including, date, time, location and participants. He and Lodi had agreed that starting with Janel being killed on Monday night, and working forward to the present from there, up to when Lilian was shot, was a good approach.

They did just that and in fifteen minutes had a concise statement. It was apparent that Lilian had thought a great deal about what she wanted to tell the police. She began her

145

statement by saying that she was completely clean and sober other than the pain killers that were being administered intravenously. She followed that by reiterating that she had not had any illegal drugs since Monday night when Janel was shot.

Then she proceeded to tell her story as follows:

> *Winthrop Jensen was a Jamaican male and he had been her "boyfriend" for two or three months. She referred to him as "Bunny." According to Lilian, the Jamaicans had been on a manhunt for a police informant, or more than one, for the past two weeks. Janel's father, Arthur Robinson, had been buying cocaine from the Jamaicans and, after establishing their trust in him, bought several ounces. He paid for half of it and they fronted him the other half. He never paid for the rest of it and they were hunting him down. Then, when the police started shutting down their operations, they at first thought that he was responsible, that he was the snitch. When they realized that Janel was Arthur Robinson's daughter, Winthrop Jensen began pressuring her to persuade her father to pay what he owed. Jensen promised Janel that "the big man" would kill Arthur Robinson if he didn't pay them back. She told them that she had no relationship with her father, never saw him and didn't know where he lived. They continued to put pressure on Janel about her father, but they still flirted with her and they wanted to have sex with her, especially "Tenny."*

*On Monday night, they were partying, ten to twelve Jamaicans including Winthrop Jensen and Tenny whom they also referred to as "Big" or "the Poet". They were in Fuller Park and had food and drinks and some pot. Janel was dancing to the music and flirting with some of the guys. Then Tenny got along side her and started to pressure her and she resisted. He was starting to talk about her paying off her father's debt with sexual favors. Tenny got distracted by two guys who approached him with a bottle of rum. They call those guys "Henry." I don't know their real names but they are brothers. One they call **long** Henry and the other they call **short** Henry but they are about the same size.*

Lilian left the party about then and ran over to Manual High School where she knew Luther Pride was watching an outdoor basketball tournament. He drove Lilian back to the park after she explained that she was afraid that Janel was in trouble. According to Lilian, Luther was going to go into the park and get Janel out of there. When they got to the park, Lilian ran ahead so that nobody would see her with Luther. By the time Luther had parked, a shot was fired and Janel went down.

Lilian was just about to the cluster of people around Janel when she heard a shot fired. At that time she could no longer see Janel. As far as who shot Janel, Lilian didn't know for sure but thought it was Tenny or one of the two Henry brothers. She couldn't say if it was accidental, as a result of a struggle, or intentional.

Lilian was grabbed hard and pushed to the ground by Winthrop Jensen—Bunny. He ran to the south edge of the park with Lilian in tow, at times almost pulling her off her feet in his haste, to where Janel's car was parked. He had Janel's keys in his hand. He then forced her into the back hatch of the Datsun, causing her nose to bleed in the process.

Bunny drove recklessly southbound for ten minutes, running through red lights and stop signs when clear, and was eventually involved in a hit and run accident somewhere around Eighth and Kalamath Street. At that point they abandoned the car and ran on foot. They made their way to a pay phone on Broadway where Bunny called the Henrys who came and picked them up in their Ford pickup truck. They eventually got back to the house at 1205 E. 23rd Avenue and she was not allowed to leave.

Winthrop Jensen shot her Thursday night. He had heard noise outside and observed the SWAT team getting out of their van. He knew they were coming for him and he ran to the kitchen where Lilian was standing. He hollered "Bitch!" and, "Informa'!" then shot her twice, in the chest and shoulder, dropped the gun on the floor and escaped out the back door.

Sgt. Sullivan asked Lilian if she knew anything about the killing of Darnell Coolidge at 16th and Lafayette. She replied that she had overheard Bunny and "the Poet" talking, on the day that she was shot, about somebody getting killed, but they were acting very suspicious of *her* by then, and they made sure that she didn't hear what they were saying.

It was Lilian's opinion that recent pressure from the police had made the Jamaican dealers paranoid. They were looking in every corner for possible informants. Arthur Robinson's unpaid debt made them suspect that he might have been informing on them to get the Jamaicans off the street before they could carry out their threats to kill him on sight. She further believed that if Janel Robinson was killed intentionally, and she could not say for sure, it was because she was his daughter, not because they thought she was informing on them herself.

Lilian had no knowledge of the attempt on the life of Detective Crowe by the Henry brothers or that they had subsequently died in a horrific accident. She did know them, however, and suspected that "the Poet" was very close to them and had known them for years, going back to their days in Kingston, Jamaica, before they all emigrated and settled, illegally she assumed, in Miami. One of the brothers had forced himself on Lilian one night at 2811½ Franklin while she was high and waiting for Bunny to pick her up. After that she discovered that she had an STD (Sexually Transmitted Disease), so she stopped seeing Bunny out of fear that there would be trouble if she passed it on to him.

She thought both brothers were evil. In her words, "If you have any unsolved rapes or murders, look at those two—nothing is beneath them."

When Sullivan and Lodi left the hospital room, twenty minutes had elapsed. They looked at each other shaking their heads. What they had just witnessed was not what they expected at all. Lilian Martinez, three days from being shot twice, was alert and confident and determined to tell them her story concisely and intelligently. They had been expecting a strung out, barely articulate doper, expressing herself in grammatically poor English and expletives. Instead, what they encountered was a bright teen-age woman, who had apparently taken advantage of her high school years and who was determined to stand up for herself, overcome her addiction and see that the man who tried to kill her was prosecuted. Because of her condition (she was obviously in some discomfort and pain), and due to the completeness and succinctness of her statement, the interview was terminated in twenty minutes.

"You know what this just did for me?" Lodi asked.

"Tell me about it," was Sullivan's response.

"Once again it made me realize, no fuckin' way is street drug dealing a victimless crime. Sometimes I think we use that term, not because there is no victim, but because the victims are 'no-count' drug users. People like Lilian are victims and they do matter and they do need our help. I feel pretty good right now," his voice getting louder, "that we're about to get this guy Tenny. I'm sure of it—just a matter of when."

"Man, I hope you're right."

They both felt a deep sense of relief. It had been a trying seven days and Lilian's survival and her statement were game changers. They would get to the bottom of this crime wave.

Lodi said that he would drop by headquarters, go to the radio room and have two copies made of Lilian's recorded statement. He would leave the original and a copy for Detective Lopez in Homicide after calling him and letting him know how well it went. Following that, they went their separate ways for the day.

Sullivan then called Eleanora to see if she wanted to go for a drive in the mountains. Not far, just above Boulder, to a picnic spot Sullivan had been going to since he was a kid. She said she would, and it was agreed that he would pick her up at two-thirty. He left her with the promise that he was going to bring the food and drink for the picnic, be it ever so humble.

He went home, changed into faded blue jeans, old work/ hiking boots and carried his baseball jacket just in case it cooled off up in the canyon. On his way out the door he called George Crowe to see how he was doing. It had only been a couple of days since he had been shot at. George said he was feeling fine, but admitted to being stressed out and nervous. Sullivan filled him in regarding Lilian's statement and Crowe was pleased to hear about it. Sullivan then called Leon Messenger, gave him an update on Lilian's statement. Leon was glad to hear about Lilian's recovery, and mentioned that he had taken his boys to the zoo.

Sullivan left his house and stopped by the Safeway at Evans and Downing where he picked up deli sandwiches and a few other things. He was feeling relaxed for the first time since Monday night and was putting police work on a side track for a few hours and trying to stay in the present.

Eleanora was ready when Sullivan got to her house. She looked better than ever, dressed in blue jeans and a sleeveless white cotton shirt, wearing a pink ribbon in her wavy, dark brown hair. She had definitely inherited both her mother's *and* her father's good looks, Sullivan thought to himself, as she got into his 1978 Dodge Power Wagon pickup. The truck had a bench seat and she slid across the seat and squeezed Sullivan's right shoulder with her left hand while kissing him on the cheek.

"Nice muscles, Popeye," she said.

"Ahoy, Ellie," he responded, then took a long look at her. "I can't believe how good you look. But what the hell are you doing in this truck today? You should have been married to the man of your choice long ago."

"Well, I don't know what to tell you. But I'm with the man of my choice today so what do you say to that? Huh?"

"Ahoy," he said again and then, "I am what I am," in his best Popeye imitation."

They both laughed a little and Sullivan changed the subject to the picnic as Ellie looked through the grocery bag that contained the food he bought.

"Mmm, this looks so good, where are we going again?"

"Well, where I was thinking is up Boulder Canyon. We could have a picnic on Boulder Creek; there are a lot of little pull-off spots where we can put our feet in the water if you want. But we don't have to go there; we could go somewhere else."

"No, that sounds great, let's go. I haven't been to Boulder Canyon since you took me there way back when."

"I forgot about that, but now that you mention it, I do remember. We went up there on a Saturday morning and I fixed you breakfast, right?"

"Right."

As they drove, police work switched from the side track in his mind back onto the mainline of his thoughts. Sullivan recapped the conversation they had with Lilian Martinez and how determinedly she told her story, and how that had encouraged and invigorated him, and Lodi as well.

"Don't you ever worry, Frank? Last week you guys came so close to tragedy but now you're rarin' to go again and probably can't wait till tomorrow night to chase down evil some more.

Aren't you afraid of burnout? Do you worry about getting hurt or killed?"

"Ellie, c'mon, that's a lot of questions. The answer to all of them is yes and no at the same time. Let's put it this way, being a cop is never easy. I know it sounds banal, but it's the simple truth. From one minute to the next you can go from heading home to being ambushed on your way out of the building. Luck and Saint Michael might keep you alive—this time. I think it would be impossible without my faith, and my belief that truth wins out, and good triumphs over evil. And working out and prayer are critical to my sanity, and to my durability. I don't want to become hateful and cynical, and it's tough sometimes.

"Plus, I feel a tremendous sense of responsibility, way more than I probably should. I want everything we do to be perfect and that's impossible. It really bothers me that Janel Robinson got killed. I feel like we should have done something about it before it happened. And then they kill somebody we're working with and we don't have a clue. On top of that, they take two shots at one of us coming out of the basement of headquarters following a raid where the dealer shot Lilian. Difference is, the two guys who tried to take out George killed themselves getting away. We arrest the guy who shot Lilian and she's going to recover. Momentum has turned in our direction. Now, when we catch whoever did the other two crimes, I'll be able to relax."

They drove on in silence while a Merle Haggard and Willie Nelson cassette played in the background. They were not paying attention to the words, but the music was easy to listen to. Out of nowhere Ellie slid across the bench seat and again kissed Frank Sullivan on the cheek. Then she slid back across the seat and looked out the window. She was blushing— embarrassed by her display of emotion. When she looked back at him she had a tear in her eye and he reached over and grabbed her hand. She looked at him again then looked out the window.

They had a nice afternoon in a shady spot on the edge of Boulder Creek. They ate the lunch that Sullivan had packed and then they relaxed on a blanket and listened to the soothing sound of the creek. For a few brief moments, Sullivan dozed off with his head on Ellie's lap.

20

SULLIVAN DROPPED ELLIE OFF AT her house late on Sunday afternoon. She wanted him to come in and he wanted to, except for a sudden feeling of panic that there was not adequate security guarding Lilian's hospital room. He decided he would call Detective Lopez and discuss it with him, so he went to headquarters after leaving Ellie and did just that. He believed that a uniform officer or a member of the investigations division should be assigned to guard Lilian on a twenty-four hour basis, supplementing, if not replacing, the hospital security guard. Lopez agreed and decided to discuss the matter with his supervisor immediately. He was pretty sure that the manpower would be authorized for the next few days at least. And it was, starting with Detail 3, the seven p.m. to three a.m. shift, that night. One uniform officer from District 1 would be assigned for the next five days. Then if more time was needed, it would be re-evaluated.

Sullivan was still in his office when the phone extension on his desk rang again. It was an unfamiliar voice asking if he were Sgt. Sullivan. He replied in the affirmative and the line was silent a moment.

Then, "This is Arthur Robinson. I don't know if you remember me or not, Sullivan. You use to play some fast pitch softball with my brother Antoine. He was a pitcher and you were a catcher on one of the teams he played on. Remember?"

"Oh hell yes, I remember Antoine. We called him Fats, like Antoine 'Fats' Domino. He could pitch a little bit, threw

155

hard. How is he? I heard he's still pitching for somebody out at Garland Park on Tuesday and Thursday nights."

"Yeah, everybody calls him that. He is still pitching, and he's fine, he's always had his shit together. He runs his own garage and he's always been good to Janel. He told me that you were a good guy. But I'm not calling about him. I'm calling about my daughter getting killed…"

Sullivan had only been half paying attention to the caller and for some reason the name hadn't registered with him. Maybe he was tired or preoccupied, or maybe he hadn't heard it clearly. Hearing the last two sentences, he suddenly realized who was calling and he interrupted him, then, "Oh okay, *Arthur Robinson*—we want to talk to you."

"Well, you don't know the half of it. I'm probably the reason she got killed and I wanna' do something about it. I talked to my ex-wife LaDonna and she tells me that you are the man I should talk to, about setting things right. That's why I'm calling."

"Okay, I'm sorry for your loss. Arthur, where…"

"LaDonna thinks I can help you get the guy responsible for Janel's death and she's right. She hates my fuckin' guts and wants nothin' to do with me. And if I help you catch the killer, she'll still hate my fuckin' guts. But I'm doing this for me, and the thing is, I can do this guy if you work with me."

"Where are you now?"

"I'm at the fuckin' po-lice building, man, in the lobby, the po-lice at the desk let me use the phone at the desk." Robinson was raising his voice now, showing impatience and irritation.

"Now settle down, Mr. Robinson, it's a stroke of luck that you even reached me here today. This is my day off. But I am here and I'm willing to talk to you, okay? Are you wanted now? Cause if you're wanted I'm gonna put your ass in jail whether you talk to me or not."

"I'm not wanted now, man, but check me out: Arthur Robinson, August 7, 1941."

"Okay, I will. If you're serious, I'll be down there to pick you up in ten minutes."

"All right, I'm here waiting, man."

"Okay."

Sullivan immediately called Leon Messenger on his cell phone. There was no answer but he left a message and within five minutes, Messenger returned his call.

"Hey, Sarge, what's happenin', man? Don't you ever take a day off, my brother?"

"Hey, I was gonna ask you the same thing yesterday, Leon."

Sullivan then explained why he was calling and Messenger jumped at the chance to come into the office and interview Arthur Robinson. Within twenty minutes, Messenger was in the office, wearing black nylon sweat pants and a gold muscle shirt and gold shoes. His muscular upper body was on full display and the bronze of his skin was accentuated by the tight-fitting gold material. He had a big smile on his face as he and Sullivan shared a hard, bro' hand shake, harder than Sullivan would have preferred, but he appreciated Messenger's vigor.

Arthur Robinson was sitting in the holding cell outside the Narcotics Bureau. Messenger looked inside the one-way glass and immediately recognized Robinson's face from so many years of working in Northeast Denver. Then he opened the door and led him to an interview room. They were joined there by Sgt. Sullivan and then they got down to business. Messenger requested that Robinson start his narrative from when he first started buying from the Jamaican drug dealers, and work forward to the present.

Robinson was dressed in nice clothes; his slacks and dress shirt appeared to be on their second or third day of use, clean, but wrinkled, and not fresh. His graying mustache needed trimming and he needed a shave. He smelled of alcohol and tobacco smoke. His eyes were watery and bloodshot although his speech and movements didn't seem to be impaired. He looked burdened—like a man on somebody's hit list who had just lost his daughter to a violent act.

Robinson's narrative flowed somewhat haphazardly, more like he was trying to cover everything quickly rather than as if he were trying to withhold certain details. Sullivan and Messenger had to question him frequently for the sake of clarity. He admitted to having bought cocaine from Jamaican dealers in Denver for the past year or so. He generally bought small amounts, eighth of an ounce—what was called an "eight-ball", or less. He had earned their confidence and was on a first name basis with several of them who were known to the dark narcs: the Henry brothers, Winthrop Jensen, and the one they called Big Tenny, or "the Poet." He also mentioned several others that Messenger and Sullivan did not know.

By his own admission, Robinson was a con man. As he put it, he couldn't help himself, he would lie and con even when being straight and truthful was more to his advantage. He had conned the Jamaicans out of two ounces of fairly pure cocaine on a scam that if they fronted him that much, he would deliver them an extra five hundred dollars per ounce. The plan didn't make sense when he attempted to explain it to the narcs and there was no reason that it should have—it was a humbug. The bottom line was that the Jamaicans thought that he owed them about $6,000.

After twenty minutes or so, Messenger and Sullivan called a timeout and offered to get Robinson water or a soda or coffee. He said he would like a soda and they agreed to get him one. They left him secure in the interview room and talked on their way to the pop machine. They were both scratching their heads at the scheme Robinson had just described, one that had gone predictably bad, and for which the Jamaican dealers, and possibly others, wanted him dead. They decided that for the next portion of the interview they should focus on how, if at all, Robinson could be of use to them.

When they reconvened, Robinson laid out his plan that involved him taking $5,000 in city funds, marked bills, to "the Poet" after having arranged a meeting with him. That amount, according to Robinson, was most of what he owed them. Questioned as to how he would arrange the meeting, he responded that he would either get word to one of the people who hung around with him or he would try and hook up with "the Poet" at one of the places he was known to hang out.

It was apparent that Robinson had been around and was somewhat familiar with the way that narcotics detectives setup deals with informants. Sullivan had already checked the informant files in the Captain's office, before Messenger arrived, to see if Arthur Robinson had ever been used as an informant, and if he was wanted. He learned that he had been used in the early Eighties but was terminated after he took $100 to buy cocaine and came back with nothing but a story that he had been ripped off for the money and had been given no drugs. He was searched and neither money nor drugs had been found, and his story could not be corroborated nor disproved. The detectives handling him decided not to work with him again. They put a note in his file to that effect. Sullivan also learned that Robinson was not currently wanted.

After hearing his plan, Messenger informed Robinson that there was no way in hell they were going to turn him loose with $5,000 of anybody's money. That would be bad police work and an invitation to trouble. He went on to explain that

Robinson had been *de facto* disqualified as a reliable informant, and any use of his information in an affidavit for a search warrant would have to disclose that fact. How they could use him, was solely as a source of information to corroborate what they already had.

Messenger reviewed his notes with Robinson, double checking names, descriptions, addresses, vehicle descriptions, weapons information and dates corresponding to events that he mentioned. The entire interview took forty-five minutes or so. When he was finished, Messenger gave Robinson his pager and cell phone numbers and told him to call him Monday night at seven o'clock, or any time if he had new information. Robinson agreed and he was then escorted out of the building.

Messenger and Sullivan sat in the sergeants' office and discussed the interview. Robinson would not be used as an informant. But he had given some good accurate intelligence information, albeit very little that they did not already have. He was a con man who was now motivated to talk by guilt, grief and fear. They both agreed that the best they could hope for was that he would get fresh information, acting on his own, that he would pass it on to them, and they could act on it accordingly.

What they feared was that Arthur Robinson would get himself killed in the process, solving nothing and creating more work for everyone.

By six-thirty on Monday night all the dark narcs were in the sergeants' office recapping what had occurred over the weekend. The major events included Messenger's time at the Kingston Corner on Saturday evening, identifying a vehicle belonging to Tennyson Cummings and tentatively setting up a "date" to go back and talk with Della on Monday night; the interview with Lilian Martinez at Denver General Hospital on

Sunday morning; and the interview with Janel Robinson's dad Arthur late Sunday afternoon.

It was their one chance in the night to talk a little, kid each other and have a few laughs before the night took shape. They invariably had a collective agenda, more or less agreed upon, but in police work perhaps like no other, "one thing leads to another." Therefore, when they had the chance to relax and talk among themselves, it was relished. Lodi had stopped by the police garage on his way to work (in fact, it was way out of his way) and picked up a disfigured motorcycle windshield that had been taken off of one of the wrecked Harleys from the Traffic Division and thrown on the scrap heap. With the garage's permission he took it with him to headquarters and stood it up on Crowe's desk, as if for protection. This got a few laughs and let Crowe know that he was cared for. Everybody knew how lucky they had been that he had not been killed. Two shots missed their target by just inches, destroying the windshield but nothing else. And the assailants did not survive to make another attempt.

After the bullshit session, it was decided that Leon should attempt to see Della again at the Kingston Corner. Before he went, Lodi was to scout the location and see if the car identified as belonging to Tennyson Cummings, aka "the Poet," was in the parking lot. The team was divided as to whether Leon should enter the store if "the Poet" was there since they had seen each other at 2811½ Franklin when Leon accompanied the informant, Darnell Coolidge, who was murdered soon after making a buy that night. Was he murdered for being an informant? That was the question. If so, did that mean that Leon was made as a cop and would therefore be in danger if he was introduced to Cummings again? Would "the Poet" confront him about being a cop or would he play him along and set him up to be killed later?

Leon and Lodi were in favor of going in no matter what. Sullivan and Crowe were of the opinion that the goal was for Messenger to gain the trust of Della and possibly work his way into Cummings, through her, or in any case gain valuable intelligence from her. The sergeant's vote was the deciding vote in this case and it was decided that it would be a no-go if "the Poet" was known to be in the store, if his car was in the parking lot.

The next issue to be decided was whether Leon should be wired for what was just to be a conversation. He didn't want to be; he had on a tight fitting, bright green dress shirt, khaki pants covering his Walther in a leg holster and shiny, size thirteen, tan, wing tip shoes. It was agreed that he wouldn't be wired and that he would leave if he sensed that he wasn't trusted. It was also decided that a uniform car would be parked nearby, if one was available, so that if "the Poet's" car was seen in the area, a routine stop could be made to identify him and to prevent him from entering the store while Detective Messenger was there, if possible.

Upon arrival surveillance was established and Lodi reported that "the Poet's" vehicle was not there, as far as he could tell. Detective Messenger entered the Kingston Corner at about eight-fifteen in the evening. There were several people in the store speaking accented English or the Jamaican patois—lots of loud talking and laughing. Reggae music was playing at a modest volume, allowing conversation.

Surveillance observed Messenger getting out of his Cordoba, after parking on the north side of the market. He entered casually and was observed greeting Della at the front of the store. She was with a customer but when finished she took Messenger's hand and whispered something in his ear. They went toward the back of the store. Surveillance momentarily lost sight of Messenger in the store but most of the store was in sight and everything seemed copasetic. Lodi had his car parked on the edge of the parking lot with the hood up and he was under the hood as if analyzing or fixing a problem. He had arranged that he would lean out from under the hood and wipe his hands on a rag when he could tell that everything was okay inside the market.

Crowe and Sullivan were in positions where they could clearly see inside the store as much as possible from outside. It was a routine surveillance. In twenty minutes or so, Messenger came out of the store and headed to his parked car, out of sight of the store.

When he got into his car he discreetly got on the radio and hastily called the sergeant. "Hey, Sarge, everything is cool in there; she has no idea who I am. We didn't talk business, I just flirted with her and we talked music and food and stuff like that. She said she's been in Denver about a year. Before that she was in Miami."

"So are we done in there for tonight, Leon?"

"No, she wants to meet me up the street at The Riviera, a Mexican food place on Kentucky and Cherry. She'll close here at nine o'clock and go up there."

"10-4, that sounds okay. What do you think of her? Can she lead us anywhere?"

"Oh yeah, man, I think so. She said a friend is meeting her at the place at nine for a minute, and then she and I are going to eat. We can set up on it now and see who shows up."

"I know the place, Leon, been eating Mexican food there for years. You and some Jamaicans in there won't fit in with their usual clientele. But it's a low-key place and good food. Let's all meet first by St. Thomas Seminary down on Louisiana and Steele by the front entrance. Nobody will pay any attention to us there."

"Okay, Sarge, I'll be there in a minute, man."

Sullivan then confirmed that the other two were clear and the four of them met quickly by the front entrance to the seminary. It was decided that Messenger would go into the Riviera, wearing a wire, to meet Della and whomever else showed up. Crowe hurried back to the office to get the Kel-Kit and transmitters so that Messenger could be wired. The kit consisted of a receiver and recorder to enable the monitoring and recording of the conversation. The transmitter Crowe chose this time was a small sending unit housed in what looked like a pager. That way, Messenger could wear it clipped to the waist of his pants and not worry about being patted down for a hidden wire. It looked perfectly normal, as so many people carried pagers.

Crowe would sit in his vehicle with the Kel-Kit and take notes as he saw fit. Sullivan would go into The Riviera with Lodi before Messenger went in. It was agreed that they would sit at the bar and order food. The last thing Crowe said on the air before they went their separate ways was, "Bring me an order of those ground beef enchiladas."

21

MESSENGER ENTERED THE RIVIERA AND looked for Della. He saw her stand up to greet him at a table to the right of the front door. Sullivan and Lodi saw him come in and meet the woman at the table. Messenger touched her lightly on the shoulder as they both sat down. They ordered drinks, then food, and then Della excused herself to go to the restroom. Messenger stood up as she left, maybe overdoing the perfect gentleman act, but she seemed to like it.

As Della returned to the table, she was met there by a tall man with a Jamaican accent. He was about as tall as Messenger but not as heavy in the chest, arms and shoulders, more the body of a tall, fit soccer player.

"Tenny, this is somebody I met at the store, Norman Preston," she says to the newcomer at the table.

The man she called Tenny, said to Messenger, "I think we might have met, *mon*, but I can't remember where."

Messenger responds, "No, man, if we had, you'd remember. Nobody forgets meeting me. I'm big and loud and I am unmistakable. How many brothers you know have this white patch in their hair?" he said pointing to his head. Anyway, good to meet you, my brother, I'm Norman." Messenger pointed this out knowing that when he had gone to 2811½ Franklin with the late informant, his permanent whitish-gray forelock was temporarily dyed black.

Messenger then gave him a hard bro' hand shake that flexed his shoulder and arm muscles in the process and made a slapping sound. The other man's grip was firm as well, as he asserted himself. "And people call me Tenny. Good food in this place, mon, and excellent margaritas." Tenny was dressed nicely in designer jeans and a loose fitting, light weight shirt. He held a book-size leather case, about the size of a bible, zipped up the entire edge. He carried himself like a celebrity athlete or entertainer. He was polite and friendly but distant— maybe wary. Tenny soon excused himself from their table, and walked to a table farther inside the bar where he joined two other men in their twenties.

Crowe continued to monitor the conversation at Messenger's table after Tenny left. Messenger and Della had dinner and made small talk about music, including Messenger's favorites from way back: Chicago and Stevie Wonder. But he was also up on Patti LaBelle and Janet Jackson and Tina Turner. Della liked the R and B stuff too, but said that Bob Marley and Jimmy Cliff were her homeboys, and Peter Tosh, who later in 1987 would be killed in what Della claimed was her hometown of Kingston, Jamaica. Della tried to shift the conversation to sports a couple of times but she was surprised to find out that Messenger, or Norman Preston as she knew him, had almost no interest in sports, only certain sports figures, like Ali, who interested him as social activists and flamboyant celebrities.

It was just a normal conversation and an observer might have mistaken Messenger and Della for a couple on a first date. After an hour, Messenger paid the bill, and he and Della left the restaurant. They both nodded at Tenny as they were leaving and he responded in kind. Messenger walked her to her car and once in her car, she reached out and grabbed his hand. She asked him to follow her home, that was nearby. He declined, and as she drove away he walked to his Chrysler Cordoba.

During the surveillance, Detective Crowe had observed where Tenny parked when he arrived at the Riviera. On the secure channel, Sullivan directed Messenger to get in a spot, from a distance safe from being observed, where he could see Tenny's car, but not to follow it when it left the Riviera. He directed Lodi and Crowe to follow Della's vehicle and assigned himself to that task as well.

"Zebra 22, she's leaving the parking lot now. She's heading east on Kentucky. Looks like she is going to turn north on Cherry."

"Zebra 23, okay, George, you can go straight on Kentucky. I'll pick her up northbound. She is northbound, no, wait a minute, she's making a u-turn in the middle of the street and is now heading southbound. I had not started following her but I'm headed the wrong way now. Can anybody pick her up?"

"Zebra 20, I got her, southbound on Cherry. She's approaching Louisiana now and she's making a left turn onto Louisiana."

"Okay, I got her," said Crowe, dispensing with the formality of his call sign, knowing that everybody knew his voice. "She's pulling into a parking lot behind the houses on the west side of Dahlia, in back of those apartments there. She parked facing eastbound, facing the backs of the houses on Dahlia. I got a good eye on her. She's standing outside of the car now, she might be waiting for somebody. She's smoking a cigarette and looking at that apartment complex there."

"Zebra 23, that address is 4705 E. Louisiana, but it will be impossible to see where she goes inside that complex, if that's where she's headed. Let me know if you need me to move into position, George."

"Okay, Lodi, I'm good for now, parked in the lot in one of these other spaces here to the west of her, and I have a great view of her. But I'm totally in the dark and she can't see me."

Just then Messenger broke into the conversation, "Zebra 21, this cat is leaving the Riviera and heading your way in that dark Camry. I didn't have to move to see that he went east, then south on Cherry."

"Okay, Leon, you stay back, okay?" was Sullivan's response.

"Right on, Sarge, I'm heading downtown to write a statement to put in the file. But holler if you need me and I'll turn around."

"10-4, thanks, Leon, good job. That had to be tough sitting in there with a pretty woman, sweet-talking her and eating enchiladas." Messenger laughed on the air, and added, "Yeah, man."

The surveillance crew watched for a minute or two after Leon's transmission before the Camry pulled into the alley and then parked next to Della's car.

"Zebra 22, I'm in a great spot with a perfect view. I can hear them talking."

"Where are you, George? How did you get in so close?" Sullivan asked.

George Crowe responded, in a soft almost inaudible voice, "You forgot, the late Henry brothers put my undercover car out of commission, so you assigned me the old blue dodge van with the dark windows and the custom interior. I'm in the back looking out the side window. No way they can see me. I'm using headphones but I still have to keep it down.

"They are in a disagreement about something, Sarge, she's doing most of the talking. I can't tell what they are arguing about. Wait a minute, I just heard her say that she thinks Tenny is wrong about Norman being a cop. She's saying that she thinks Norman is cool. Then she said that she did invite him over but that she didn't want Tenny to meet him in the parking lot."

George was repeating the conversation as close to word for word, as he heard it. Lodi was writing notes as fast as he could write them, as was the sergeant.

"Zebra 20, we're getting it, George." And then he added, "Lodi, let's play this especially carefully, I don't want to follow him when he leaves. We don't want to get burned."

"10-4, Frank."

"Zebra 20 to Zebra 21, are you listening to this, Leon?"

"Right on, man, I can't believe my ears."

They kept the meeting, tense as it seemed, under surveillance until Tenny gave Della a lukewarm or half-ass hug and then got back into his car and left the area, and Della went into the apartment complex. As Lodi had noted, the complex was fairly large, making it impossible to keep an eye on her to determine which apartment she entered. They would work on that later, discreetly, through investigative means such as checking utility subscriber information, DMV records, etc.

The team agreed to meet at their office. Lodi drove there by way of 28th and Franklin, and Tenny's Camry was parked in the rear of that address in a parking spot off the alley. He made note of the time and took that information to the office with him.

A meeting that had started as an informational fishing expedition or a hunch on Messenger's part on Saturday afternoon had netted several key pieces of valuable intelligence. Della was identified as a new player in the group, with a connection to the suspected main man. A name, alias or otherwise, had been linked to the man and the vehicle matching the information received from Lilian and Luther. Most importantly, they had learned that the two of them had discussed whether Leon Messenger was a cop and that they were possibly playing him along with a potentially deadly end game in mind. Based on all of that, Sullivan decided to contact Lopez and Mathis in Homicide and see if they could come to the office for yet another meeting. He also called the lieutenant,

Hugo Connors, as the new intel added still more bona fides to the intelligence reports that the Jamaicans intended to kill one of the dark narcs. Sullivan brought him up to date on all details of the Jamaican criminal investigations.

When Mathis and Lopez showed up in the Vice and Drug Control Bureau, they both looked fresh, as if they had had a restful weekend. The homicide detectives dressed in business attire: suits, ties, nice slacks, etc. They were both dressed nattily on Monday night. Lopez in a blue sport coat, white shirt, red and blue striped tie and gray slacks. Lola Mathis looked stylish in black slacks and a light-weight yellow knit, short-sleeve top. She stayed in shape and didn't mind letting it show.

Sullivan promptly started the meeting by apologizing for calling another meeting. But, he explained, he considered it imperative to get everybody up to speed on the development of the various pieces of the case.

Lopez and Mathis informed the dark narcs that they had officially finished the case on the Henry brothers: Attempted Homicide of a Police Officer. The suspects were deceased and the case was closed in the *exceptionally cleared* category. Most importantly, it was a matter of record that an attempt had been made on Detective Crowe's life by members of a Jamaican drug gang.

They then went on to say that there was no ballistics match on the 9mm rounds removed from Lilian Martinez's body and the round recovered from the body of Janel Robinson. They were prepared to file Attempted First Degree Murder charges against Winthrop Jensen for shooting Lilian Martinez. The two of them agreed, that based on their experience investigating homicides, they liked Winthrop as the shooter of Janel Robinson. The impulsive way he attacked Lilian Martinez seemed to fit with the way Janel Robinson was killed so suddenly. But Lilian says he did not do it; she thought Tennyson Cummings did it, although she did not see him do it.

Regarding the ballistic tests that had been completed by the crime lab on the distorted rounds recovered from the body of Darnell Coolidge and the crime scene, they could not match them with the weapon recovered from Winthrop Jensen. However, Lopez reiterated that the rounds were badly distorted, but there were some indications of a possible match to the weapon recovered from Lorenzo Walters, aka Robert Grant—possible was as far as it went. The lab technician's report was inconclusive. Likewise, none of the prints found at the scene were a match with those of Lorenzo Walters.

Next to report in the meeting was Detective Lodi who was in an unusually grumpy mood and it was showing. He suggested that if Tennyson Cummings had made Leon as a cop, and from the sound of it had wanted Della to lure Messenger to her apartment to set him up, it substantially raised the stakes of the game and added a sense of urgency to "getting his ass off the street." Lodi's frustration with not having any success developing some kind of case against Cummings was evident.

Next, Sullivan asked Lodi to recap their interview with Lilian Martinez on Sunday. He did so succinctly, and promised written statements as soon as they were transcribed. He verified that Mathis and Lopez had received the two copies of the tape recording of the interview. They both nodded affirmation.

At that point, Sullivan summarized the conversation he and Leon had with Arthur Robinson on Sunday afternoon. He ended his synopsis by saying that the best that they could hope for Robinson was that he would develop some information on his own, while not becoming the next homicide victim, and that they wouldn't use him as an informant.

It was then Messenger's turn. His input was based mostly on his recent introduction to and conversations with Tennyson Cummings and Della. Messenger had two main points to make. One, Della needed to be identified, as soon as possible.

Leon Messenger had extensive undercover experience in a variety of situations. He thought he had her wrapped around his finger when they were at the table but when he went to her car with her, and she invited him to follow her home, her manner had changed and he wasn't sure exactly how or why. He had learned to pickup on subtle changes in an unwitting's way of talking to him. In their conversation at her car, she was telling him to come over to her house, but the unspoken message he was receiving loud and clear, on what seemed to be an inappropriately personal level, was "No! Don't come over, not now, not tonight."

Messenger then summarized his opinion of Della as a source of information, or as a player to be targeted. He said that he thought she was connected to the Jamaican drug trafficking operation in Denver, but not necessarily as a player, or possible co-conspirator. He was not sure that Della and Tennyson Cummings knew each other that well and, further, that they even liked each other, but there was definitely some connection and he wanted to identify it.

That brought Messenger to his second point. "Man, I'm starting to sweat, look at my head, man. As unsure as I am about Della, I'm just the opposite about Tenny, 'the Poet'. I feel like we really need to take this guy down or the body count is going to rise. The killings will continue."

As he finished saying that, he wiped sweat off his forehead, on the edges of his full afro, with a paper tissue that he had in his hand. His grayish white forelock (a condition known clinically as poliosis), glistened for attention. Then he stood up, turned, and threw the tissue in a trash can next to the sergeant's desk. Messenger regularly dyed it black with varying degrees of permanence.

This break in his narrative coincided with George Crowe's re-entry to the meeting. He had left and gone to his desk for a few minutes when Messenger had mentioned the positive identification of Della as a priority.

"Hey, Sarge, can I interrupt Leon for a minute?"

"Heck yes, George, please do."

At that point Leon reached his right fist up and Crowe gave it a casual bump without even looking at him and then spoke.

"Okay, well, I started working on the computer before we went to cover the meeting and I also went to the Records Bureau. She has no local record, but through NCIC, I think I've identified her as a woman named Celeste de la Sala Brown. She is thirty-three years old, and she isn't from Jamaica. She is from Cuba, by way of Miami. But she has been in this country a long time. I checked for the licensing on the Kingston Corner, which is in Glendale by the way, and the owner is listed as Della Brown. She gave her home address as the one on Louisiana where we followed her: Building 1, apartment 111.

"On her NCIC record she has one arrest by INS for an immigration hold, but that was dropped and she was released as 'legal resident.'"

"Wow, George, *my* man! That's some good work brotha'. She is a mystery woman then," interjected Messenger.

As he began speaking again, Detective Crowe's voice was rising in pitch showing excitement in what his investigation, to this point, had revealed. "Yeah, I mean, I'm thinking there's a lot more to this. I intend to call the Miami INS office tomorrow and see if I can find out more information about this arrest. Sounds fishy to me. Maybe they had her on a case and they tried to work her, or maybe they found out she was legal and they had no case. Anyway, I'll call them tomorrow and find out."

"Okay that's fantastic, George. I can't wait to hear what the rest of her story is." That was Sullivan's comment, and as he was about to speak up again, he wiped both hands down his face as if trying to remove the weariness he thought must be showing through. They were no closer to getting a drug case on Tennyson Cummings, and they didn't have him solidly connected to the homicides, the threats, or the attempt on George Crowe's life that resulted in two suspects dying. They didn't even have him positively identified yet. He looked at Lopez and Mathis as he started to speak.

"My first point concerns Lilian Martinez. She's gonna be a rock-star witness against Jensen, that is if we can keep her safe, and I might add, sober. But she does not think he killed Janel Robinson. She thinks it was the Henrys or Tennyson Cummings. And I think she's right. Furthermore, Tennyson Cummings thinks Leon is a cop and there's no way Leon's going to get into him undercover. But I want Leon to stay in touch with Della just to see what we can learn. In the meantime, Lodi can try and get a buy at 2811½ Franklin using Lorenzo Walters, if we can find him, and then we'll time the warrant to make sure that Cummings is there when we hit it. If Walters is out of pocket now, either because he won't call us or maybe he's a yet-to-be-discovered victim, then we'll try and come up with another informant to get us the probable cause we need for a search warrant. The problem with that is, there's no way we're gonna' catch Cummings holding or be able to link him to that address and tie him to any dope we find that way. He's too smart for that.

"The next point I have is that Eleanora Mathews may be able to identify Tenny if we can find a record on him or even a DMV record and picture. I want you, George, to keep working on identifying him and when you contact the INS guys in Miami, see what they might know about this guy. They might know of him through association with Della. Check with ATF and the FBI too—it's possible that they may have something. If all else fails, we'll set up on him and try and get a photo of him coming and going from that Franklin address."

"That all sounds good, Sarge, Al and I will help George identify him as well. What about Janel's father? Is he totally out of the picture as far as trust goes? Could you use him?"

"No, Lola," began Sullivan, and then continued, "it's not solely a trust deal as much as I'm afraid they'd shoot him on sight. But we can use what he has given us, in a search warrant affidavit to corroborate other information we receive. He has told us a lot about Tenny, says he doesn't know his real name. He has bought drugs from him and from that house on Franklin, so that's all good."

Messenger laughed, "I'm sorry, man, that'd almost be entrapment, sending him in as bait and daring those guys to kill him. Then Robinson goes to the morgue and we put the people that did it in jail. End of story."

"You are cold, Leon," was Lodi's response, "but I think we should do it—the end justifies the means, right?" Everybody laughed a little bit. Nobody was taking such an idea seriously; neither were they totally dismissive. What continued to trouble Sullivan's mind was that Robinson would probably do something on his own, trying to redeem himself, and possibly get himself killed in the process.

The meeting had run its course and it was time to get back to work. The way Sullivan left it was that the dark narcs would continue to focus on this group of Jamaican drug dealers until the homicides had been cleared by arrest. Lopez and Mathis expressed their gratitude to the dark narcs for all the work they had done since last Monday when Janel Robinson was killed.

22

IT WAS ALMOST MIDNIGHT WHEN the case meeting concluded. The homicide detectives had been working since that morning and they headed home after the meeting. Each of the dark narcs went about finishing up what he had to do before calling it a night. The phone on Sullivan's desk rang and he answered immediately. It was not who he had hoped it was.

"Sergeant, this is LaDonna Robinson, do you have a minute?"

"Of course I do, LaDonna, Do you just want to talk or is there something in particular that's on your mind?"

"The thing is, I found a couple of photos in Janel's room that I think might be helpful to you. They are of Janel and Lilian with some of the Jamaicans and she made some notes on the back of them. I don't know if they are important but they might be. The two guys who came over here to talk to her that time, and to basically threaten her, they are in one of the pictures."

"Do you want somebody to come and get them right now or would you rather wait until tomorrow?"

"I was thinking maybe you could come and get them right now. I can't sleep anyway."

"Okay, I'll do just that. Do you want me to bring you anything, maybe something to eat?"

"What I could really use is a drink, but I know the liquor stores are closed."

"They are, but let me see what I can do. What do you want, if I can get it?"

"I would sure like some vodka, and I have something to put with it."

"Okay, let me see what I can do and I'll get over there as soon as I can."

Sullivan then told the others about the call and the photos she had found. He explained that he needed to find some vodka to take over to her and asked if anybody had any ideas. Messenger spoke up.

"Hey, Sarge, I'll ride with you and I know where we can get a pint of vodka. It won't be legal and it won't be that expensive kind, man, but I'll get it for her."

With that, Messenger and Sullivan left the office and headed northeast. Messenger directed Sullivan to drive to the 2500 block of Washington Street and when he got there, had him pull into the alley and stop in a particular place. Messenger got out and went to the back door of what looked like somebody's house. He disappeared inside and in a few minutes came back to the car with a pint of Smirnoff vodka in a brown paper sack.

"Ask me no questions and I'll tell you no lies," he said to Sullivan.

"Right on, thank you, man," was Sullivan's response as they drove five more minutes to LaDonna Robinson's house where she met them at the door. Her dark mood lightened somewhat when Messenger introduced himself and handed her his purchase with his compliments.

"Well, thank you, my brother," she replied and then asked the two of them to sit down. Her living room was cluttered with what looked like might have been Janel's effects, but she cleared room for them to sit down on the couch. She handed Sullivan the photos. There were three of them. The first was of Janel and Lilian and Winthrop Jensen.

"Well, he's ours already," was Messenger's comment.

The second depicted Janel and Lilian and two other women and two men. LaDonna was returning from the kitchen with some vodka and orange juice in a glass when she explained, "Now those two guys there are the ones who came here to pressure Janel into helping them find Arthur."

Sullivan flipped the photo over and it read, "Della, some other woman and the Henrys."

"Look at this, Leon," Sullivan said to Messenger as he handed him the second photo.

"That's Della?" he asked dubiously as he looked at the back and then the front. And then he added, "And those two are the fuckers that shot at George." Messenger immediately apologized to LaDonna for what he had said and her response was, "No offense taken. That might be how I'd describe them anyway."

On the back of the third photo it said "Della and Tennyson." He had his arm around Janel and Della. He and Della were smiling broadly; Janel was not smiling.

After a few more minutes of conversation, Sullivan thanked LaDonna for giving them the pictures and promised to return them when the investigation was concluded. She declared that she didn't want them back and thanked them for the vodka, raising her glass to them as she said it. Both Sullivan and Messenger expressed their condolences again and politely shook her hand before leaving.

When they got to headquarters, they showed the pictures to Crowe and Lodi. Crowe said he thought he could identify the Henry brother who had been in the pickup shooting at him. After looking at the photos, Crowe made some notes in his notebook and then went to the copy machine and made three sets of copies. The notes he made were a reminder to question INS in Miami about the Henrys as well as Della and

Tennyson, and to fax them copies of the photos, and Winthrop Jensen's mugshot also.

Then Sullivan again brought up that Eleanora Mathews said that she saw at least one more woman in the crowd at the shooting that night in addition to Lilian and Janel. "One of these two could have been in the crowd, both of them for that matter. It's unlikely, but maybe one of them shot her. I'm gonna take the photo and see if Eleanora can identify either one. Then, if we get a better photo of any of them, I'll show her those. But at least we have a photo now. And I was going to call Luther tomorrow anyway, and see how he's doing, so I'll ask him about other women there when Janel was shot. I might have to figure out a way to get him copies of the photos and see if he knows Della and the other woman."

After a little more discussion, Sullivan typed up the nightly letter and the four of them left the building together. Before leaving, Sullivan called Eleanora to see if it was all right if he came to see her. He didn't mention that he had the photos to show her. Her response was, "By all means." Then she said she had baked something special for him after work, hoping that he would call.

It was a clear, warm night and after getting out of the El Camino in front of Ellie's house, Sullivan paused to take it in. Some stars were visible, as was the waxing crescent moon. As he thought about that, Ellie walked out the front door and stood next to him, then put her arm around his waist. Sullivan responded by putting his right arm around her shoulder and squeezing her closer to him. Neither said a word. After a few minutes, Sullivan took her hand and they walked into the house.

When he entered the house, Sullivan immediately recognized the aroma of pineapple upside-down cake. Ellie locked and bolted the door as Sullivan made his way to the kitchen.

"Mmm, that smells so good, Ellie. It's pineapple upside-down cake, isn't it? To what do I owe this special treat?"

"To yourself, I guess. What do you want to drink? I can make instant coffee or tea and of course I have water and a couple of those little bottles of ginger ale."

"Instant coffee sounds great." Sullivan said this as Ellie had already cut the cake and put two pieces on separate plates. Then she started to heat a worn teapot of water on the stove. She put the plates and forks on the kitchen table along with two cloth napkins, and motioned for Frank to sit down. He did so and she sat next to him. He was facing the back window and she was on his left facing the wall. When the water was hot, Ellie got up and fixed Frank a cup of instant coffee and one for herself. Then she sat down again. Frank had been thinking about how fabulous she looked in blue jeans, a pink T-shirt and sandals as he watched her fix his coffee.

But when he took his first bite of pineapple upside-down cake, Sullivan's thoughts transformed to visions of his mother and her exceptional baked goods, any kind of cake included. He stared peacefully ahead.

"Where'd you go, Frank, is the cake that 'out of this world'?"

"It is that good. So good it made me think of my mom, whom I thought had no equal in the baking department. Then I looked back at you and my mom was gone—with a smile on her face, I might add. Now it's just me and you and your pineapple upside-down cake."

They both laughed a little bit and continued eating. Then, as they finished, Sullivan brought out the photos.

"Let's get this out of the way, Ellie. I got these photos from Janel Robinson's mom, LaDonna. She found them among Janel's things. I want to know if you saw any of these people in

181

Fuller Park last Monday night." Then Sullivan handed her the photos and told her to take her time and look at them carefully.

"Okay, Frank, I recognize all of these people except two. I've never seen this woman." She said that while pointing at the woman—the unidentified woman—in the picture with Janel, Lilian, Della and two men.

"I've never seen that one before either, and she wasn't there when it happened." She said that pointing to Della's picture. "The Mexican girl was there and of course Janel. Those two guys in that picture were there also, right smack dab in the center of it. Is the Mexican girl the one who got shot at that house you guys raided the other night?"

"Yes, it is. That's Lilian Martinez and it looked bad at first but now it's almost certain that she is going to recover. She gave us a good statement yesterday, especially about the drug dealing and her shooting. She maintains that she isn't sure who shot Janel, but she thinks it's the big guy in that picture with Janel and the pretty woman. His name is Tennyson Cummings."

"Yeah, he was definitely there in the middle of everything. I'm pretty sure he's the one who had the gun, but I didn't see him shoot her. And the guy in the other picture, with Janel and Lilian, that's her name, right? That guy was there too."

"Okay, thanks, Ellie, I'll write a brief statement tomorrow regarding your identification of the photos of the people who were at the shooting. If you need to make a statement at some point, I'll let you know."

Sullivan placed the photos back in a small notebook that he put in his pocket. Then he changed the subject.

"How are your mom and dad doing, Ellie?"

"They're just fine, Frank, I told them that I'd run into you and a little bit of what happened down there last week, but not all the details. That'd just worry them. You know, they don't live around here anymore. They moved out to Highlands Ranch and really like it there."

"How about your North Denver family, do any of them still live over there?"

"No, you know my Nonna and Nonno passed on a few years ago. They always tried to teach me a little Italian and insisted that I use the Italian words for grandma and grandpa. I still think of them as Nonna and Nonno. They were truly the salt of the earth and I loved them so much. I run into some of the old-timers from that neighborhood when I go to Mass at Mount Carmel."

"You're right about your grandparents, they were the salt of the earth. And of course, your nonna's cooking was, like the ads use to say about Mounds bars, 'indescribably delicious.'"

Ellie stood up and offered Sullivan some more cake. He declined, so she put the cover on the cake plate. Then she put the dishes in the dishwasher, wiped off the counter and turned off the kitchen lights. She moved toward Sullivan and slipped her right hand in his left. She whispered in his ear, "Come with me, we have some catching up to do." He followed her without reservation.

23

DETECTIVE CROWE HAD TO GO to court on a different case on Tuesday afternoon at one o'clock. He went to the courtroom and met with the prosecutor who informed him that there would be a continuance in the case. He was relieved as he didn't want to spend all afternoon waiting to testify. Instead, he made his way to a deli in a food court near the courthouse, grabbed a sandwich and headed back to his desk. Every officer he ran into in the City and County Building and Headquarters, who knew him, wanted to talk about the close call he had experienced the previous week. Nearly all of them congratulated him on the outcome—two suspects dead in Cherry Creek—even though Crowe had had nothing to do with deciding their fates.

As he ate his sandwich, he got his notes regarding Della together, so that he could ask the right questions when he called INS in Miami. He had gotten the phone number and the name of a contact person from the Denver INS guys with whom the police worked. He was nothing if not organized as an investigator. On the top of a legal pad, he wrote the name, Celeste de la Sala Brown, date of birth, 08/10/53, aka Della Brown, Cedella. Then he started another column on the pad and at the top of that column, he wrote the name, Tennyson Cummings, aka Tenny, Big Tenny, "the Poet," date of birth unknown; age, middle to late thirties.

He called the INS contact number and talked to Greg Lynch, INS agent in Miami. Crowe took a few minutes to introduce himself. He told Lynch that he had eight years on the job, that he was working in a street narcotics unit, called the dark narcs, working nights, targeting violent street-level dealers. He added that they were currently working some violent Jamaican drug dealers and went into some detail about the recent homicides. He briefly mentioned the attempt on his own life last week, without going into detail or mentioning the Henry brothers. Crowe wanted to get to the main point of his call, that he was primarily seeking information about two people, and he gave Lynch the names of Tennyson Cummings and Della Brown, complete with known variations.

Upon hearing the names, Greg Lynch responded, "I hope you have some time, George. The good news is that I know of both of those; the bad news is that I have a ton of information and it's a long story."

Crowe responded, "I've got all afternoon, if it's convenient for you now."

"Now is perfect for me. I've been working with Miami Narcotics and ATF and the joint task force at Miami International Airport for the past three years or so. Many of our targets are Jamaican, but not all of them of course. As you can imagine, we have drug dealers coming here and passing through here from every country in the world, especially Latin America, Cuba, and Jamaica."

Lynch went on to tell Crowe that Della, whom he originally knew as Della Brown or Cedella Brown, was being looked at as a known associate of Tennyson Cummings and other Jamaican drug dealers a couple of years ago. Then he interrupted himself to clarify that he would tell Cummings' complete history in a minute. Della was thought to be a runner for Cummings and maybe a part-time girlfriend.

Then he started from the beginning. "About eighteen months ago, Miami was working a case on Jamaicans dealing grams and eight-balls of cocaine; they were also capable of some weight to the right customers. The main target was thought to be part of Cummings' crew, but they could never get a hand-to-hand from him with their u/c (undercover) officer. One night they sent the u/c officer into a house close to downtown, which is a rough area. It was supposed to be a routine buy/walk, no problem. The u/c officer had been introduced to people at the house by an informant. On this night, he entered the house, not wearing a wire, but no problem. You know we do it all the time on these small-time dealers, I'm sure you guys do too, and there were four guys covering the deal in separate vehicles.

"Well, the u/c officer made the buy and headed down the dark street to his car. Everything seemed cool. Before the officer could make it to his u/c vehicle, a blacked out Mustang convertible appeared on the cross street at the corner, close to where the u/c vehicle was parked; someone in the passenger seat opened fire with a 9mm semi-automatic pistol, hitting the officer twice in the chest and killing him almost instantly.

"The Mustang sped off into an old industrial area a few blocks away, at an extremely high rate of speed."

Crowe interrupted him at this point, "Wait a minute, I remember this case. We all heard about it when it happened and talked about it a lot, man. You never caught the guys, right?"

"That's right. What happened was, the closest cover car went to aid the officer who was down, and the next two closest cars took off in pursuit. But within blocks the car had disappeared and they couldn't find it—never have found it. Not long after surveillance reported that the u/c officer was out of the house, shots rang out. The fourth cover officer, who was at the back of the location, saw a woman run out the back of the dope house. She practically ran into him and he grabbed her and put her in his car. He joined in the short search for the shooting suspects, with her in the car. I say short because it was like the car got swallowed up never to be seen again. It was determined that the woman would be arrested since she had been in the house just before the officer was killed outside of it. She told the officer that her name was Della Brown and that she was Jamaican. She had no ID, and since I was on the task force with them, they called me. She refused to talk and I eventually put her in jail on an INS hold as she told me she was illegal."

Crowe interrupted him at this juncture. "Man, I can't get over this. These people here are tied to the murder of that narcotics detective down there. This is even heavier than we thought."

"Well, wait till you hear the rest of it, George. I had to be at a hearing at ten o'clock the next day, and at her appearance she tells the hearings officer that she is not illegal and asks to talk to me. He allows it and we go into an interview room. She tells me that she is Cuban-American but that she has been in Miami most of her life. She volunteers that she has nothing to do with the drug dealing at the house she was seen leaving, that she was just there to get some coke, that she was hard up, she didn't have money, and they would not front her any.

"At this point I asked her if she saw a man come in and get some cocaine while she was in there. She responded kind of casually, as if she had something to hide, that she heard somebody come in, but she didn't pay too much attention. I wondered if she was withholding something." Lynch paused for a second, then let his breath out, sounding as if he had just lit a cigarette. He continued with emphasis.

"Then I told her that the man was an undercover police officer named Fabian de la Sala and that he had been shot and killed as he left the location. Her reaction caught me off guard.

"She jumped up screaming and lunged at me while crying hysterically. Half of what she was trying to say was in Spanish and the rest in English. I had my arms around her to restrain her and talk to her, and after a few minutes she settled down and I realized that what she was trying to tell me was that her real name is Celeste de la Sala, and the undercover officer, Fabian de la Sala, was her brother. She then explained to me that Brown was their mother's maiden name and she uses it sometimes as well. But legally, she is known in this country as Celeste de la Sala."

Crowe jumped in at that point. "Oh man, so the undercover officer was her brother. So is she connected to Tenny in some way other than just being in his place buyin' some dope?"

"Well, that's a good question. Let me answer it by way of telling you what we have on Tennyson Cummings, aka Tenny, aka "the Poet." The Miami narcs were working on him but never made a case on him. They had received information that he was in charge of Jamaican street level cocaine dealing and that he controlled it with an iron fist. There had been two or three drug related homicides that he was supposedly mixed up in and, as in your case, there had been threats against the narcs and agents who were working the Jamaican dealers. They have never solved the murder of Detective Fabian de la Sala. The Mustang used in the drive-by shooting of de la Sala was a stolen car and, as I mentioned, it has never been recovered. It was probably chopped or sent to Mexico or Colombia or some other damn place, with an altered VIN and a false title. Because threats, attributed to Jamaican dealers and specifically Tennyson Cummings, had been made on officers' lives, we are all pretty sure that they murdered Detective de la Sala."

INS Agent Lynch went on for the next few minutes providing what background information he could, regarding

Tennyson Cummings, "the Poet." The first point he made was that Tennyson Cummings was his real name and that he was a Jamaican, in this country legally. He had a record in Miami, having been arrested for CCW (carrying a concealed weapon) three years ago. Lynch assured Crowe that he would fax him the record and mug shot as soon as they got off the phone. He also suggested that INS should be an active participant in the case. Crowe informed him that his sergeant, Sullivan, had already spoken with the command officers in the Narcotics Bureau about getting federal participation in the case and filing the drug cases that resulted in Federal Court.

Lynch stated that Celeste de la Sala had been seen with Cummings but that no nexus to his drug dealing business had been established. She was, by her own admission, a frequent cocaine user who had bought cocaine from his places. The most interesting point he made about Celeste de la Sala, or Della, as she was known to the dark narcs, was that after her arrest the night her brother was killed, and her release from custody the next day, she had disappeared. She did not attend her brother's funeral and no mention of her was made in the stories about the officer's family. However, through immigration records obtained by INS, it was firmly established that she was indeed who she said she was and that she was Detective de la Sala's sister.

Crowe's mind was racing and he asked a question that he was anxious to have answered: "Do they have any people that they suspect did the killing? You know, names from informants and stuff like that, but not enough to charge and convict anybody. Does anybody say that Cummings was directly involved?"

"They have nobody saying that Cummings did it, but they have heard that it was his people. In fact two brothers, Clive and Glenmore Henry were being looked at. They are close associates of Cummings. But we never came close to getting enough to charge them."

"Well you can stop worrying 'bout those two," interjected Crowe. "Those are the two who shot at me last week, and in tryin' to escape, they both ended up dead in Cherry Creek after a short chase and a spectacular, fiery crash of their vehicle."

"You're shittin' me!" blurted out Lynch. "Do you have any fuckin' idea how happy the cops, well, all of us involved in this, are going to be hearing that the Henry brothers met their demise after trying to ambush a cop? Everybody down here who dealt with them says they are stone cold assholes. Every field contact card on them stressed how hostile and uncoop- erative they were."

"Do you guys have mug shots of the Henrys? We don't have any photos, and the homicide dicks could use them on two of the unsolved cases they have. Same with Tennyson Cummings, we need a mug shot of him as well."

"Okay, I'll put the case documents together and talk to the Jamaican Task Force here and let them know the good news. I'll also coordinate with the INS office up there so if there's anything we can do to help, we'll be ready to do so."

Then George Crowe and Greg Lynch exchanged phone numbers and pager numbers so that they could keep each other up to date. When Crowe got off the phone he stood up, shot both hands straight up in the air before clapping them together and enunciated an elongated, "Yessss."

He explained the basis for his glee to the other detectives in the office at the time. Then he called Sergeant Sullivan's pager and asked that he call him right away at the bureau. Sullivan, who was giving his baseball team a workout at South High School, ran over to District 3 police station nearby and called him. He was excited to hear what Crowe was telling him about the connection of the Denver Jamaican players to the Miami cases, particularly the possibility that the Henrys may have been responsible for killing the narcotics officer down there, and that the officer who was killed was the brother of Celeste de la Sala or Della Brown as they knew her. The two of them discussed the possible role that Della was playing and her relationship to Tennyson Cummings, and both admitted to being baffled. They were missing something, and more would be revealed.

Sullivan congratulated Crowe on his good investigative work and let him know that he would be in the office by six-thirty or seven o'clock that evening. He then went back to the ball field and finished a light round of batting practice for his team and bullpen sessions for his pitchers. They were scheduled to go to Laramie, Wyoming on Saturday for a weekend tournament. Although he hoped to be free to go, Sullivan made arrangements with the players and some parents who assisted him with coaching logistics, to carry on without him. He explained, though not in much detail, that he was under a heavy workload and might not be able to get away. What he didn't tell them was that he wasn't going to Laramie on a baseball trip unless they had Tennyson Cummings rolled up tightly on drug and homicide charges and safely in jail—or in the morgue.

24

ALL THE DARK NARCS WERE in the sergeants' office by seven o'clock on Tuesday night—the official time that their shift began. They had all been at their desks working and talking about the case at least an hour earlier and were ready to get going. The information learned by Detective Crowe had ratcheted up their already high intensity. It confirmed that they were onto something big: cop killers probably. The threats made against them, and manifested in the attempt on Detective Crowe's life last week, were casting long shadows. Hearing that Della Brown, one of their targets, was at the downtown Miami drug house just before the Miami undercover detective was killed in 1984, and that he was her brother, could not have been more astonishing. And that the drug house where it had happened was one operated by Tennyson Cummings, and that two of the prime suspects in the police officer's homicide were the now deceased Henry brothers who worked for him, was soul stirring. This brought them to the conclusion to which the facts had been leading—Tennyson Cummings, aka "the Poet," was not somebody to trifle with.

Now the question was, as Lodi so directly put it, "It's as simple as this: Does he get one of us, leave town and win the game like he did in Miami, or do we get *him*—dead or alive?"

"That is the long and the short of it for sure, Lodi, couldn't have said it better myself." Sullivan said this, then grabbed his agenda out of the inbox and flipped to the current date, June 30, 1987. The agenda had been given to Sullivan as a Christmas present. Each date had the name of the patron saint of the day

192

written at the top and a brief description of what he or she had done, according to the Catholic Church, to establish canonization. Believing in and trusting the Saints, and sharing his life with them, was part of who Sullivan was.

"Let's go over the possible roles Della Brown, or more correctly, Celeste de la Sala, has in this case. Is she an innocent bystander who uses cocaine, and runs a Jamaican grocery store? Is she Tennyson Cummings' girlfriend? A cocaine addicted slave to him? Is she his boss by any chance? What is a Cuban doing posturing herself as a Jamaican? We definitely need to find out more about her. Maybe she set up the murder of her own brother."

"Here's what I think she is, Sarge," chimed in Detective Crowe. "I think she's the key to this whole case. We either catch her dirty and get her to tell us everything she knows, which would be unlikely to happen. Or we need to keep Leon close to her so she begins to confide in him." And then looking at Leon directly he added, "You should drop by tonight and just bullshit with her, and if she asks you to her apartment, you should go with her. That's assuming that we have the exact location nailed down between now and then so that we can come and get you quickly in case she starts jumpin' on ya', man." Crowe and the others, including Messenger, laughed a little at that.

Crowe then added, "Of course we'll make sure that no one is in the apartment before you get there and that Cummings' vehicle isn't parked outside the building. How does that sound, Sarge?"

"It sounds good to me, George. What's your take, Leon?"

"That's what I want to do, get close to her, but here's my thing. We have two associates of Tennyson Cummings, people we know who, at the very least buy from him, and/or are in business with him, who are relatives, father and sister, of people he is thought to be responsible for killin', man. I'm talkin' about Arthur Robinson and Della. In addition, man, we are all brothers here, and Cummings' close associates, the Henry brothers, tried to kill one of our own. According to my view of the world, that puts karma in our corner and we can do no wrong. I want to play, and I mean play, as in control, Della Brown or Della Salad or whatever the fuck her name is, get Cummings and finish this thing."

At Leon's misunderstanding of Spanish, the other three laughed aloud.

"No, man, it is *de la Sala*, her last name. Her first name is Celeste, Celeste de la Sala." That contribution was made by George Crowe. Then Lodi added, "I like de la salad better, let's put her ass in jail and put Cummings right next to her. I agree with my man Leon, karma is on our side and we're close to finishing this thing."

It occurred to Sullivan, that their planning meeting had turned into a pep rally of sorts and it was his responsibility to get back to planning.

"Okay, we all want to wrap this case up before anyone else gets hurt or killed. The main objective now is to get a case on Cummings. We can do that by turning up a credible witness who will testify against him in the murder cases. We can do surveillance on his places; 2811½ Franklin is the only one we know of now."

"Hold on, Sarge," interrupted Lodi, then continued, "I haven't mentioned it yet, but I just got a call from a woman who wants to work for us. A while back we arrested Gwen Moran, remember her? She was from Colorado Springs. We arrested her at that crack house up on 13th and Cook. We didn't put her in jail because she had nothing on her, but she had been there doing crack and ended up telling us she was hooked and needed help. She was twenty-seven years old and she asked us to call her dad in the Springs to come and get her. He's a retired Air Force colonel or something."

"Hell yes, I remember her. About two weeks later there was a story in the *Rocky Mountain News* that she was killed in a crack house in Colorado Springs."

"That's right. Well, her sister called me shortly after that, just pissed off as hell that the cops weren't closing down crack houses everywhere. Remember that?" he asked looking at Sullivan, who nodded. Then he continued, "She thanked me for saving her sister temporarily by arresting her up here, and told me she was going to make a crusade out of saving other people from becoming crack heads and dying because of it.

"Tonight, she called me again. She had read about the drug house murders up here and has come up here to help us solve them. Her name is Gretchen Moran. She is staying at the Residence Inn at Speer and Zuni and she wants to meet with me. She's confident that she can buy from any drug house in Denver. She fancies herself pretty sly and believes she can bull-shit her way into, and out of, any place she wants."

"Have you set up a time to meet her, Lodi?"

"I told her we had a meeting till about eight o'clock and then I would drive over there and meet her. I was thinking that you could go with me. Well, for that matter, George or Leon or you, whatever you think. I just don't want to meet her alone, you know what I mean?"

"I understand completely. Why doesn't George go with you? If you think it'll work, bring her down here and document her and then put her to work. After we do what we're going to do with her, we can have Leon call Della Salad (snickering) and maybe hook up just to get closer to her."

"Hey, Sarge, I'll go ahead and call her while those guys are out setting up their thing. From now on I'm going to record all my calls to her and I should be wired when I meet her. Anyway, if I can, I'll meet her later tonight; let's see what she says."

"Good plan," said Lodi, "just don't call her Della Salad (more snickering), that would probably blow your whole thing with her."

Everybody seemed loose and confident as the meeting broke up. As with every project undertaken, everything built or studied, there is a point where the tide changes and momentum carries it forward. That point seemed to have been reached in this case and the dark narcs could sense that they would soon have this case finished. The nervous energy was palpable as each started getting big-game ready.

Detectives Lodi and Crowe headed out across Speer Boulevard to the Residence Inn at Speer and Zuni. Gretchen Moran was staying in room 124 and the officers went directly there. She answered the door and let them in. She was an attractive, passively sexy woman about thirty years old with reddish brown hair and blue eyes, medium height and weight. She looked fit—not at all like a crack user or alcoholic or addict. She didn't look like a street person and the detectives soon learned that she didn't talk like one either. She was dressed in nice blue jeans and a white sweat shirt, and dress sandals, which wasn't at all out of place on a June summer evening in Denver.

She shook hands with the detectives, then mentioned to Lodi that she remembered talking to him on the phone after her sister died. She reiterated to the detectives that she wished to work with them, that she had no police record but that she had been to crack houses with her sister when she was trying to help her kick her crack habit and change her life. She stated that she was naturally street wise and had learned as a young woman how to talk men into anything she wanted. She always knew that she was sexually attractive to men and she played it to her advantage. She admitted that her attitude about men was jaded because she had been hurt badly and so altered; her only use for men now was to get something she wanted or go somewhere she needed to go. She admitted to using sex to get ahead in school and at work.

She informed Crowe and Lodi, in no uncertain terms, that she was doing this to avenge her sister's murder in a crack house. While she understood it wouldn't bring her back, it might save somebody else from getting hooked, surrendering their life to addiction and then losing it violently, as her sister had.

After about fifteen minutes, it was decided that they would go to headquarters and document her as an informant, and then try and make a controlled-buy from the Franklin address.

"Are you guys parked in the lot right outside the door?"

"Yeah, right outside the door," responded George Crowe.

"Okay, go wait in the car. I have to put some street clothes on and change my hair and makeup a little bit. It won't take too long. The last thing I want is to be mistaken for an undercover policewoman."

While they were in the car waiting for her, Lodi and Crowe discussed her. They both were of the opinion that she was too pretty and too clean to ever get into a crack house. But then Crowe brought up the obvious, that she was quietly, but distractingly sexy, and how that might be her key to getting in—anyplace.

She came out of her room carrying a small gym bag and got into the back seat of Lodi's undercover ride, a 1978

Thunderbird, dark blue in color. When she got in, she asked them to look her over. The difference was startling. She looked like a street person. Her designer jeans had been replaced by some raggedy-ass cotton work pants. She was wearing a dirty baseball type undershirt with black sleeves. And she was sporting scuffed, black work shoes. Her hair was ratted a little, giving it an unkempt look. Her face had been made up to give her the appearance of a crack addict and, in addition, she smelled like urine.

"What the hell did you do to yourself?" asked Lodi.

"Well, the makeup is the main change I made. I put on a yellow-based foundation that is a full shade lighter than my skin tone. I put on mascara and got it wet to black out under my eyes and used a glue stick to mat down my eyebrows. I burned some incense in there and got close so it went directly into my eyes and *Voila*, they are red and worn out looking. Then for the finishing touch, I put flour caked in vaseline around my lips, not too much, just a little bit, to make these little goobers here.

"As far as the smell goes, I peed in these pants and then put them in the dryer and have not washed them since—they will smell like urine *for evah*! I had to pretend I was a crack whore to get my sister out of a place the night before she went back to a worse place, where they killed her, so I have experience. Then I use my attitude and my sexuality, mostly the way my tits look in this baseball shirt, to overcome the piss smell and the dirty appearance. I bet I get what I want on one try. I have my clean clothes, makeup remover and fresh makeup in my gym bag so if we can go to your office when we are done, I'll change there. I don't want to be seen in the real world looking like this.

"And by the way, I'll go to court if I have to. If you can't do your thing and keep me out of it, then so be it. I'm a witness."

25

LODI AND CROWE TOOK GRETCHEN Moran to headquarters to fingerprint her and otherwise document her as a confidential informant. They checked for criminal records and driving histories. In addition, they had a female officer search her to make sure she was not armed or carrying other contraband or currency. All that checked out okay. Lodi asked her to pick a code name and she chose Josie, and it was the name she would use, if asked, when buying cocaine. She was then wired with a pager transmitter and given one hundred dollars in marked bills. She was told to buy a full gram of cocaine. She was fully briefed on who might be inside the house at 2811½ Franklin, particularly Tennyson Cummings.

The sergeant was already out in the area as were Crowe and Messenger in the van Crowe was driving while the windshield was being replaced on his regular unit. It worked out well as Messenger was able to ride in the blacked out customized part of the van, invisible from outside the van.

Lodi dropped the CI off on 29th Avenue east of Franklin. He parked a little to the north where he could have an eye on her all the way up the street to the house. Sullivan had a clear eye on the front door of the house from south and east of it, and Crow and Messenger had the back of the house covered.

The CI staggered up the street, nervously jerking her shoulders and neck and gave the appearance that she was tweaking. She made it to the front door, and Lodi, monitoring the kel-kit, said that she was knocking. Then he reported that an unknown male had opened the door and asked her what she wanted. The conversation, which was being taped for later review and possible use as evidence, went as follows:

CI: "I'm hurtin' I need a full one, man."

UM1: "What you mean, who *da* fuck are you?"

CI: "My name is Josie, my sister Gwen knows you guys. She probably does whatever she has to, in exchange for the shit. She's a crack ho'. I bet you're the one been gettin' you some. Sound familiar?"

UM1: "Oh yeah, I know Gwen, but I ain't seen her round here in a while."

CI: "Well, she's fucked up all the time so maybe she's got a steady gig going somewhere else. But I got money, you ain't getting none of *this*, so how 'bout it? Hey what's *his* problem, the big guy with the gun?"

UM2: "Just mind your own fuckin' bidness sista."

CI: "You ain't gonna need that tool for me, mister. I pay my own way and when I can't pay, I figure out something else if you get my drift."

UM2: "Do it and get her the fuck outa' here, Pea."

UM1: "Gimme da money."

Then there was some shuffling, sounding like an exchange of money and product followed by the CI saying, "Thanks, maybe next time I won't bring any money and we'll see what happens," and the first unknown male replying, "You do that and I'll wear that *punani* out, sista'. You won't need no drugs when I'm done *wid yuh*."

The footsteps of the CI were heard and Lodi called out that she was leaving the front of the place and that he had an eye on her, that she was heading his way. Shortly, Lodi reported that the deal had gone fine and that they were heading to the office.

The team regrouped in the conference room at their office. Gretchen was followed into the restroom where she was thoroughly searched by a policewoman again. It was determined that she had nothing on her and she quickly cleaned up and changed her clothes. The sergeant and Leon hardly recognized her when Lodi escorted her into the conference room where they all met. She was shown a picture of Tennyson Cummings, one of the photos LaDonna Robinson had given to Sullivan and Messenger. She immediately identified him as the person who had been holding a gun inside the house while she dealt with the unknown male called Pea.

Crowe headed out of the room like he had an emergency of some kind but returned nonchalantly a minute later with a mug shot of a Jamaican male. He looked at Lodi and showed him the mugshot, then showed it to the CI. She immediately identified the person in the mugshot as Pea.

"This is Dexter Campbell; he's wanted right now on your case, Lodi. I wondered if it wasn't him because he has a head the size of a fuckin' grapefruit and they could call somebody like that 'Pea' or 'Peahead'. I haven't seen him on the street since he failed to appear on your case." He said that addressing Lodi, seated next to where he was standing, and the two bumped fists.

"You don't forget an ever lovin' thing, do you, George?" Lodi said this shaking his head and smiling.

"Nope."

Sullivan piped up at that point, "Okay, it's time for you to tell us what you observed inside the place, Gretchen."

"Okay. Do I call you sarge or sergeant or what? By the way, my sister told me that you and Lodi gave her a big break, and I think she was close to getting her shit together after that, but the addiction was too rough."

"Yeah, well, we didn't have a case on her. Might have been better for her if we had. Anyway, I was sorry to hear about her getting killed. And you can call me whatever you want, Frank, Sarge, Sullivan, whatever."

"Okay, I like Frank. First of all, Frank, this was about as easy as falling off a log. Neither one of those jokers could stop looking at my tits. The big guy was talking tough, but he was thinking with his dick. He was holding what looked like a nine millimeter automatic. But I'm no weapons expert, even though I've been around guns my whole life. I do know for sure it wasn't a Colt 45.

"Could you hear me, Lodi? I was trying to let you know he was there and that he was holding a *tool*. That's Jamaican slang, street slang for a gun, but I guess you knew that already."

"Yeah, I was hearing you fine," replied Lodi, "and I heard you saying that he had a gun, and then you said something about his tool. You did great."

"Not *his* tool, Lodi, I said tool—meaning gun."

"I know, I'm just kidding you."

"Well, all right, let's go back tomorrow and I'll buy some more."

"I need you to write a statement before you leave, because if all else fails, we will file these buys you make, and you will have to go to court."

"Okay, I already told you I'll go to court if need be. I'm ready to go write it, then I'd like you to take me back to the Residence, if you don't have another place you want me to try. This was too easy."

"Not tonight, we're in good shape with this, thanks to your guts and moxie." Lodi then asked the sergeant if he had anything else, to which Sullivan responded that he did not.

It was almost eleven o'clock at night by this point, too late for Messenger to meet Della Brown, but he decided to call her from a recorded line anyway. He had two numbers for her. He tried the first and got a message that he had reached Kingston Corner, our hours are…, so he tried the other number and she answered after two rings.

"Hey, baby, how you doin'?"

"Norman, is that you? I can't hear you very well."

"Yeah, it's me, I meant to call you earlier to see if you wanted to go get a drink or a bite to eat, but I had to take care of one little thing and it turned into something else, and by then it was too late."

"Oh, that's too bad. You wanna' come over to my place, I've got some rum and coke?"

"Ah man, I'm beat now. I'll call you tomorrow or else I'll make it by the shop before you close."

"Okay, that sounds good. Let's plan on going out for a while and then coming over here."

"Oh man, I like the sound of that for sure."

The call ended and Messenger came out of the undercover recording room giving the thumbs up sign as he carried the tape to his desk to mark it as evidence.

The dark narcs spent the next couple of hours finishing up paperwork and getting their investigations updated in general. The sergeant did his administrative paperwork and wrote the nightly activity letter. The last few minutes of the work night were spent sitting in Sullivan's office discussing Gretchen Moran. She was not a crook working off a case, not a typical informant. Her explicitly expressed motivation was to be part of the effort to reduce drug related violence. And there was the element of avenging her sister's murder behind her willingness to get involved as well. Her courage to act as an agent of the police, and be a witness, if necessary, impressed all of them, and frightened the four police detectives at the same time, knowing how dangerous this group was. Nothing stopped self-righteous vengeance like an armed and violent drug dealer vindictive in his own cause. Could the opposite be said as well?

Sullivan summarized the concerns of all as he discussed the challenges that they faced by using her. She was not a trained law enforcement officer and her zealous involvement had to be tightly controlled. If she were hurt or killed, acting on their behalf, it would be unacceptable on several levels. They hoped they could minimize her involvement, make one or two more buys and then hit the place with a warrant—soon.

When the paperwork was finished, everybody left the office before Sullivan, who took time to call Ellie. She was unwinding from a night's work and she asked him to come and see her. He asked if she wanted something to eat, she said no, she had eaten a peanut butter sandwich when she got home. Sullivan asked her if she would make him one and she said she would.

"No, wait a minute, you use peanut butter without sugar, right?"

"Of course I do, nothing less. The kind I use is Adams®, the nutty, rather than the smooth. And I have dark rye bread. I know what you like."

"Perfect, just right," was Sullivan's response. "I'll be there in ten minutes, God willing."

"Okay, I can't wait."

Sullivan started directly to Ellie's house. He tried to relax a little on the drive as he had a stiff neck, undoubtedly tension related. He was intense on the job, especially when he was in charge of operations: search warrants, undercover meetings or buys, or controlled-buys made by a cooperating witness as was the case on this night. It took him time to unwind, and to give himself a little extra time, he stopped at the all night Kings Soopers at 9th and Downing to buy a small bunch of flowers consisting of dahlias, carnations, baby's breath and greenery. The flower purchase changed his mind set and put the night's activities in their own space, allowing him to think of other things, like a beautiful woman waiting for him with a peanut butter sandwich on rye bread.

He always drove, aware of a possible tail, but on this night there were very few cars on the street at all, let alone one following him with ill intent. He was relaxing by degrees as he had trained himself to do since he quit alcohol. He arrived at Ellie's house and the street was quiet. He parked in her driveway and she was standing near the gate to the rear yard waiting for him. She was wearing a short, dark blue silk robe and flip-flops. It was another beautiful summer night—cool and dry under a clear sky.

They kissed at the gate and Sullivan followed her into the house. They sat at the kitchen table while he ate his sandwich and drank a glass of unsweet ice tea. Ellie drank hot herbal tea. She talked about the events of her night at work. Sullivan sat there listening to her, thinking how easy it had been for them to reconnect. Until little over a week ago, they hadn't seen each other or been in contact for years. He hadn't even thought about her too much in the last fifteen years or so. Now, he was smitten with her; he had no idea if it was love or infatuation.

For the time being, he was not preoccupied with that or with the uncertainties of police work. Not after she slipped over onto his lap and he realized that all she was wearing was her silk robe. He was off duty now.

26

LODI WENT TO THE OFFICE at about one o'clock on Wednesday afternoon. He had an envelope in his back pocket, from which he had removed and thrown away the contents. On the top half of the envelope was a short list of nonperishable household items he had scribbled down before he left home and had picked up on his way to the office. On the bottom half of the envelope was a list of things he wanted to accomplish at the office. At the top of that list was to get a copy of the arrest warrant for Dexter Campbell and a copy of his mugshot. Next, was to get a copy of Tennyson Cummings' mugshot that Crowe had received from INS Miami.

Lodi then headed to Denver General Hospital to talk to Lilian Martinez. He was met in the hall outside the room by her mother, Sofia. She seemed glad to see him and immediately let him know that Lilian was greatly improved and would soon be released from the hospital. Lodi entered the room and was shocked to see how much better she looked, just since Sunday. She was about recovered from her near-death trauma and had been clean and sober for several days. He showed her the mugshots he had and she identified both, Tennyson Cummings, as Tenny, and "the Poet," and Dexter Campbell as "Pea" or "Peahead."

Asked what she knew about "Pea," she said that he was a "rude asshole" who often carried a gun. She went on to say that he had been in the park the night that Janel was killed. Speaking of Janel, she said that Janel's mother had come to see her and had brought her some flowers that had been left after

Janel's funeral. She offered that LaDonna Robinson had good things to say about the police officers who had been trying to solve her daughter's murder case. She specifically mentioned the narcotics officers.

After Lodi left the hospital room, he checked with her mother in the hallway to see if she had made any plans to get Lilian out of town for a while before she was needed for court, suggesting it would be a good idea to keep her safe—and sober. Sofia agreed and said that she planned to have Lilian stay with her aunt in Greeley for a couple of weeks.

Lodi sat in his car outside the hospital and made some notes about his interview with Lilian and her positive identification of the photos she had been shown. Then he decided to call Gretchen Moran and see if she was still at the Residence Inn. He asked for room 124 and she answered immediately. He said that he was just checking on her to see if she was still in town, and she scoffed at the idea that she would have returned to Colorado Springs. He said that he needed her to sign the typed statement regarding the controlled-buy she made last night.

"You can bring it over now," she said.

When he got there, Gretchen was cleaning the windshield of her car that was parked in front of her room.

"Hey, Gretchen, how you doin'?"

"I'm fine, Lodi, how are you today? Let me see that statement."

He handed her a typed copy of the statement she had made, including detailed descriptions of the suspects, the inside of the house as far as she had been able to see it, the gun Cummings was holding, the recorded bills with which she paid for the cocaine, and the disposition of the evidence she purchased.

"This is a great statement and we will need it if we ever go to court. By the way, the lab test came back positive for cocaine

HCl (cocaine hydrochloride), and the package weighed almost exactly a gram. The shit's not great quality, percentage wise—we don't care about that, but they might get some complaints from customers. In fact, if you go back, you can tell them that the stuff was nothing to write home about."

"What do you mean *if?* You want me to go back tonight, right?"

"We do, but we are also troubled. You are not a trained police officer and neither are you a drug-buying customer turned informant to work off a case. Therefore, our concern from an ethical position as well as from a vicarious liability standpoint, is that something might happen to you. It's our job to take those risks, not yours." He hesitated, then added, "I have to go to the office now. Call me at seven o'clock and I'll let you know what the plan is."

"Okay, but I'm telling you, don't worry about me. At least let me go back one more time so you can arrest those guys and maybe put them together on those homicides."

"'Put them together'! You sound like a cop. What's your background?"

"No more than you already know really. I've lived in the real world and I know what people sound like, including cops."

"Okay, that's fair enough. I'll talk to you tonight."

With that, Gretchen went into her room and Lodi headed back to headquarters. At headquarters he typed an affidavit for a search warrant based on the circumstances of Gretchen Moran's buy the previous night and other relevant background information. He made sure to include some of the corroborative details that Sullivan and Messenger had extracted from their interview with Arthur Robinson. He took the affidavit across the courtyard to the County Court Judge in the city jail building, who read the affidavit and signed it without question, giving Lodi a friendly caution to be careful. The warrant, once signed, had a seventy-two hour window in which to be served. Lodi was not sure when they would be ready to hit the place, but if everything went right it would be in that time frame. And if something happened that called for it to be done sooner, the warrant was signed, sealed, and ready to be delivered.

By six o'clock on Wednesday evening, all of the dark narcs were working. Sullivan was in the Homicide Bureau briefing Detectives Mathis and Lopez on the latest developments. Detective Lopez grunted a loud "Fuckin'-A!" upon hearing that the Tennyson Cummings Jamaican crew was strongly suspected of killing an undercover Miami police officer. They were both astonished that the officer's sister, known in Denver as Della Brown, real name Celeste de la Sala, was at the drug house just prior to the execution-style murder of the u/c officer outside of it.

Sullivan also informed the homicide detectives that they had a buy from the house at 2811 ½ Franklin, that Tennyson Cummings was in the house with a 9mm pistol overseeing the transaction, that the person who made the buy was willing to testify, and that she would make a good witness. He told them she may go back and try to get another buy and they were also going to have Detective Messenger meet Della Brown again, just to see if it could lead to something. He let them know his feeling was that they were about to break this thing wide open.

With that, Sullivan promised to keep in touch and headed back to the Narcotics Bureau. They all got together in his office to plan the night's activities. Leon surprised the group by speaking first. "I want to go to the Jamaican grocery, spend some time sweet talking Della and then tell her I'm in need of a little product and see what she says. She'll probably blow me off, but I want to check out three or four hundred dollars and tell her to get me an eight-ball. I wasn't sure she was a doper, but after the info my man Crowe got, we know she's got some connection to it and them, meaning the Jamaicans. The worst she can say is no, man, get the hell outa' here. I just think it's time for me to hit her up. Maybe she'll do it thinking she and I can get a thing goin'; that might be what she wants."

Next, it was Lodi's turn. "I like the idea, if she goes for it. Why don't you tell her that you have something to do and that you'll come back later and pick it up. We're only risking a few hundred dollars at the most if she rips you off. But if you tell her to call you when she has it, then we'll keep an eye on the Franklin address and hopefully Tenny will be there.

"After your initial meeting, we can send Gretchen back in and she can tell us if he's in there or not. If he is, Gretchen does her thing, gets out of there and we wait for Della to come and get your dope. From that point we could finish it anyway we want, because we'll have both of them tight in our grasp. We could hit it while Della's in there, or we could let her bring it back to Leon and go from there."

Messenger interjected his opinion, "Oh definitely, let her bring it to me and we have a sales case on her, and we get our money from Tenny's house and we got him rolled up in it as well. The main thing is, man, we get him off the street, whether we pin the murders on him or not. I'm not going to call her, I'm just going to drop in at the Kingston Corner and see how it goes."

"That all sounds good. You take the kel-kit, George, and wire Messenger up. Lodi and I will go set up, but I want you to go by the Franklin address on the way, Lodi, to see if the Camry is there. Otherwise, we'll look for it to be in the parking lot at the Kingston Corner. If it *is* there, we'll decide then if Leon should go in or not. You cool with that, Leon?"

"Yeah, man, let me know if he's there."

At that point, Messenger checked out four hundred dollars from Sergeant Sullivan, made copies of the bills, folded the money, put it in his pocket and headed to his car. The other guys grabbed their equipment and headed out of the office.

Lodi drove by Franklin, and the Camry that listed to Tennyson Cummings was parked behind 2811½ Franklin. He notified the other guys and then went and setup on the Kingston Corner. Sullivan and Crowe took complementing surveillance positions, and Messenger drove into the lot and parked a few minutes later. It was about eight o'clock and still daylight.

Messenger went into the store and found Della ringing up a customer at the cash register. As soon as the customer took her purchase and left the store, Della approached Messenger and gave him a big hug and a kiss on the cheek. As Leon looked more closely at Della, he became aware that she was wearing heavy makeup and could see that she was black and blue on the left side of her face, though the makeup had faded it into her natural tan coloring.

"Hey, baby, what the fuck? What happened to you? Don't tell me you ran into a door."

"Okay, I won't, but it's a private matter, let's say a family matter, and it's something I have to take care of. Don't let that come between us."

"Oh, man, I don't know. Are you sure you're all right?"

"I am all right. How do you like my outfit by the way?"

Messenger looked at Della. She was wearing a short black skirt, black nylons and a silver knit top looking as if it were made of rows of safety pins. She looked trashy—especially with the heavy makeup covering her black eye. And she looked a little out of place in a Jamaican grocery store.

"I really like your outfit. How much longer are you gonna' be here?"

"I have to stay here until nine o'clock and then I have to take care of something."

"Ah, man, that's a shame. I wanted to party a little bit. Maybe get high and, you know, see what happens."

"You know I've been wanting that to happen, but not tonight. I have a little business to take care of."

"All right. Well, can I do anything for you? Do you need something to eat or drink or anything?"

"Aren't you the sweetest thing, Norman. Where the hell you been all my life?"

"Tomorrow's a new day, baby. Let's see where it leads us. If you get done what you got to do, call me later." Messenger said this while his voice trailed off to barely above a whisper as he finished, and he had moved closer to her face as he said it. As he did so, he could see that her eyes were a little glassy and streaked with red. She was not herself; she seemed nervous and wanted him to leave. After giving her a kiss on the cheek and a promise to see her soon, he did leave.

After he had driven a few blocks away, he called surveillance.

"Zebra 21, to 22, did you hear all that, brother?"

"Yeah, loud and clear," responded George Crowe. "Let's meet down by the seminary where we met last time."

Lodi and Sullivan acknowledged and the four dark narcs met in the parking lot of St. Thomas Seminary, inconspicuously out of the way.

"Man, somebody beat the shit out of her, and she's acting differently than I've seen her the other times. She shut me down before I had a chance to hit her up about the coke—like she's on to me. And she looks like she's on something herself now; maybe it's just pain killers. The damage to her face looks fresh, man; she's gonna be a mess tomorrow. And she was limping a little bit."

"Okay, well, that's interesting. There's definitely more to her than meets the eye. Let's just wait and see if she gets ahold of us tonight or tomorrow." That was Sullivan's take on the unexpected reception Leon Messenger had received in the Jamaican grocery store. As he said it, he was a little relieved. He had thought more and more lately that Della Brown was a dead end, that getting a criminal case on Tennyson Cummings through her would be time consuming, and not a sure thing at all.

"Okay, as soon as it gets dark, let's try and get Gretchen into 2811 ½ Franklin again. I mean, I've been thinking it over and if she wants to do it, let's do it."

"I was pretty sure that was what you were thinking. I called her, and she said she'll be ready in a while. I'll head out there now and get her and bring her down to the office for the briefing."

27

AFTER DETECTIVE MESSENGER LEFT DELLA Brown in the Kingston Corner, having posed as Norman Preston, Della went into her office at the back of the store and straightened up some paperwork. Then she waited on a couple of customers making small purchases, and when they left, she contemplated closing early. She had been running the store for a few months and had made an all out effort to stay clean and sober in a new city and to make a success out of her new business venture. Her father in Miami had loaned her the money for a new start in a business specializing in Caribbean products. He had initially tried to encourage her to start a Cuban cafe featuring "*Cubano*" coffee, sandwiches and snacks. Maybe that would become part of the business expansion plan.

Celeste de la Sala, aka Della Brown, was thirty-three years old and had been born in Cuba. She fled Cuba with her parents during the Castro Cuban Revolution when she was an infant. Her father had owned a successful shipping company in Cuba and had continued to be successful in that business in Miami. He resembled a great many of the Cuban immigrants from that era: Catholic, conservative, and fiercely anti-communist/anti-Castro. He had raised his son and his daughter to be well-educated, fluent in Spanish and English, successful, and patriotic Americans proud of their Cuban heritage.

In her college years, Celeste began experimenting with marijuana and alcohol and later with cocaine. She had managed to stay pretty much in control, and after her graduation she was welcomed into the family business. That worked for a little while, but her appetite for the shady nightlife had been whet during her college days. She had been introduced to an illicit after-hours scene in Miami, and there she was introduced to Jamaican culture, Reggae music and cocaine. She was also introduced to Tennyson Cummings. He was tall and good looking, spoke perfect American English when he wanted to impress, and walked like the man in charge. He was *treated* like the man in charge as well, among his Jamaican peers. She soon became a regular at the scene, drinking rum and doing a little coke in the Ladies room.

From the after-hours scene to coke parties at some Jamaican places, she also became acquainted with Dexter Campbell, The Henry brothers, Winthrop Jensen and countless other Jamaicans from the Miami scene, who subsequently ended up dealing cocaine in Denver. She had been intimate only with Tennyson Cummings and soon realized that there wasn't much chemistry there. Frankly, she considered herself, as a Cuban-American, *above* Cummings.

Celeste de la Sala had been raised among recent Cuban refugees living in America, people her parents' age and young Cuban-Americans. It was a group segregated by language, culture and circumstance. The contrast between the Spanish speaking Cuban culture, music, food and religion, and the mostly illegal immigrant Jamaican culture could not have been more striking. Flirting with it a while, she may have moved on to something else were it not for the cocaine factor. She had not expected to get addicted and when she did, she lost her independence. She probably would not have

215

continued to associate with Tennyson Cummings were it not for her increasing addiction to cocaine. He was useful when she was in need and short on money, as she possessed, and he accepted, her own medium of exchange. And he was never physically abusive though he disdained her addiction as a fatal weakness and derided her for it.

Celeste de la Sala was devastated by the news of her brother's death at the vengeful hands of cocaine dealers going after law enforcement, specifically narcs. She heard various stories after the fact, regarding why he had been killed and by whom. The doper scene pointed at Jamaicans, for the most part, as being responsible for it. A certain faction credited Marielito gang drug dealers as having done it as revenge for cases de la Sala had made over the years. The Marielito gangs were made up of recent Cuban refugees, "boat people," who came to Florida in 1980, and contract killing was known to be part of their repertoire.

Celeste had met a couple of her brother Fabian's partners from the police department, but she didn't know them well enough to call them. That was especially the case since the police knew that she was in the house, though unwittingly, at the same time her brother was making an undercover-buy just prior to his death.

Upon learning of his death, she had gone into hiding—from herself, her family and everyone else.

She lived a miserable street existence consisting of prostitution, and alcohol and drug usage. This went on for several weeks. She had no contact with Tennyson Cummings (who only knew her as Della Brown) during this time, as she deteriorated into a distressing silhouette of her former self. But it wasn't because she knew that he was responsible for her brother's death; he had no idea that the cop he had ordered killed was her brother.

Celeste's father Antonio was heartbroken by his son's death and further devastated by the lack of contact from his daughter after that happened. He had heard from some of Celeste's friends that she was mixed up with Jamaican drug dealers, but he nevertheless anticipated that she would reunite with her family and grieve with them. After several weeks he went looking for her to no avail. Before he could find her, she hit rock bottom and sought her father's help. He responded by helping get her into rehab and nursing her back to health; after several months of sobriety, they began planning for her future. He had purchased a trucking company in Denver and had spent quite a bit of time there. He really enjoyed his time in the fresh mountain air and offered her a job in the management of the trucking outfit. She liked the idea of a geographic change but didn't want to work in the family business. Instead, he set her up in the Kingston Corner grocery store. After rejecting her father's idea of having a Cuban place, they agreed on a Caribbean-themed grocery store featuring food, music, and other imports from the Caribbean.

Celeste de la Sala, or Della Brown as she was known in this contemporary context, looked in her compact mirror surveying the damage to her face as she sat in her office deciding what to do. She had made a terrible discovery earlier in the day and it had led to an ugly confrontation, followed by a postponement of a decision as she met with Norman. She thought about her options and then made a decision: she would close

at the normal time, nine o'clock; she would stop by her apartment to pick up what she needed; and then she would do what
she had to do.

28

IT WAS ABOUT NINE O'CLOCK when the dark narcs gathered for a briefing. Normally, they would not have a briefing for an informant-buy that wasn't planned as a buy-bust—that very rarely happened—but this case was different. Gretchen Moran, a cooperating witness/informant was going to make another buy, and it was being done with an abundance of caution due to the known violent tendencies of the target, Tennyson Cummings. He was always armed and he was implicated in several murders and attempts to date.

Sgt. Sullivan had arranged for two uniformed officers to be on standby and they would be assigned to cover the back of the residence in the event that an immediate entry had to be made. They were present at the briefing that was conducted by Sullivan. He started with an overview of the case that brought everyone up to date, including Detective Messenger's latest undercover meeting with Della Brown. That was a potentially important officer safety issue as it appeared to be a brush off, indicating that Messenger had been burned as a cop, or maybe just that the group had become overly suspicious in an effort to keep cops out of their business.

The plan came down to Sullivan, Lodi and Messenger being in separate cars as close as they could get without being burned, and Crowe in the old van, monitoring the kel-kit for the safety of the informant; he would give the other officers a play-by-play of what was happening. He would also have a video camera on a tripod documenting the outside of the scene as well as possible.

In the event that immediate entry was necessary for whatever reason, Sullivan had a one-man ram for his use on the front door. Messenger and Lodi would be the entry team and Sullivan would drop the ram and follow them, after accessing his sidearm, a Smith and Wesson Model 66, stainless, with a six inch barrel. Crowe would secure the front perimeter, preventing anyone's entry after the officers had entered. If Crowe heard on the wire that the informant was in danger, he would relay it to the sergeant who would give the word. The command the dark narcs used was "ball, ball, ball." That came directly from Sullivan's baseball background being used by players to aggressively call for a ball in the air. Better than "go, go, go" on the radio because it couldn't be misheard as "no, no, no."

The informant would be given a verbal distress signal to use as well, which was, "This is no way to do business!" If those words came over the wire, the team would make immediate entry to ensure the informant's safety. Having the search warrant already signed could become an important legal issue— immediate entry.

The dark narcs were accustomed to stressful situations and they had learned that planning, careful implementation of the details of the plan and contingency planning to deal with unexpected events, were the keys to survival in rough situations.

When everybody was clear on the plan, the informant, who had been excluded from the tactical briefing, was wired, given one hundred dollars in marked bills, and was taken to the area in Lodi's vehicle. He took her to a dark, secluded alley near the Franklin address where he dropped her off after checking to see that all the surveillance people were in place and testing to see if Crowe was reading her on the kel-kit. Crowe said that he was and it was a "go."

Gretchen Moran had once again donned the makeup and attire that transformed her appearance into that of a cocaine addict in need of a dose. She walked unsteadily and even stumbled to her knees in some bushes at one point near the target address. She was thinking about the precautions that the police had taken on her behalf and she was hoping that it was enough. She had managed to put up a nonchalant front, but the truth was, she was nervous as hell. She mumbled a couple of little prayers, and as she got close, said, "This one's for you Gwen," and pounded on the door. She had been hoping that the one Crowe had referred to as "Peahead" would open the door. He would remember her from last night and wouldn't give her any shit other than trying to get in her pants, and she was used to deferring those advances. She was pretty sure she could promise him some later and tell him she was "too busy now to handle a fine specimen of a man like him," and buy herself some time that way. As her mind went over those things, she realized that she was glad that she was wearing a wire and that all she had to do was say the word and she would be rescued.

It *was* Pea who answered the door.

"*Yuh* come back see me, *wha yuh a luk fah* tonite sista'? *Dis*?" He says the last word grabbing his crotch.

"Nah, I'll need that later, but first I need some to put myself together. Another whole one is what I want, I have a customer that needs it before he can get his dick hard for me. I'll share it with him. Understand?"

"I *unna stand dat*," is Pea's response and he looks toward the back of the house. The big man is standing at what seems to be the doorway to the kitchen. He has a gun in his waistband. He is smiling at Gretchen.

She smiles back at him and says, holding eye contact, "I'm glad to see you more at ease than last night, man." She has worked it out with Crowe and Lodi, that she would say something to that effect if she could see he was armed but wasn't holding it as he had been the previous night.

"Zebra 22, okay, he's armed but not holding it." Crowe puts that on the air for the benefit of the others, then adds, "She's doing fine. Pea recognized her and hopefully his one-track mind will work in our favor."

Gretchen continues to talk casually, as if she hung out in situations like this everyday. "So what about it, can you throw in a little extra if I promise to come back when I'm done? And by the way, that shit last night was a little sorry, man. I mean somebody cut the shit out of that."

Tennyson Cummings speaks up at that time, "Well maybe we'll have to do a little test this time to make sure you like what you are getting. *Yuh dig*?"

"Yeah, I dig, that's cool but I got a customer waitin' on me, and it's his money at stake here, so I don't want him to think I backdoored him." She then adds, "Y*uh dig* that?" She is mimicking him.

"Backdoor?" asks Tennyson Cummings somewhat perplexed.

"Yeah, you know what that means, or are ya' some kind of Ivy League brother? I'm talkin' about takin' a fool's money and leavin' him waitin' at the front door while I haul ass out the back door, never intending to give him nothin.'"

"That's why the brothas' deal with us, because we don't 'backdoor' nobody. *Wi a* honest businessmen here." Cummings has shifted into his patois spiced English to more accentuate his Jamaican-*ism*.

"Well, that's nice to hear. My sister recommended that I come to see you guys to fix my troubles."

"Well how *bout ih?*" Pea asks this holding his left hand out, palm up, and Gretchen responds by putting two fifty-dollar bills in it.

Then she persists, "Why not give me a little extra for my trouble and when I come back I'll make it up to you."

"Maybe *yuh gimme sum pussy fos?* How *dat soun'?*"

"Forget it. My way or I go someplace else. You hook me up now and I come back later."

Then Tennyson Cummings takes a step toward the other two and speaks up again, "I decide who does what here." As he does so, he pulls the gun out of his waistband. "And right now I see that *Massah* Pea is holding your money, and if he wants to hold it till after he gets what he wants, then that's the way it's gonna be."

George Crowe is hearing the conversation loud and clear and passing it on to surveillance. They are getting butterflies in their stomach as they can feel the tension rising in the house.

"Zebra 22 to surveillance, she just told him that she ain't giving Pea what he wants now, and if she doesn't get her dope, she's leaving, with or without her money because her customer is waiting for her. Standby."

Surveillance continues to wait, all of them wishing they could hear what is going on.

"Look, I'll fuck your brains out *Massah* Pea, and that shouldn't take long," she says, trying to add levity. And then goes on, "But only after I take care of my customer. He's paying for *your* dope and he's paying *me* for sex. And if he was the skittish kind he never would've agreed to bring me down here anyway. I don't think he's scared a' being in this neck of the woods. So why don't I just go on back to him, with his coke, and when I'm done, I'll come back here to you and we can party all night." As Gretchen says this, she realizes that, contrary to what she told the narcs, she is scared. She's afraid of being killed in a dope house like her sister was. That fear notwithstanding, she has composure enough to sound light-hearted and joke a little bit.

"Okay, baby, just come over here and let me have a lil' squeeze," pleads Tennyson Cummings in a way that makes it sound mandatory.

Gretchen goes to him. She realizes that he wants to pat her down and see if she is wired. He now has his gun in his right hand. She puts her arms lightly around him and feels that her body is sweaty, hoping he does not pick up on it. He moves his left hand from the small of her back to her butt, then between her legs. He pauses there, "Hmmm, this is a nice little package here." He then continues back up the contour of her butt and follows her spine to her upper back, across her shoulders, down to her breasts and then to her waist band in further search of a wire. Then he pulls her to him so that she can feel his excitement.

She is relaxed again now; he has missed the transmitter which has been skillfully mounted wirelessly in an ivory colored barrette clipped to her matted down hair. He has been talking right into the transmitter as he fondled her and searched for it. She gives him a little extra hip thrust before breaking away with a promise to be back soon. Pea walks toward her and he hands her a crisply folded deck of what he said was a "*lickkle more dan ah gram.*"

Gretchen sticks it down the front of her pants and starts to head for the door.

"She's got it and she's coming out," George Crowe reported, and then, "Hold on, what the fuck! Is that Della going up to the door right now? Standby."

"Zebra 20, okay, George, let us know. Talk it up."

It *is* Della Brown approaching the front of the house. She must have parked down the block as nobody saw her get out of a vehicle.

"Zebra 22, Della is inside and she's yelling at Tennyson and calling him names." As Crowe is relaying this to surveillance, gunshots are heard coming from the house.

"Zebra 20, ball, ball, ball." Sullivan grabs the ram from the back of the El Camino as he runs by it and heads to the front door. Messenger and Lodi fall in behind him. Crowe takes a position behind them, covering their backsides. The uniform officers hustle into positions covering the back door.

Sullivan hits the door with the battering ram, which is shaped like an implement for driving T-posts into the ground, except that it is not hollow, it has a solid body and a rounded front end. He hits the door right at the position of the deadbolt and the door flies open, making an angry, powerful statement. Sullivan steps aside and Messenger and Lodi enter the house, guns drawn.

Messenger hits Della Brown as he charges in, knocking her up against the wall to the left of the door. He holds onto her while taking in the entirety of the situation. He has his weapon in his right hand. Lodi sees that Pea is lying wounded on the floor to the right of the door. He's in a fetal position hugging his own stomach.

Sullivan, seeing the scene in front of him, calls for George Crowe to enter the house behind him. He can see that Gretchen is face down next to the body of Tennyson Cummings. Cummings is not moving and a 9mm Sig Sauer P226 is still loosely in his hand until Sullivan carefully relieves him of it. Sullivan is still wearing the skin tight leather shooting gloves he wore for the ram duty, and he maintains possession of the Sig with his left hand, while he and Crowe make their way through the house, ascertaining that nobody else is inside. Crowe then calls the uniform officers covering the back of the house on the radio, and informs them that the inside is secure and that he is about to open the back door. He does so, and they stay on their post, turning their attention away from the house.

Sullivan calls for an ambulance, Code 10 (red lights and siren), a couple more District 2 cars to assist, and the homicide detectives. Then he turns his attention to the details of the scene. Tennyson Cummings has no vital signs—he has been taken out of the game. Sullivan makes a quick sign of the cross.

Dexter Campbell has been shot in the stomach and is groaning with pain. There is no weapon near him, nor on his person.

Della Brown is uninjured. She is handcuffed by Detective Messenger and he quickly advises her of her right to remain silent and advises her to do so in no uncertain terms. "Just shut the fuck up now and stay face down on the floor. This is a murder scene and we are calling the shots." He can tell that she is not totally shocked to see him handcuffing and arresting her, and he knows that she wants to say something. Plenty of time for that later. No time for it now. She has dropped a Glock 9mm pistol as he knocks her against the wall in the process of securing her, and he takes and maintains custody of that weapon.

The ambulance arrives and confirms that Cummings is dead, having been shot twice in the chest, and they call for the medical examiner to respond. Their initial treatment of Dexter Campbell reveals a single gunshot wound to the stomach. It is serious but in all probability he will fully recover.

Gretchen Moran has been knocked against the corner of a coffee table as Tennyson Cummings fell. She has been rendered unconscious but is being revived thanks to Lodi's attention—some basic first aid. There is some redness around her right eye, probably caused by the fall. The ambulance crew checks her over and concludes that she may have suffered a concussion; however, her eyes are not dilated and her pulse is normal. They advise her of warning signs, that if they were to appear, they would warrant a trip to her own physician for a checkup. She is visibly shaken and is trying to make sense out of what has just happened. Her ears are ringing from the close proximity of the pistol reports. She heard them and that's the last she could remember. How long was she out? She has no idea. Two people with guns were shooting at each other, then she blacked out; now she is still alive and the situation is under control.

Sgt. Sullivan pauses to survey the situation and takes a few deep breaths. He's holding the battering ram with one hand, before hauling it to the El Camino and picking up his raid kit and paperwork. The words of a Warren Zevon song come to mind: "Send lawyers, guns and money, the shit has hit the fan." He feels his heart beating in time with the song—hard and fast.

29

WHEN THE HOMICIDE DETECTIVES ARRIVED at the scene, Dexter Campbell, aka "Pea" or "Peahead" was just being placed in the ambulance. Before he was taken, the two fifty-dollar bills that Gretchen had used to make the buy were taken from him as evidence along with another three hundred and some odd dollars. Sullivan had called for a uniform car with a policewoman aboard to search Della Brown at the scene and transport her to a holding cell near the Narcotics Bureau. She would standby with her until Detective Messenger could get down there and interview and process her. She was being taken from the scene just as Detectives Lopez and Mathis arrived to take over the investigation.

Sullivan greeted the two at the front of 2811½ Franklin Street and gave them a quick synopsis of the events leading to the homicide of Tennyson Cummings in a shootout with Della Brown. It was by then nearing midnight; it was going to be another long night, coming off the adrenalin rush and facing hours of tedious paperwork, decision-making, and interviews.

Once at the scene, the homicide detectives took charge of it and went about their investigation. Because of the complexity of the case, the two asked Sullivan if his team would serve their search warrant, search the house thoroughly, inventory the evidence and place it in the Property Bureau.

Sullivan, Lodi and Crowe undertook the systematic search of the house, starting away from the soon-to-be-moved body of Tennyson Cummings and the pre-shooting position of Della Brown. The house was dirty, dishes in the sink, towels on the floor of the bathroom, dirty bed clothes on the bed in one bedroom and a filthy mattress on the floor in the other bedroom. There were no clothes in the closets, very little food in the refrigerator and no cleaning supplies anywhere.

In one bedroom closet, a foot square section of the hardwood floor boards had been carefully cut from their place making an accessible hiding place. A hole in the subfloor had been made and a canvas bag about the size of a ten-pound flour sack had been tacked on the edges so that the bag protruded below the floor into the crawl space. It was a pretty neat job as the tongue and groove hardwood pieces were glued together and fit tightly into the cut out space covering up the stash hole. Lodi found it as he searched the room that had the dirty mattress. He was often the one to find stash locations of carefully secreted evidence or money, as he was a relentlessly methodical searcher. A large magnet had been attached to the underside of the cover boards and a paired horseshoe magnet under the dirty mattress. The horseshoe magnet was used to lift the cover when placed in the proximity of the magnet under the boards. The only giveaway was the visibility of the lines on the edges of the cover, perpendicular to the way the floor boards ran. Removing the cover boards, the canvas stash bag was obvious. In the stash he found cash, a small photo album containing several photographs, several ounces of cocaine and packets of deck papers. In addition, there was another Sig Sauer Model P226, 9mm, semi-automatic pistol and a box of 9mm ammunition.

Lodi carefully bagged the evidence to be taken to headquarters, where it would be carefully examined and inventoried. The exception to that was the money; it was inventoried at the scene and amounted to $17,454. In accordance with departmental procedure, it was counted and witnessed by one other officer, both of whom signed the evidence package.

From Cummings' clothes, homicide detectives removed $150, the keys to the Toyota Camry, his billfold containing a Florida driver's license in his name, and house keys fitting the locks at 2811½ Franklin Street (which no longer worked since the detectives had forced entry).

It was two o'clock in the morning when Sullivan got his tool box out of his truck and repaired the front door to the extent that it could be closed and the house secured. At headquarters he would make out a report for the people in the Civil Liabilities Section, who would deal with complaints from the owner of the house. Sullivan and his crew would work with the District Attorney's office to see if the house was seizable under Public Nuisance Statutes.

Detective Messenger had written up the paperwork necessary to put Della Brown in jail under her true name, Celeste de la Sala. He had formally advised her of her rights at headquarters and she wished to speak to him immediately. He did not interview her, waiting, as he had been instructed, until the homicide detectives could be present. While waiting for them, he took her to the crime lab where GSR tests were performed on her hands, verifying that she had recently fired a weapon. Lopez and Mathis arrived and began a videotaped interview with her at about one o'clock in the morning and Detective Messenger monitored the interview from the observation room. When the interrogation pertaining to the homicide of Tennyson Cummings was complete, she was released to Messenger's custody.

Next on the list for the homicide detectives was the interview of the eye witness, Gretchen Moran. She had been patiently waiting her turn in an interview room near the video interviewing location. Lodi had brought her a sandwich and a soda but she was not hungry. She admitted to being in a state of shock. She had never witnessed anything like what she saw that night, of course—few people had—and she was literally speechless for a while. But when her turn came to talk to Detectives Lopez and Mathis with Lodi monitoring, she had no problem; she had recovered some of her confidence and swagger. Yet the experience had been a humbling one and, as she thought about it, she was pretty sure she would not do it again.

Detective Messenger and Sgt. Sullivan sat down with Celeste de la Sala, after she had been interviewed by the homicide detectives, and that interview was videotaped as well. The two of them decided that what they wanted was, in essence, a limited autobiography from her drug days in Miami to present.

When they sat down and the tape was rolling, they advised her of her rights again and then asked her to start with an introduction of herself and develop her story from her drug association with the Jamaicans in Miami, specifically Tennyson Cummings, to her relocation in Denver and her association with the Jamaicans and Cummings again, to the present moment. Celeste looked tired and a little sad. She wiped her nose with a tissue, took a drink of water from the plastic cup she had been given and sighed pensively as she closed her eyes, then she began.

> *My name is Celeste de la Sala. I was born in Havana, Cuba and have lived most of my life in Miami and other parts of South Florida. I was raised in a bilingual Cuban refugee household. We were not refugees in the more common sense of struggling financially, or with the language or religion or things of that nature. We were well off in Cuba and we continued to be affluent in Miami.*

I was raised with conservative values, went to an all girls Catholic high school and then FIU (Florida International University) in Miami where I got a degree in Criminal Justice. I had started using drugs in college and had become enamored with Jamaican culture and music, and that led to experimenting heavily with alcohol, marijuana and then cocaine.

I didn't think it was possible, but I did become addicted to drugs and alcohol. I met Tennyson Cummings at some Jamaican cultural and music events in 1984. I soon learned that he ran several Jamaican cocaine dealing locations. He hustled all the good looking women and made them think they were getting a special deal on their drugs. All he was interested in was sex, but it was so easy for him that he didn't have to do anybody any favors.

I gave in to his charm a few times when I was really high and I had some fun. I started spending lots of money at his places and by the time I got my degree, the last thing I was thinking about was law enforcement. My brother Fabian had become a cop in the late Seventies and he loved it and he adored me. He had really hoped that I would join the Miami P.D. where he was. He watched me go downhill in my senior year of college, but I don't think he knew where I was hanging out or he would have warned me to stay away from the Jamaican drug dealers. They have a notorious reputation for violence, vengeance and bigotry. The only white people they trust are women and then only if they look halfway decent.

My dad had been generous with me and kept me in spending money through college, but soon after that he could see that drugs had a hold on me. And I didn't want to dishonor him or other 'Cubanos' by becoming a coke whore.

I was at a drug house in Miami, near downtown, one night and I had no money. I was giving the Jamaican running the house a blowjob in one of the bedrooms in exchange for a half a gram of shitty cocaine. I heard a man come in and make a buy from Peahead, that same asshole that got shot in that house tonight. I heard that man leave about the time I finished the guy, and I ran to the kitchen, washed my mouth out under the faucet in the sink and ran out the back door. I ducked into the shadows and snorted most of whatever it was that he gave me. Then I heard gunshots and I made my way out through the back yard of the place, between some houses and on to the next street, where I was picked up by a cop in an unmarked car. I'd had time to toss the cocaine deck with what little might have remained, before he confronted me. I asked him what was going on and he said he didn't know. Of course he knew, he just didn't want to tell me. I could hear his police radio but I couldn't tell what they were working on. He asked me what I was doing and I told him that I was down there looking for cocaine. I gave him the name of Della Brown, that I had been using for some time, and I told him I was from Jamaica and didn't have any ID. I ended up in jail for an immigration hold because I didn't want them to know my real name.

The next day I found out that it was a cop that was killed outside the Jamaican drug house and that it was my brother Fabian. I went crazy.

*I was released from custody because they had nothing to hold me on, and I spent several months drunk and high and keeping myself that way by prostitution. I wanted to die, but was afraid to kill myself. I stayed away from my family while they grieved and buried my brother. I blamed myself for being part of the problem and supporting the assholes that killed him. I tried to find out who did it so I could kill **them** but I was unable to do so.*

Eventually my father found me on the streets, and he and a couple of other old Cubanos forcibly removed me from the street and kept me locked up in a 'safe house' until I made it through withdrawal. It took a while, but he got me clean and sober and healthy again. We started talking about my future and he wanted me to go to work in his shipping business. That wasn't for me but I listened to him. I know he loves me and I know he knows plenty about business. He mentioned his trucking company in Denver and that led to the idea of opening the Caribbean Store where you found me, the Kingston Corner.

I came here for a fresh start and things were looking up for my business. Jamaican food and music is popular but so is Cuban food and music and stuff from Bermuda and other Caribbean Islands. Sales have been gradually increasing and I met lots of nice people. I was staying sober, attending meetings and taking care of myself.

I had no idea that Tennyson Cummings was here in Denver. In Miami, they called him 'the Poet.' After that night that my brother was killed, I found different sources, mostly Marielitos gang places—they speak Spanish of course and I felt more comfortable, but why, I don't know. They can be every bit as ruthless as the Jamaican drug gangs are. I quit going to the Jamaican places and never saw Cummings again until I had been in Denver a little while. One afternoon I saw a Jamaican guy that looked familiar but he didn't say anything or let on that he recognized me. Then, a couple of days later, Tennyson Cummings comes into the store, that was shortly before you came in (pointing and nodding at Messenger), maybe a month or so. He is friendly at first until he finds out that I have changed, that I am sober and no longer have to trade sex for cocaine. We went out to eat a couple of times. I did it just to be polite and because I am afraid, well, was afraid of him. I didn't want him near me.

He saw you in my store (again nodding toward Messenger) and he knew that you were a cop and he told me so. The night that you and I went to The

Riviera, he wanted me to get you to come back to my apartment. I don't know what he was thinking, but I'm pretty sure he wanted to hurt you. I only saw him once or twice since then, but yesterday, well Wednesday, that was yesterday, right? Anyway, he came to my apartment before I went to the store. He was angry about something. And asked me if I had seen the cop again, meaning you (points at Messenger). He said that maybe I was a snitch, and that was why I had gotten close to a cop. I told him he was crazy. And he said, "Check this out; I've killed cops, or had them killed and I'll kill this one if I get a chance." I told him to get out of my face and to leave me alone, that I wanted nothing to do with him and I called him 'hijo de puta' in Spanish, meaning son of a bitch. He turned and hit me with his fist and knocked me to the floor and said he would not hesitate to kill another fuckin' Cuban, just like the Cuban cop he had murdered in Miami. I tried to get off the floor but he put his foot on the side of my head and told me, "Don't let me find out you're a snitch, Della, trying to get that cop next to me." He left and I sat on the floor and cried my eyes out. Then I got myself up, put makeup on my face and finally got to the store to open it up.

I sat in the office after you left, Detective Messenger, and I thought about what I should do. He would bully me and ruin my new life here in Denver, if I didn't stand up to him. And he had just admitted to killing my brother, but not knowing it was my brother. I decided that I would go home and get my gun and go confront him at his place. I knew where it was. He had given me his address when he invited me to a barbecue there last week, the night there was a shooting across the street from his house. I never had any intention of going to that barbecue by the way.

I knew if he said you were a cop, that he was probably right, and I thought about trying to talk to you earlier tonight, then I decided I had to confront him first. The one thing you should know, Detective Messenger, is that I didn't care if you were a cop or not. I'm not into drugs anymore. I'm a legit businesswoman and I thought you liked me and could tell I was attracted to you. I would never have let him set you up.

I went in his house; the witness can tell you this. I had my gun in my hand and I told him, 'Don't you ever hit me again you mother fucker or I will kill you dead.' He raised his gun and fired it twice; one shot hit Peahead. I then raised mine and fired twice at him and he went down. Next thing I know, you, Detective Messenger, are slamming me against the wall.

He was going to kill me so I defended myself.

Look at my face; he hurt me and he would have eventually killed me. I think you may charge me with murder but I'll beat it.

In Miami, in Little Havana, I'll get an award or they'll name a park after me or something, for ridding society of this asshole, in the process of defending my own life. Check him out thoroughly; you'll see, you guys will all get a commendation for getting this guy off the street, one way or another. Look closely at that gun he had. Well, I'm sure you will anyway. Check mine out too for that matter. It's registered to me in Miami.

That's all I have to say unless you have questions.

"Thanks, Celeste, that's a heckuva story. Is Celeste what you like to be called?" That was Sullivan's lead-in question.

"Well, actually, Celeste is what everybody who knows who I really am calls me, family and old friends. I told Detective Messenger that my name was Cedella when I first met him; that's what my brother always called me when we were growing up. He liked the way it sounded 'cedella sala', kind of combining my first and last names in some way. He babied me and spoiled me my whole life and I was crushed when he was killed."

Sullivan followed up, "I'm sure you were, Celeste. Homicide may have talked to you about these things but I want to ask if you had any knowledge of the homicides possibly connected to Tennyson Cummings, the *late* Tennyson Cummings, I should say?"

"Well, here's what I do know. I wasn't there when the girl was killed in the park, but he told me that there was an argument and she was accidentally killed. One of the other Jamaicans, Peahead, the guy that got shot by Tenny tonight, told me that Tenny killed her. There was an argument about something, I guess. Peahead was telling me, kind of warning me, that Tenny was liable to do just about anything. He told me that he was super paranoid about people close to him snitching and that had made him tense as hell lately."

Sullivan continued, "Do you know anything about the murder of a guy at 16th and Lafayette? Did the homicide guys ask about that?"

"They did, and I told them that I don't know anything about it."

"How about the attempt on a police officer's life recently, did you hear about that?"

"I didn't, but I bet he had somebody do it for him. He's the kind that would kill you in a moment of rage, but to plan and setup a killing, I think he would get somebody else to do it. Just like my brother, Tennyson Cummings killed my brother but he didn't pull the trigger. To him, that would be like Don Corleone doing his own dirty work. He thought of himself as a big shot."

"Okay, thanks, Celeste. How about you, Leon, you have anything?"

"I do, Sarge, but just a couple of things about my dealings with her. First of all, did you think I was a cop when I first went into your store?"

"No, the thought never crossed my mind. I just thought you were a cool looking dude with a big smile, and I liked you when we started to talk."

"When did Tenny tell you that he thought I was a cop? Had he seen me out at your place that first time?"

"He came and picked me up that Saturday night after you and I first met. He saw you crossing Colorado Boulevard on foot, as he pulled out of the driveway after he picked me up. He said to me, 'See that big man crossing the street back there behind us? He's a cop. What's he doing out here by your place?'

I turned to look and I saw you. He asked me if I knew you and I told him, 'No, I did not.' He looked at me kinda funny. Like Peahead said, he was getting tense and paranoid about cops and snitches."

"Well I'll be damned," was Messenger's response, shaking his head. "I thought I was totally cool keeping an eye on the place to see who showed up. I was trying to get his license plate, which I did, but, man, I'm gonna have to be even more careful than I am. He recognized me from the jump. That fuckin' blows my mind. He had only seen me that one time at the house with the CI."

Celeste de la Sala added, "When he saw you in The Riviera, he knew who you were right away. And when you said that nobody forgets you, he actually wondered if he was right about you being a cop. If you would have denied it, he would have been sure you were covering up. The way you played it was cool.

"I think what happened was that he didn't trust the guy who took you to his house. Somebody probably convinced him that he was a snitch and not trustworthy."

"Well, you know that the informant ended up being murdered at 16th and Lafayette. That's the one I asked if you knew anything about." This from Sullivan.

"No, I didn't hear about that murder. I did hear about Lilian Martinez getting shot by Winthrop; she was his girlfriend. I talked to the other guys about him and her too, the Homicide detectives. I had seen Lilian a couple times before, and I guess I had seen Janel, the girl that was killed. They told me that they had pictures of me with them. I know Lilian was using a lot and had gotten pregnant and all that. But they were so young."

Sullivan decided it was time to wrap it up. "Okay, that's about all for now, Celeste. Do you have any questions for us?"

"My only question is how you knew that I had anything to do with that group? Why did you target me?"

Messenger answered, "I just decided to go in the place and look around since we had no idea what clientele in legitimate Jamaican businesses is like. I wondered if the drug dealers hung out there. Then I met you and decided to watch the place to see who came and went, and Tenny showed up. After we saw that you two knew each other, we decided that I would try and get close to him through you."

"Well, I wish I hadn't known Tenny at all—ever. And then maybe you and I could have become friends. I like cops. Maybe I would have even tried to join the Denver Police Department. I would be a good cop, just like my brother was."

"I think you would have been," was Leon's comment on that. Then he added, "I'm just glad that you're a better shot than Tenny was, and under fire too, damn!"

"Me too," was her only response.

When Messenger and Sullivan had finished getting a statement from, and talking to, Celeste de la Sala, she was placed again in the holding cell. Detective Lola Mathis came into Sullivan's office and informed him that she had contacted the on-call Deputy District Attorney and went over the situation carefully with her. She made the decision to have de la Sala placed in jail, Investigation First Degree Murder, but brought up the distinct possibility that she would not be bound over for trial at the Preliminary Hearing, as self-defense looked like perfect legal justification for what she did. At that point Mathis took the paperwork from Messenger, and she and Lopez walked the prisoner next door to the city jail.

30

WHEN GRETCHEN MORAN HAD FINISHED her statement, Lodi, suggested that he take her back to the Residence Inn. She asked if it would be okay to sit in the office with them. Nobody else was in the Narcotics Bureau at that hour so he told her that would be fine. She had experienced a stunning trauma and didn't want to go to the hotel and be by herself. She asked permission to use the phone to call her father in Colorado Springs. They directed her to a desk in the corner with more privacy and dialed the number for her. She spoke for a few minutes and when she returned to her chair near Lodi and Crowe, she had tears in her eyes. They asked if she was okay and she nodded that she was. She sat there quietly and contentedly, while they worked. She was coming down from a prodigious adrenaline rush just trying to level out.

Lodi and Crowe had continued to inventory and examine the evidence recovered from 2811½ Franklin. The cocaine and the money were important evidentiary components in the construction of a posthumous case against Tennyson Cummings. The recorded buy money from the previous night would later be found among the bills that were recovered from the stash location as a result of a diligent bill-by-bill serial number comparison. They would proceed to put the case together as if it were to be filed against Tennyson Cummings and Dexter Campbell, though obviously only the case against Campbell would go forward.

The other weapon recovered from the house was the one that Cummings had fired twice in the direction of the front door of the house, hitting Dexter Campbell once: the Sig, Model P226, 9mm with a round in the chamber and seven in the magazine when it was removed from his lifeless hand by Sgt. Sullivan. Ballistics comparisons would be done to ascertain if that weapon, and the other Sig P226 recovered by Lodi in the stash location, had been used in previous shootings and homicides on file. In addition, a GSR examination would be part of the post-mortem examination of the body of Tennyson Cummings.

Crowe would contact Greg Lynch from the Miami Task Force and arrange ballistics comparisons with the rounds that killed Detective de la Sala. For that matter, the 9mm Glock recovered from Celeste de la Sala would be tested as well.

No public service bills, phone bills, or water bills in the name of Tennyson Cummings were recovered from the house, nor were there any rent receipts. Nothing was found indicating that 2811½ Franklin was his residence. Nothing whatsoever with Dexter Campbell's name was found either.

Perhaps the most informative evidence found at the scene was the small photo album. In it were photos of all the dark narcs that appeared to have been taken at scenes of various search warrants and street operations. They had been taken from a distance, apparently, but the faces were circled and identified by last names. There were several of Messenger in which he was easily identifiable. There were some of Crowe and two or three of Lodi and Sullivan. There was a picture of Darnell Coolidge, the informant who was killed at 16th and Lafayette, a couple of pictures of Arthur Robinson and several unidentified men, possibly Miami police officers. There were also pictures of several women. Among the women in the pictures was Celeste de la Sala, in a photo apparently taken on the

243

beach somewhere in Florida; she was wearing a bathing suit and posing, but she wasn't smiling. On the inside cover of the album he had written, "Michael Corleone: Keep your friends close but your enemies closer."

Lodi and Crowe had just finished processing the evidence and were about ready to take it to the Property Bureau. The evidence no longer needing their undivided attention, they engaged in small talk with Gretchen Moran, hoping that talking about the experience would help her start the healing process. She admitted that she had been scared when Tennyson Cummings had patted her down, looking for a wire, while feeling her up for his own gratification. Then she relaxed after he didn't find it and thought she had it made, at which point Della Brown burst into the house with a gun, the shooting started, and she was panic-stricken.

Sgt. Sullivan and Detective Messenger walked back into the office about then. It was four o'clock in the morning. They sat down and listened just as Gretchen talked about how everything seemed good until Della Brown walked in and she and Cummings started shooting.

"That's the nature of this undercover stuff, man. One minute everything is cool and then in an instant it changes and it's all upside down." That was Messenger's expert opinion.

Sullivan added, "That's the thing: all the planning and contingency planning in the world cannot account for every possibility. The one eventuality we didn't talk about at the briefing was the possibility of somebody showing up to have an armed confrontation with Cummings while you were in there. Crowe saw her approaching the house and we were surprised, but there was no way that we could have anticipated what she would do. And we had no reason to think that we should stop her from entering.

"Let me tell you, there's no worse feeling in the world, hearing gunshots in a place and thinking that one of your own is in danger," said in a no-nonsense tone by Sgt. Sullivan.

"I disagree, man," spoke Messenger, laughing. "We're crashing that door down, and then we're going through it not knowing who was shooting at what, that was a terrible feeling. Am I right, Sarge? And you being right next to the guy shooting," he said, nodding at Gretchen, "and right in the line of fire—that had to be a terrible feeling, girl."

"I thought that I was going to die, I'm serious. It's a good thing that I fell and knocked myself out or I might have had a heart attack or something. But emotionally, I'm stunned and saddened. I feel like I have witnessed something awful, no matter how bad the guy was who got killed. I didn't expect to feel like this at all."

Sullivan stared blankly while he let that sink in. Then he went on. "But as bad as you feel, it could have been much worse if Cummings had shot Della rather than the other way around. In that case we might have had a shootout and God only knows how that would have turned out. Shiver me timbers. That's all I can say," said Sullivan, borrowing an old pirates' phrase.

"Before Della got there, it seemed like they were reluctant to let you leave. It sounded like they were about to get rough with you. I was almost ready to give the command to hit the place, before the shots were fired. That forced our hand—we had to hit it as rapidly as we could. There's a good chance we would have been heavily criticized if one of us, or an innocent person—you, Gretchen—had been injured or killed. No doubt about it, this was the worst case scenario we contemplated— gunfire with you inside. It's exactly why we seriously considered not sending you in the place again, except that you were not the shooter's targeted victim.

"But our plan was to get you out of there if you were in danger and that's the plan we stuck with knowing it was high risk. It worked! I don't want to second-guess it, or what-if it, beyond learning from it. And we all move on."

"Well, like I said, I was getting scared, but after he searched me and didn't find the wire, I relaxed and regained my confidence a little bit. I wasn't too worried; I trusted you guys, and with good reason. When I came to, you guys were there and I was safe—but I don't know how or why.

"What has made me miserable in the aftermath of the violent explosion that literally knocked me out, is thinking how fearful Gwen must have been before she was killed. I wonder if she suffered as her life was ending, or was she blessed with unconsciousness as I was. It makes me sick to my stomach and my sense of loss and grief are worse than ever.

"I thought I would feel better but I just feel sick, and I want to go back to the Residence Inn, I guess. But I don't want to be alone."

Messenger went to her and took her right hand, placing it in both of his strong, warm, brown hands. "Look, you did a courageous thing, going in there, and you saw, up close, what most people don't even think about—the danger that always lies in wait, just below the surface in the illegal drug trade. Man, 'victimless crime' my ass. Why do you think we take so many guns out of these places? Because these guys are hunters? Uh-huh. Right! You did good, you should get a commendation for that, from the Kiwanis Club, or the Mayor's Office or somebody."

Sullivan had called the lieutenant immediately after the incident and let him know that a drug dealer had been killed just after their informant had made a buy from him; that guns, dope and money had been seized and all of the other details that in the long run would make this an extremely successful night's work. Implicit was the distinct possibility that three homicides had been solved in the process. Sullivan then put all of those details in the nightly activity letter.

There was nothing more to do until the next day, so at four-thirty in the morning they called it a night. Crowe and Lodi decided to get something to eat and Gretchen was amenable to that on her way back to the motel. Lodi made it clear that it was her choice; he would take her back first if she wanted, but she said she was hungry and would like to go with them. They decided on an all-night place at Speer and Colfax and headed out.

Messenger said that he was beat and was going straight home. After some thought, he decided he wanted to go and socialize a little bit.

Sgt. Sullivan went to his office for a few minutes to clean up his desk and to check his phone messages. He had one message from LaDonna Robinson, one from Luther's mom Gina Pride and three messages from Eleanora.

LaDonna Robinson said she had heard about the shooting and arrests and just wanted to talk to him about it. She asked that he call her tomorrow and then told him "Thank you, Sergeant, thank you for all the hard work you guys have done."

Gina Pride's message was short and sweet, "Hey Frank, Lilian Martinez called Luther tonight and said that you guys arrested suspects in Janel's murder. He really wants to talk to you about it and I want to hear about it as well. Call me some-time Thursday, maybe around noon, please. Thanks, Frank, talk to you then."

Eleanora had called three times and asked that he call her no matter how late it was. She said she had heard news reports about a police shooting at 28th and Franklin and was "worried sick, and praying for you, all of you." He called her back and it rang four or five times before she answered breathlessly. She said that she had fallen asleep on the couch and had slept two or three hours. She asked that he come over. They ended the call, and he was on his way.

It was five-fifteen in the morning by the time Sullivan pulled into Ellie's driveway. It was a soft, daylight savings time pre-dawn and Sullivan stretched when he got out of his car and took it in. Ellie was standing by the gate on the side of the house, watching him through tears of joy and relief. She approached him and he started to speak as she put her finger to her closed lips making the universal *shush* sign. He remained quiet as she hugged him and held him as tightly as she could. She kissed him, pushing her tear-moistened face against his beard. She cried softly a moment before finally releasing her hug and grabbing his hands. "I love you, Frank," she said, looking him in the eye.

"And I love you, El," he whispered as he pulled her close again with a silent prayer of thanksgiving in his heart—for her and the dawning of another blessed day.

31

JUST BEFORE NOON ON THURSDAY morning, Sullivan was at his house getting ready to go for a run up to Washington Park and back, when he got a page from Detective Lopez in Homicide. He called him back immediately.

"Hey, Sarge, thanks for calling me back. What a night, huh?"

"You can say that again. Are you at work already?"

"I am, I came in early to get started with the ballistics tests on those two Sigs that you guys took out of that place last night. You ready for this?"

"Can't wait, let me have it."

"Okay, the Sig found in the stash with the money and drugs *is* the weapon that killed Janel Robinson and Darnell Coolidge. They printed it before testing it, so we'll see what they come up with. I really hope they come up with Tennyson's prints so we can clear both of these cases."

"That is amazing, man, even better than I hoped for. I don't suppose you've tested the other one, the one that Tennyson Cummings had in his dead hand when we got in there?"

"We have tested it and George Crowe is sending the reports on both to his contact in Miami this afternoon to see if they have a match on either one of them. Now on that one, we did lift his prints off of it and the GSR test on him was positive so we know that he shot at Celeste de la Sala, then she shot him twice."

"What about Dexter Campbell, the guy who got shot, 'Peahead'? Any news on his condition?"

"No, not yet. Lola and I are going to go over there and talk to him this afternoon or tonight to get a statement from him about the shooting. I'm not sure he'll have much to say. You guys don't mind do you? I mean, the drug sales cases are all that we have on him so far, so if you want us to wait, we will."

"No, go ahead, but get ahold of Lodi and see if he can go with you for the interview. Knowing him, he's probably in the office already, and he's good at getting these guys to talk, as a rule."

"Okay, Sarge, I'm gonna let you go. I'll get in touch later as we get more information."

"Thank you very much, Al. Good work!"

"You guys too. I've never seen a crime scene quite like that one last night. Everything and everybody exactly in place as when it happened. A suspected cop killer was dead on the floor, the person who killed him was sitting on the floor in handcuffs, and another drug dealer had been shot twice and was being attended to on the floor by paramedics. How do you guys keep up the pace, Sarge?"

"Yeah, it's exciting, I'll say that for it. We were just lucky last night that the right person got shot, otherwise it might have been a mess. How many rounds did Celeste de la Sala fire, just the two that hit him?"

"No, it looks like she fired four times. She admitted to us that she lost track. But we only recovered four shells; there were two bullets in him and two in the wall behind him. Apparently, she only missed as he started to fall forward. She's good with a pistol. And the thing is, I think she'll get away with it. We'll have to see what Dexter Campbell says, but her story looks pretty good. The recording you guys made from the wire indicates that the guy had his gun in his hand. When she tells her story about how her brother was killed and how this guy as much as admitted to doing it, and to other killings as well, how Cummings beat her and threatened her—no way she's going down for this. Just between you and me, maybe she should get a medal for it."

"I agree, but I'm still in shock that she did it. We saw her approaching the place and we recognized her of course, but the last thing we expected was that she was there for revenge. Then we heard the shots; we got inside and it wasn't her who was down but him—down for good. I don't know what we expected, but what we feared was that Cummings had shot our informant."

"We've never had anything like this, five related shootings in a little over a week, counting the attempt on Detective Crowe, and all of those cases are now cleared. And on top of that we might have cleared the murder of a police officer in Miami a couple years ago."

"I'm sure of it. Thanks again, Al, I gotta run now."

"Okay, Sarge, I'll call Lodi right now. See you later I'm sure."

Sullivan hung up the phone and went into the kitchen to get a cup of coffee. He poured it and was buttering some toast when the phone rang again. Sullivan decided to let it go to the answering machine and monitor it.

"Hey, Frank this is Hugo Connors, I'm calling to pass on the gratitude of the Captain and the Division Chief, along with my own…"

At that point Sullivan picked up the phone. "Hey, L-T, I'm here, just took a minute to get to the phone. We had a long night and I haven't been up too long."

"No problem, as I was saying you guys are to be commended for all the work you've done in the last ten days and you've done it without any of us getting hurt or you guys hurting anybody. That's incredible Frank! Are you guys caught up on your paperwork?"

"I think after tonight we will be, by tomorrow night for sure. Lodi is filing a sales case on Peahead, Dexter Campbell, for both of the informant buys, and he may have to do a little more on that tomorrow if the lab reports aren't back yet. This afternoon he and Al Lopez are going over to the hospital to interview Campbell as well. George Crowe is going to run down the ballistics comparisons with his contact in Miami and see if either of the weapons we recovered last night was used to kill Detective de la Sala down there two years ago."

"All right, that sounds good. I want to be sure you guys take the weekend off. Saturday is the fourth of July, so why don't you all take Saturday, Sunday and Monday. I'm worried about how much stress you guys have been under and all the hours you have been putting in."

"Well, I appreciate it, that's pretty much what we decided to do. Next week we'll get started on some of the other complaints that have been piling up while we worked on these guys. If those guys want, I'm going to give them tomorrow night off also. I want tomorrow off so I can take my baseball team to Laramie for a baseball tournament, our last one of the year."

"Sounds good, Frank, I really do appreciate the hell out of you guys. I'll talk to you later."

"Okay, thanks, L-T."

Sullivan then spent the next hour firming up travel arrangements for his team to go to Laramie on Friday afternoon for the tournament, and coordinating everything with players, parents and the other coaches. He assured all of them that he was going with them and looking forward to it.

When he finished that, he did go for a run, and used the time, as was his custom, to clear his mind and let go of the stress that had been building in him during the last ten days. He pushed himself hard and stopped several times on his trip through the park to do sets of twenty pushups. He was totally soaked in sweat when he got back to his house. He breathed deeply, intentionally letting go of everything but the present moment, extremely grateful that he and his team had made it through last night without shooting or being shot.

Sullivan put on the The Band's *The Last Waltz* album and listened to Van Morrison and Richard Manuel and the Band sing "Tura Lura, Lura" over and over again while he cooled down. He then took a shower and got ready to go to the office early.

But before he left he called Eleanora at home. She was just about ready to go to work.

"Hey, Frank, how are you feeling today? You couldn't have gotten too much sleep; it was morning when you left here and went home."

"Yes it was, and a good morning at that. One thing we didn't talk about last night was Laramie. You know, I'm taking the boys up there for a tournament tomorrow and I'd like you to come with me if you want to."

"Hmmm. Let me see if I can get the day off tomorrow. I'd love to do it. I'll call you in a little while, after I get to work. I'm pretty sure it will be okay. I've never been to Laramie. It'll be great to be together."

"Well, it's kind of a charming old cowtown and we're going to be playing at the University of Wyoming, so we'll be in an interesting part of town. Just a Holiday Inn, but it's a new one, nice pool, good restaurants nearby. I think you will enjoy being around the boys too. They're about ready to start college and are full of optimism and ready to change the world. And they'll love you."

"Okay, I'm so glad you asked me. I'll call you back in a little while."

"Call me at the office. I'll be there about six or so."

"Okay, bye, bye.

"Bye."

32

SULLIVAN WAS IN THE OFFICE at six o'clock when Ellie called him to tell him that she got Friday off and was ready to go. They agreed to talk later.

All of the dark narcs were in the office by then, so they sat down in the sergeants' office to plan the night and discuss what had happened during the day.

Lodi was the first to speak and he informed the others of the interview that he and Detective Lopez had with Peahead. They were only allowed a few minutes with him as he was in a great deal of discomfort. They advised him of his rights and limited their questioning of him to the shooting of Janel Robinson. He said unequivocally that Tennyson Cummings had shot her, unintentionally, as he pushed her away, while engaged in an argument with another Jamaican. According to Peahead, the group, almost entirely made up of Jamaicans, most of whom were not drug dealers or crooks, was gathered in the park listening to music, drinking beer and eating barbecue. Cummings and another Jamaican, whom Peahead referred to as Willow, got into a heated argument and Cummings pulled a gun. People, including Janel Robinson, tried to intervene. Cummings forcefully pushed them away from him and in the process the gun discharged, killing Robinson.

The team listened intently as Lodi recounted their interview with Dexter "Peahead" Campbell. At this point in his narrative, Lodi emphasized that Peahead was passively cooperative and not at all hostile toward Lopez and him. He further related that Campbell had no intention of identifying Willow by giving up his real name or anything else about him. He said that Willow had no culpability in the shooting. He refused to say what the argument was about, only that Willow had nothing to do with drug dealing and that he was a Jamaican legally in the country.

When Lodi had finished saying that much, he said, "I asked Peahead about the intel report that we got that stated that he was threatening to kill the dark narcs. He flatly denied it. He did say that when he was in jail, he ran into another Jamaican and told him that *Tennyson* wanted us dead. That, he said, is probably where the report came from. And after talking to him, I tend to believe him. I think he was probably repeating Tennyson's threats and it got attributed to him."

Lodi went on to explain that he intended to file two cases of sale against Campbell and that he hoped to interview him again after he had been moved from the hospital to the county jail. He could see a great deal of potential in Campbell's possible use as an informant.

Messenger spoke up eagerly at this point. "Hey, Sarge, I wanna run over to the jail and talk to Della, I mean Celeste de la Sala, and see if she can give me any information on Willow."

"Good idea, Leon. Is your buddy working over there tonight?"

"Yeah, man, he is. He'll make sure I get to see her right away. I'll be back in fifteen minutes."

"Okay, she probably knows him, so try and get everything she can give you."

"Right on, brother."

The meeting continued without Messenger present. Crowe informed Lodi and Sullivan that he had spoken again with Greg Lynch in Miami and had faxed him the ballistics reports so that they could compare them with the rounds removed from Detective de la Sala's body. Lynch could not believe that Celeste had walked into Cummings' place and killed him in a shootout. He admitted to wishing he had been there. Crowe related that Lynch had promised to expedite the ballistics comparisons and went on to say, "I told him there was no hurry; Cummings isn't going anywhere." This coming from the stoic George Crowe moved both Lodi and Sullivan to hearty laughter.

Next, it was Sullivan's turn to speak and he brought up the fact that the Sig recovered from the stash location at 2811½ Franklin was definitely the weapon that killed both Janel Robinson and Darnell Coolidge. Both Crowe and Lodi had already been informed of that by Detective Lopez.

At that point the meeting was interrupted by a uniform officer wishing to speak to Detective Lodi. Lodi left the meeting to talk to him.

The officer, John Asher, had been in the same academy class as Lodi and they were friends. The two shook hands and Lodi started the conversation. "What are you doing here, John? Don't tell me that you made an arrest."

Asher responded, "Ha ha ha, well, as a matter of fact we did, and we have him in the holding cell. His name is Lorenzo Walters and he is wanted for Parole Violation. He says he's working for you, and that you'll take care of it. That was the first thing he said when we arrested him, 'get a hold of Detective Lodi, I'm working for him.'"

"Well, we arrested him at a house on a search warrant, and he said he wanted to work, but he was shootin' me through the grease and never got back to me, so I sent the paperwork through on a charge of Weapons by Previous Offender, and his Parole Officer violated him (revoked his parole). Where is he? Let's go talk to him."

With that, they walked to the holding cell where Asher's partner was filling out paperwork. Asher opened the door to the holding cell, and Walters, who was handcuffed to a retainer ring for his own safety, blurted out, "Oh man, Lodi, thank God you were here tonight. I've been trying to get ahold of you, man. I have some good stuff for you."

"Hold on, Lorenzo," started Lodi, "you never called me back after that one night and I have tried to find you. We had a deal. You were too fuckin' lazy to keep your end of it and now you'll go back to prison. Think about this while you are there: you had a chance to get yourself together and stay out of prison and couldn't bring yourself to do it. Simple as that, you let yourself down, not me. I'll see you later."

With that, Lodi signaled for Asher to close the door to the holding cell, as Walters pleaded frantically for another chance. Lodi went back to the meeting and Asher and his partner escorted Lorenzo Walters to jail.

When he got back to the meeting, Lodi explained that Walters had been arrested and was on his way to jail. He didn't come through, they got the job done without him, end of story. Sullivan recapped what he had been saying in Lodi's absence, including that the team was going to be off for the three-day weekend and that he himself was going to be off Friday as well. Anybody else who wanted to, and didn't have any pressing deadlines on paperwork, could take Friday off. Messenger, who had just walked back into the room, and Crowe both took him up on it. Lodi said that he had to come in during the day to file the case on Peahead.

That resolved, Messenger had some important information to share. "Check this out fella's, Celeste does know a Jamaican nicknamed Willow. His real name is Edison Willoughby and she gave me his phone number. She was emphatic that he is not a dope dealer, or any kind of crook for that matter. She says he is legally here. He participated in the Pan Am games with the Jamaican soccer team in 1983 in Caracas, tried out for this year's team, but didn't make it. She says he is in his late twenties, is a grad student at Denver University, and is active with local youth soccer teams. She must know him pretty well; she knew his phone number by heart. I'm going to call him right now if it's okay with you, Sarge."

"Do it. He was probably afraid to come forward but maybe he'll talk to you now. And then go share what you learn with Lopez and Mathis."

"All right, man, I'll let you know."

Messenger did manage to contact Edison Willoughby, arranged to meet him at his apartment by DU, and he and Detective Mathis went out to get a statement from him shortly thereafter. Willoughby turned out to be a dark Jamaican male about six feet tall and of medium build. He appeared to be in excellent shape. He admitted to being at the scene of the murder of Janel Robinson. He and Tennyson were acquainted but not overly friendly. Willoughby was as anti-drug as could be; he had seen numerous lives ruined by drug usage and the reputation of his people in this country damaged by the drug-dealing, drug-smoking stereotypes.

He had gone to the park for a barbecue on the night Janel was killed and had intervened when Cummings got aggressive with her because she rejected his advances. Willoughby and Cummings started shoving each other and an enraged Cummings pulled a gun out of his waistband. He pushed Willoughby with his left hand while raising his right holding the gun. He turned and pushed Janel with the right and the gun discharged. When asked if he thought the gun went off accidentally, Willoughby said he wasn't sure. From the side, the physical movement could have been either accidental or intentional. He went on to explain that he couldn't see Cummings' face; otherwise, he could say for sure.

Willoughby admitted to being ashamed of himself for not coming forward on his own. He stated that he had gone back and forth about it and had about convinced himself that he would have eventually gone to the police to tell his story. He shuddered to think that Janel Robinson got killed and everyone, including himself, ran away and let her die alone in the park. He referred to her as "just an innocent kid."

He went on to make the case that law abiding Jamaicans would be very disappointed in him, a national celebrity of sorts, acting like a coward and running away and letting a murderous drug dealer go free. Then Messenger quoted him as he had written it down in his notebook: "When I heard he had been killed, I celebrated like I had just scored a goal, pumping my fist and yelling, 'Yes, yes, yes!' I was afraid he was going to kill someone else and I was celebrating that he had not."

Messenger concluded his report by noting that Willoughby would like to establish some dialogue between the legitimate, legal Jamaican community, and the police. He finished by saying, "I told him you'd call him as soon as you had time, Sarge, maybe next week. He wants the Jamaican community to develop trust in the police, and he would like the police to learn more about them and their culture. I told him, 'Right on man!'"

The meeting ended and Sgt. Sullivan went to his desk and called LaDonna Robinson.

"Hey, Sarge, how are you doing? I heard about all the action last night. What the hell happened?"

"Hey, LaDonna, that's why I'm calling. We hit that place at 2811½ Franklin last night and the man that killed Janel was in there. He was killed by someone in the house before we could get in. The bottom line is that we have interviewed two more witnesses and can now say unequivocally that Tennyson Cummings shot and killed Janel. We recovered the gun that was used and other evidence. He was a bad man who had bragged about killing people, make no mistake about it. We'll never know for sure, but killing Janel might have been accidental. He had a gun in his hand for some reason. I guess we'll never know."

"Oh my God, I feel so much better, Sullivan, I am so relieved to know this. Can you come over here and talk to me in person? I could use somebody to talk to."

"Let me see what I can do. I'll call you back in a little while after I finish up some stuff."

"Okay, Sarge, goodbye."

When Sullivan got off the phone, it dawned on him that he had not called Luther back in Bradenton, so he did just that before it got too late. Luther had a room with a host family that had a separate phone in the ballplayer's room. They had been a host family for years and Luther was glad to be with them. Minor League baseball players were underpaid, and the room and board provided by host families were a very important part of minor league infrastructure.

Luther answered after three or four rings and said he wasn't asleep yet. They had played a night game and he just got home. He told Sullivan that everything was going great. He was set to get his first start on the mound on Sunday and would probably go at least three innings, depending on pitch count. Frank Sullivan was very happy to know Luther was doing well and to think of him in a safe setting with a bright future. He was blessed. Luther informed him that his mom was flying down tomorrow for the Fourth of July weekend and he couldn't wait to see her. He said she had taken the night off and was home getting ready for the trip.

Sullivan gave Luther a brief, clean explanation of how they had solved Janel's murder, and at least one other case, if not more, and that the suspect was dead. He explained that he was going over to talk to Janel's mother in a little while as she seemed to be having a rough time, understandably enough. Luther asked Sullivan if he would call his mom and maybe take her to see Mrs. Robinson so she could spend some time with her. Sullivan said he would, wished Luther good luck on the weekend start, and assured him that he would be coming to watch him play as soon as he could get time off.

"Take care of yourself, Luther."

"Likewise, Coach. I'll call you next week. I'm really happy that you got the guy who killed Janel."

"Me too, Luther. Play hard and we'll talk soon."

Sullivan called Gina Pride immediately, apologizing for not calling her earlier in the day. Then at Luther's request, he asked her if she would like to make a late night visit to LaDonna Robinson. She said she would be delighted to do so and Sullivan arranged to pick her up.

Sullivan called Ellie at work just as she was leaving. He explained what he was doing and she too wanted to go. He told her he would pick her up at her house as soon as he could.

Sullivan asked Crowe, Lodi and Messenger if they wanted to go with him and console LaDonna Robinson, and provide her a little company. He expressed his hope that they would, as she seemed down in spite of being relieved that Janel's killer had been identified and captured, so to speak. They were all in. Lodi said he would go by King Soopers and pick up flowers and soft drinks and snacks. Crowe and Messenger agreed to go by the bootlegger at 25th and Washington and pick up some vodka for her. They finished what they were working on and headed out.

At half past midnight, the four narcs, Ellie and Gina were gathered with LaDonna Robinson at her house. She was glad to see Messenger come in with a pint size brown paper sack and she gave him a kiss on the cheek. Lodi put the flowers on LaDonna's table in her modest living room, and Gina and Ellie arranged those and some snacks and drinks on the table as well. Everyone took a seat.

Gina and LaDonna talked about what good "buddies" Luther and Janel had been. Much of the next hour involved just listening to LaDonna talk about her daughter, interrupting herself with sobs and tears as she went. Gina repeated good things about Janel from Luther's point of view and what he had told her.

At one point LaDonna looked at Ellie and asked, "And who are you, Ellie?"

"I'm an old friend of Frank's and I was at the park the night Janel was murdered. I wanted to come and hold your hand a minute and let you know how heartbroken I am about this. My aunts live near Fuller Park and we were having a picnic in the park when it happened. Frank and George were the first detectives at the scene, and at first I couldn't believe it was Frank—I hadn't seen him in years. Back in high school he was my boyfriend for most of our senior year and then we went our separate ways. When I saw him, I let him know that I was a witness and he's interviewed me several times since it happened."

"I bet he has." When LaDonna said that, everybody, including herself, shared a good laugh. Then she added. "Don't let that man get away again, Ellie, he's a keeper. And you know, all these guys have been so good to me. These are good people. This thing wouldn't be solved yet without them; they're street cops." Sullivan thanked her for the compliment but down-played it.

When the time came, the gathering broke up with tearful goodbyes on the part of the women, and hugs and good wishes all around. LaDonna stood at the open door until everyone had left, feeling, for the first time in days, some hope in her heart.

EPILOGUE

FRANK SULLIVAN AND ELLIE ENJOYED the drive up to Laramie on Friday for the baseball tournament. He took his '78 Dodge truck and she sat next to him on the bench seat. They talked about old times, they talked about last night, they talked about tomorrow. What they didn't talk about was them, as Frank and Ellie. That was developing on its own and neither of them wanted to jinx it by analyzing it or planning it.

The tournament was sponsored by a Laramie V.F.W. post, and before it started, the announcer dedicated the weekend to a "fallen fellow ballplayer and hopeful young spirit, Janel Robinson." He then very briefly explained why she was being remembered and, after a moment of silence, the crowd of players, coaches, parents, and baseball fans cheered. Sullivan had arranged this with the tournament director after getting the backing of the other coaches participating in the tournament, many of whom were friends of his. At the end of competition, Sullivan was given one of the bats awarded to the all-tourney team, to take to Mrs. Robinson as a keepsake. Janel Robinson's name, and the words, "All-Tourney Team" had been engraved on the barrel.

On Tuesday night, after the holiday break, Detective Crowe received a faxed message from Greg Lynch of the Miami Task Force. Lynch followed it up with a phone call. He explained to Crowe that the ballistics comparisons revealed that the 9mm taken from Tennyson Cummings' hand by Sgt. Sullivan was the weapon used to kill Detective Fabian de la Sala. That was a big deal, as the case could be exceptionally cleared: weapon recovered and three suspects, Tennyson Cummings and the Henry brothers, dead. No case filed.

The case against Celeste de la Sala was dismissed at her preliminary hearing and she was released from custody. She decided to stay in Denver and continue operating her business.

The dark narcs received commendations for their work in solving the homicides of Janel Robinson and Darnell Coolidge, and the shooting of Lilian Martinez. And they had dismantled a violent drug trafficking ring. Those accomplishments were listed in the commendations. But what they were really recognized for was their relentless dedication to serving the citizens of Denver; they were commended for their solid, "blocking and tackling" police work—in the trenches—night after night—*in* the community, *with* the community, in the best interests of all.

ACKNOWLEDGMENTS

My wife Carol, and our family,
have loved, supported, and encouraged me
in everything I have done.
I am eternally grateful for that.

Thanks to Barb, my editor,
for all her hard work and patience,
improving the manuscript
at every stage of the process.

I am blessed and very proud
to have been a member of the
Denver Police Department for 25 years.

ABOUT THE AUTHOR

 **PAUL MAHONEY** has a B.S. in Criminology and Law Enforcement (1970) from Metropolitan State University in Denver and an M.A. in American Studies (1975) from the University of Notre Dame. During his law enforcement career he had articles published in professional journals and also wrote a textbook on narcotics investigations. In his time as a Denver Police Officer and as a member of the American Embassies in Ecuador and Peru, he thrived on strong relationships with his co-workers and those with people in the communities he served.

Paul is married with four children and six grandchildren. He has spent his best days in retirement, being a grandfather while devoting a good deal of time to his custom woodworking and cabinet-making business. He is an avid baseball fan and has been known to stop and watch a Sunday Morning League game or a high school game or a sandlot game. He and his wife have traveled extensively across the U.S. and internationally as well. They lived in the Tucson area for many years and currently reside in the Great Lakes region.

www.ingramcontent.com/pod-product-compliance
Lightning Source LLC
Chambersburg PA
CBHW031608240626
47153CB00002B/676